Summer at Serenity Bay

Summer at Serenity Bay

Helen Bridgett

Stories that inspire emotions!
www.rubyfiction.com

Published 2021 by Ruby Fiction
Penrose House, Crawley Drive, Camberley, Surrey GU15 2AB, UK
www.rubyfiction.com

A CIP catalogue record for this book is available from the British Library

ISBN: 978-1-91255-052-4

Printed and bound in Great Britain by Clays Ltd, Elcograf S.p.A.

For family and friends
– always an inspiration!

Acknowledgements

I'd like to thank everyone at Choc Lit and Ruby Fiction
for giving me the opportunity to share this story with
you – particularly the Tasting Panel readers who
passed the original manuscript and made publication
possible: Cordy Swinton, Alma Hough, Carol Fletcher,
Deborah Warren, Dimitra Evangelou, Donna Morgan,
Fran Stevens, Gill Leivers, Hilary Brown, Jo Osborne,
Lucy Mouland, Maureen Webb, Melanie Russell,
Vanessa Wick and Wendy Stevens. Finally, as ever,
I thank my Mam and Dad for giving me a life-long
love of books and Jason for always being there.

Chapter One

A cock crowed and a female voice yelled for it to 'shut the feck up'.

Chloe took a moment to get her bearings. The light coming through the window was on the wrong side, the pillow smelled of outdoors, heavy blankets covered her rather than a light duvet and the mattress was very soft. Then she remembered – it was over and as she lifted her head from the pillow, it was still heavy from sobbing herself to sleep. She tried to put all the pieces together; the humiliation and agony of yesterday stabbed at her sharply. She couldn't quite process all that had happened, how someone she'd loved could have treated her like that but he had and she'd run to the only person she wanted to see. As Chloe threw back the heavy blankets, her whole body ached as if someone had literally punched a hole in her chest and ripped out her heart. She stepped unsteadily onto the cold wood. In the apartment she'd left behind, she'd have been getting up to the glorious warmth of underfloor heating and deep pile carpet. The cool smooth texture she stood on now was another reminder that this was all real and not just a bad dream. Outside of the mass of wool and feathers, the room felt cool so she rummaged through the carry on suitcase she'd hurriedly packed, looking for something suitable to wear and one by one tossed each item of clothing aside. All of it belonged to a former life.

What on earth am I going to wear? She grabbed a blanket and wrapped it round her shoulders then, still in her pyjamas, found her way down to the kitchen that Roisin had pointed out to her last night – she opened the door and it was exactly how she imagined it would be. The floor was practical hard-wearing stone, worn by centuries of boots tramping across it – and was even colder on bare feet! The large wooden table that ran the length of the room was rubbed smooth by plates and elbows. Spices, a mixing bowl and bags of flour stood tidied at one end. A glamorous elderly woman with long wavy grey hair piled loosely on top of her head looked up from the sink where she was drying dishes and gave her a huge smile as she walked in.

'There she is,' cried Chloe's best friend, appearing from behind her gran. 'Consciously uncoupled from man and job in one day – now that takes some doing.'

Chloe gasped with hurt. Roisin was the only person in the whole world who could say something like that and usually get away with it but it was too much too soon. To her horror, a big fat tear escaped and she hurriedly wiped it away.

'I'm sorry.' She sniffed. 'I'm being stupid.'

Roisin looked mortified and before she knew it, Chloe was wrapped in her arms and being hugged until she thought she might pass out.

'No, I'm the one who should be sorry,' said Roisin. 'Not quite time for my warped sense of humour is it?'

'Not yet,' replied Chloe, clearing the last of the tears and then looking up in astonishment at what she was now seeing. Roisin caught her glance and let go of her grip.

'So what do you think?' Roisin asked holding her arms out wide.

Across the beams of the kitchen were streamers, bunting and tinsel. Propped up on a chair at the head of the table was a big cardboard banner shouting *WELCOME HOME!* Adorning the message were lots of love hearts fashioned in glitter.

'I made it myself.'

'I can tell,' replied Chloe and this time the tears were from laughter. Roisin always managed to make any day seem brighter. She really did love her crazy friend. 'Thank you, it's ... *unique*. And I love the Happy New Year bunting.'

'Well we didn't have "forget the loser" and it is a new start so kind of a new year and being back with me means you're home don't you think? Anyway, we need to feed you – come and meet Gran properly.'

Chloe wasn't exactly sure how to greet Gran. A handshake would be too formal – should she wave? Her quandary was answered by the woman holding out both arms and inviting her to take part in the second hug of the morning.

'I heard what happened and I'm very sorry. You can stay here as long as you like. And I'm Heather by the way – Gran always sounds so old.'

'Thank you. Your home is lovely. The aga looks original do you still cook with it?' Chloe pointed to the huge stove which dominated the outside wall of the room.

'Of course not darling – I dry my hair with it.' The woman laughed, her eyes twinkling.

Chloe took a second to realise she was being teased; Roisin and Heather were obviously cut from the same cloth when it came to their sense of humour. And the strength of their hugs. Feeling every inch the city interloper, Chloe blushed while Roisin gave her gran a friendly punch.

'Gran, be nice or Chloe won't help us with all the work that needs doing round here.'

Heather smiled and held out a chair for Chloe. With Chloe and Roisin sat, she proceeded to place before them a loaf of fresh fruit bread, still warm from the oven, butter in a strange dish shaped like a spouting whale with an Icelandic flag on it, and a jar of homemade jam. Roisin cut some chunky slices from the loaf, spread them with butter and handed one to Chloe. It was melt-in-the-mouth delicious; the warmth brought out the cinnamon flavor making something very ordinary, very special indeed – it even surpassed food from Chloe's favourite deli. To Chloe it felt like a big doughy-embrace and the first real food she had tasted in years.

'Good isn't it?' asked Roisin after they'd both sat eating in silence for a while, apart from the occasional groan of pleasure.

'Good doesn't come near, it's … *ohhh*. I don't think there's actually a word to describe how gorgeous this is.'

From her rocking chair by the window, Chloe saw a little smile of pride on Heather's face – she waved an "oh be gone with you" hand at Chloe but the smile stayed on her face.

'Gran was a bit of a rebel as a teenager so was sent to bed with bread and butter most nights,' Roisin explained. 'When she grew old enough, she started baking her own bread and developing the recipes. It's kind of a thing in this house – fantastic bread. After this, I'll show you round. Wear something casual.'

'I didn't really bring anything.'

'Well you're not wearing the suit you arrived in – it'll look as if the bailiffs have turned up,' said Roisin. 'No worries, I've loads of stuff you can borrow while you're here.'

'Could we not go shopping?' blurted Chloe just a little too quickly – horrified she might actually have to dress like Roisin for even a few days.

'Ha – got you. At least you're smiling now.'

'What is that you're wearing anyway?' Chloe was taking in Roisin's brightly coloured harem pants and waistcoat. 'Are you planning on starting to tell fortunes or to just run away with the circus?'

'Maybe both. I can tell yours for a start – you're about to have a huge adventure with your gorgeous and talented friend. So eat up and let this glorious coastline start working its magic on you'

It already was. Chloe smiled softly knowing she was in exactly the right place to recover. Roisin had a way of making things better and although she'd never visited Roisin's home before, her friend was right – just being with her felt like coming home. They'd clicked from the first moment they'd met in Fresher's Week at Liverpool University and realized they had a lot in common. They were both studying English

Literature, they were both Scorpios and they were both from the same county albeit opposite ends.

'Like we were separated at birth,' Chloe remembered Roisin saying.

In those three years, they saw each other through bad boyfriends, impossible exams and terrible haircuts. After graduation they shared a flat in Newcastle city centre – Chloe working for a local advertising agency and Roisin at an independent theatre. London called after a couple of years with an amazing opportunity for Chloe and they went their separate ways. They visited each other every couple of months and took holidays together at least once a year to begin with but then work priorities took over and they saw less of each other. With their thirtieth birthdays just around the corner, both their lives turned on a sixpence. Roisin lost her mother and retreated from her old life completely to India while Chloe, unable to comfort her friend in any way, looked around for someone who might need her.

Roisin left some of her "plainer" clothes – cropped purple jeans and a tie-dyed T-shirt – out for Chloe while she was in the shower. They had once shared each others' clothes all the time but that was ten years ago and now everything was a bit tight. Chloe struggled to fasten the top button; seven years in London, sitting on the tube, then at a desk, and finally on a sofa had taken their toll. Chloe looked at herself in the mirror – the woman staring back at her looked like a slightly podgy farmhand. In fact the only signal that she'd ever held a professional job recently was her gorgeously shaped eyebrows. She ran her fingers over them, smoothing the perfect arch, happy that, however trivial, there was something good to cling on to. Chloe brushed her dark wavy hair straight and scraped it back into a tight ponytail; that was more like it – at least she could control her hair. Lord knows she'd had no control over things yesterday; everything seemed to spiral into freefall so quickly. She'd needed to escape immediately.

Here. To Roisin. Somewhere she could curse Jonathan, drink too much wine and sing *I will Survive* until the wee hours of the morning. Just for a couple of weeks. She knew she'd have to go back eventually, to pick up the pieces of her career and her disastrous love life. But one day, not yet. This was her time-out.

Chapter Two

Chloe hadn't been able to see much when they'd arrived last night but she remembered looking up at the stars and thinking back to her childhood. She'd grown up in rural Northumberland, in the market town of Hexham which was about an hour from here. The skies always seemed so vast there and once she'd asked her dad if their town had more sky than anywhere else. He'd smiled and told her that certainly it did then pointed out the Plough and Orion's Belt. She could still recognise both of them but that was pretty much the extent of her knowledge. She'd decided on the drive here from the station that this place had to be twinned with the Milky Way – it had felt so ethereal. Now as she stepped out into the bright June sunshine, the sky was just as vast but instead of indigo it was a glorious cornflower.

Chloe inhaled the sea air and looked around. The main farmhouse was a little tired around the edges but it could be picture perfect; a traditional stone building with four windows placed symmetrically around a door whose peeling paint looked to once have been red but which was now faded into a kind of puce pink. It stood at the head of a courtyard flanked on either side by the former stables which were now evidently converted into living accommodation. The farmhouse and its buildings were set in miles and miles of fields which stretched like rolls of green velvet until they reached the sand dunes and over them, the bay. The house had uninterrupted views of the sea and a horizon that seemed infinite.

'Wow.'

'Spectacular isn't it?' said Roisin now standing beside her.

Chloe nodded, shaking herself out of her thoughts.

'Wait till you see the sunrise we get here. There's nothing like it anywhere in the world – but then I'm biased.'

'We used to get gorgeous sunsets in London. I'd usually be working late enough to watch them from the office and the whole building would be swathed in this orange glow.'

'Sounds more like a nuclear explosion to me. Come on, I'll tell you the plans,' said Roisin, leading her away from the view and back into the house. 'It's been in Gran's family for years. I used to come here as a kid and we always had a brilliant time.'

Chloe listened to the memories as they strolled from room to room. She could see it was a well-loved home, one where Roisin had felt comfortable chalking her height on the wall and wearing shoes indoors. It reminded her of something Jonathan had said early on, that he wanted to live somewhere messy with kids and dogs free to run around. Chloe pushed that thought away and bit her lip to stop it trembling; even if he had been telling the truth, he wouldn't be living there with her. Roisin showed her the paint on the doors, chipped from being barged through and slammed during play while the carpets in the hallway were threadbare from roller skating. It wasn't surprising Roisin had come back.

'Gran used to host painting retreats here when I grew up – she loved having the place full of people. So that's what I plan to do.'

'Paint?'

'No – bring back the people,' replied Roisin. 'I'm going to open it up as a wellness retreat.'

Chloe raised her eyebrows discreetly but said nothing – it might be a spectacular setting but calling it a wellness retreat was stretching the power of fresh air a bit far. They kept walking. The ground floor of the house was divided into two halves and they'd reached the right hand side: a huge space which ran from the front of the house to the back with French windows overlooking the bay.

'And this was the guest dining room where Gran held the painting classes if the weather was too bad to be outside;

I'm going to convert it and use it as my yoga studio.' Roisin waved Chloe in with a flourish.

'You teach it now?'

'Yep, I qualified when I was in India,' replied Roisin. 'So what do you think?'

While she was unquestionably impressed with what she could see of the view, the rest of the room was a bit of a mess. As she studied the overflowing cabinets down one side of the room, Chloe spurted out, 'Jeez, what's all this crap?' She instantly regretted it.

The so called yoga studio was like one of those strange museums they have in small towns the world over. Shelf after shelf was filled with the likes of plastic Eiffel Towers, Grand Canyon snowdomes and dolls in national dress; faded and dust covered, they spoke of an era before selfies became reminders of holidays and adventures. Chloe guessed that wherever this lot had come from, the whale butter dish had a similar origin.

'Hey, less of the crap, thank you very much. The guests brought them for Gran. It was kind of a joke – she always gave them a little something from here and asked them to bring something for her. There's a book in her bureau with the names of everyone who stayed here and what they brought. It's lovely and a bit mad all at the same time – a bit like Gran really.'

They walked through a side door which led to a small lounge where mountains of cushions, vases, photographs and ornaments added to the collection of clutter. Chloe picked up a few pieces and looked at them more closely – Roisin was right, they were all a little bit mad but the sentiment behind each of them had been lovely.

The lodge bedrooms in what had been the stables were much the same, in fact worse as Roisin explained that her gran kept each room for a specific person so they were able to leave personal belongings. With someone's family photos on the walls, throws on the beds and coats and jumpers in the wardrobes, entering each room felt like an intrusion.

'But none of these people come here anymore, right?' asked Chloe.

Roisin shook her head. 'Many of them were older than Gran anyway so for all I know they might have passed on. I know she did get an invitation to the funeral of one of them.'

Even worse than clutter: a dead person's clutter. Chloe could see this place had some potential when she stood outside, but coming in was a whole different ballgame and she wondered whether her friend realized that.

'At least there are no dead animals on the walls,' she said, voicing one of her major dreads on entering the house.

'Err, there is one.' Roisin opened the door to the next bedroom to reveal a very old, very worn weasel mounted in a glass cage. Both women grimaced then burst out laughing.

'Did you spend a lot of time here then? I remember at Uni you said your gran lived on the coast but I don't remember you coming here.'

'Oh we came every summer when I was a kid but as soon as I hit sixteen I was a bit embarrassed about the place to be honest; an old farmhouse with my mad hippy mother and gran. It's sad really. I didn't appreciate what they had until it was too late but like all of us back then I was desperate to see the world and "have a life".'

'I know what you mean.' Chloe sighed. 'But I remember your mum and she always followed her own path and wanted you to do the same. I bet she'd be happy that the path led back here.'

'She would. She'd say it was serendipity. Come on, I'll show you the rest of the place.'

Everywhere they went, the song remained the same. Chloe could see that Roisin was building her dream in a piece of paradise that had fallen from grace somewhat. There was potential everywhere but it was undoubtedly going to be hard work; the type of work she imagined her friend had never attempted to tackle before. Roisin explained that they had hired someone to do the structural work but the builders had left a mountain of rubble to clear. The stables had been well converted but several years of neglect had crept into each corner and started to breed. Chloe didn't have to look for the mould as they walked around; she could smell it the moment she walked through a door.

'How did it get so … tired?' Chloe asked. 'If your gran had guests to stay?'

'In the year after mum died, neither of us could face being here. When I went to India, Gran left for France and lived with one of her artist friends. This place was locked up until a few months ago but … You don't escape pain, wherever you go, and this year I just needed to be here for the anniversary of mum's passing.' She smiled ruefully before continuing, '*Anyway*! We will get it back in shape. It'll be a labour of love won't it?'

'We?' From the way Roisin now smiled at her, there could be absolutely no doubt what she was hoping for.

'Come on! Some manual work will do you good. You can bash that man right outta your hair while you're beating the carpets.'

Roisin had that big daft grin on her face and Chloe knew she simply couldn't say no. Her friend had picked her up when she'd most needed it and besides, she was right. Hammering and scrubbing like crazy for a couple of weeks would certainly stop her fretting.

'You're right. It'll be cathartic, and I'd be glad to help,' said Chloe before gently adding, 'but you do know that I can't stay too long don't you? I just abandoned everything in London and there'll be so much to sort out with the flat. Plus I'll need to find another job sooner or later.'

'I hear you. Sooner … or later.'

Chapter Three

Over the next fortnight, they worked liked Trojans to clear out the clutter. Having got Heather's blessing – *we have to look to the future now girls, not dwell on the past* – they began with the creepy dolls in national dress. With no money to hire a skip, rubbish was cleared by the carload and driven to the tip. Finding that Roisin was more of a problem than Heather as she told Chloe the stories behind the souvenirs she recognized and speculated on those she didn't, Chloe took charge and insisted they get themselves into a rhythm or nothing would get done. Every day, Chloe decluttered the bedrooms and threw the rubbish into the yard, then they both loaded Roisin's jeep before Roisin took everything to the tip and unloaded it. Chloe had carte blanche to throw out anything at all and after negotiation, Roisin was strictly forbidden from bringing any of it back.

'Let me keep one thing for each lodge, please,' begged Roisin.

'One,' replied Chloe wagging her finger at her friend. 'And I'll know if you've kept more.'

The simple rhythm of working together began to ease Chloe's pain. At the end of each day they showered their aching bodies then took a short walk on the beach before eating a home-cooked meal, and retiring to bed. Chloe hated the moment everyone said goodnight as that was when her mind became free to ponder. Emails and messages from friends dragged her back into her London life and while she was there she couldn't help going over and over the last weeks of their relationship, looking for signs she'd obviously missed. She only slept when she'd exhausted herself trying. The days were so much better; Chloe made sure she had no time to think about life outside this declutter, and the problems she'd arrived with were no match for flaking paint and the cost of new flooring. Any time her brain tried to replay the events of that day, Chloe turned up the playlist that accompanied their work and while scrubbing even harder, she belted out their favourite songs until she could no longer hear her own thoughts.

One day, she and Roisin pulled up a corner of the threadbare carpet in the hall where, under layers of old linoleum and ancient decaying underlay, they found the original parquet. All it would take was a few hours of polishing and it would look fabulous.

'Are all the rooms on the ground floor like this one?' she asked her friend.

'I have no idea,' she replied. 'Let's find out shall we?'

Together they dragged up all the carpets and to their delight found beautiful wooden floors underneath. Heather joined them afterwards and all three grabbed brooms and mops, throwing themselves into the dusting, sweeping, scrubbing and polishing. By the end of their efforts, they were completely worn out but the potential of this gorgeous place was literally starting to shine.

Later that same day, Chloe and Roisin drove into the village centre with a list of things they needed and as Roisin parked up and headed to a farm supplies store to buy paint, Chloe took a proper look around. It was Friday afternoon and she couldn't help but contrast the quiet street in front of her with how London would be right now, how it had been on the day she'd left. They were chalk and cheese. She decided it was the kind of place elderly aunts would drive to on a Sunday afternoon, possibly dragging reluctant young children. She could imagine them complaining that it was small and boring; begging to go home, back to their bedrooms where they'd lie on their beds chatting with friends on the phone or on social media. But it really was a very pretty place and she wondered why her parents never brought her here.

The bay housed a small harbour with the local pub at one end, brightly painted shops and houses on the front street overlooking the sea and the track to the farmhouse at the other end. Tattered bunting in the Northumberland flag colours of red and gold was strewn from the lampposts while hanging baskets proudly displayed their summer flowers and a plaque declared Kyrrby the winner of the Best Kept Village back in 2015. Neat blackboards with menus and funny messages stood outside the bars and shops to tempt people in. The village was certainly trying it's best but there was no getting away from the fact that it was quite simply deserted.

Chloe walked towards the beach hut that housed the tourist information office and saw a man with his arm in a sling turning the sign on the door over to open. Outside the building was a box of magazines tied up with string. The man tried to pick them up with his good arm but couldn't so started shuffling the box along the pavement with his foot.

'I'll help you with that,' said Chloe trotting forwards to pick the box up – then struggling herself to lift it; it was far heavier than it looked.

'Or maybe I will,' said a voice behind her. An arm reached in front of her and picked it up with ease. Chloe's eyes followed the arm upwards towards the body and then a face; a tanned face; a tanned face with sparkling eyes and long lashes; a tanned face on top of a muscular body, and a mass of wavy, dark blond hair to finish it off. Chloe realized she was staring and that her throat had gone dry.

'You don't look as if you've any strength in you.' The face laughed.

What a cheek! Chloe was about to protest and tell him why she hadn't any strength left in her – that she'd been scrubbing floors all morning.

'I'm Andy by the way – I run the Surfshack.'

Instead she found herself taking the outstretched hand and shaking it very firmly, hoping to change this man's opinion of her. She didn't know whether or not it worked but her fingers were aching from the effort.

Andy from the Surfshack put the box of magazines down on a shelf and picked up some scattered flyers that lay on the floor of the hut. Chloe noticed that some of them were advertising Roisin's yoga classes.

'That Roisin is always posting these things through the letterbox,' said the man running the hut. 'I don't know why she bothers – they always get trampled.'

Chloe sighed and took them from Andy, smoothing them with her palm and removing the most dog-eared. It was an incredibly tight space and the old man seemed to have no spatial awareness; Chloe had to pull herself tight against the walls and hold her breath just to avoid brushing up against Andy. The shelves of the little hut were overflowing with leaflets but many were obviously out of date. Chloe took out the leaflets inviting visitors to book their Christmas lunches and stacked Roisin's in their place. Andy opened the box with a penknife.

'So where do you want all these, Charlie?' he asked, holding up some free lifestyle magazines.

'You might as well leave half of them in the box for them to collect next month,' said the injured man, evidently Charlie. 'I keep telling the publishers that they're sending too many. With the number of visitors we get, they'd have to take a dozen each to empty a box that size.'

He smiled at them both as if he was expecting a little laugh at his comment. Chloe offered a rueful smile before pursing her lips; a village with no visitors and an information centre that was still advertising the previous Christmas wasn't exactly a promising set-up for Roisin.

Andy voiced her thoughts exactly. 'Then we need more visitors not a smaller box of magazines,' he said. Looking at Chloe, he added, 'You're here to help Roisin aren't you?'

Chloe was slightly taken aback that the guy facing her with

his hands on his hips knew her business. 'Yes, I'm helping her get the place ready. We're giving it a fresh coat of paint tomorrow.'

'It'll need more than a coat of paint to get people in.'

Despite thinking exactly the same only a few days ago, Chloe now felt the need to defend her friend's dream and told him she was sure it would be a great success.

'Nah, he's right,' said Charlie. 'Everyone needs more customers here. Visitors like the castles you see – and we don't have one.'

He told her that Kyrrby, despite having a stunning beach, was nestled between two of the most famous castles in the county and the coastal road meant you could drive from one to the other completely bypassing the village. And that's what most people did. As he spoke, she realised that would be why her parents never brought her here as a child. Her dad liked to go to nearby Bamburgh and Dunstanburgh to explore the castle walls and she loved to play on the huge beaches so they'd never ventured further.

Chloe muttered something about being sure the village had lots of attractions before she left the hut. She couldn't help but wonder how on earth Charlie ever got the job of promoting the village. As she walked along the front street, Andy caught her up.

'I hear you used to work in a big London ad agency.'

'You seem to have heard a lot about me,' replied Chloe, certain that there was a hint of disdain in the way he'd said "ad agency". She started to walk a little quicker but to her annoyance he stepped up the pace too. Chloe knew if she walked much further at this speed, she'd be out of breath and didn't want to add to his seemingly low impression of her.

'I care about Roisin,' said Andy as he stood in front of her. 'And I know that this place means a lot to her. I wouldn't want her to get hurt.'

'And why would I hurt her? I've known her since Uni.'

'And I've known her since we were kids, and you might not mean to hurt her but I know your type – you'll dump her as soon as London comes calling again …'

Chloe opened her mouth to tell him how arrogant he sounded – really how dare he! – but was interrupted by the woman they were talking about.

'Ah good, you've met,' Roisin said cheerily. 'This is the marketing guru I was telling you about, Andy, and Chloe, this hunka hunka burnin' love runs the surf and kayak place, as you can probably guess.'

'He is kinda the clichéd poster boy for it,' replied Chloe, hoping he'd pick up on her jibe.

'Then we can put him on the poster,' declared Roisin. 'He's offered to give our guests lessons – when we have guests that is.'

'Just let me know when you need me,' said Andy, high-fiving Roisin and nodding a goodbye to Chloe.

'You told him I worked in an ad agency,' said Chloe, sounding just a little bit accusing. 'He seemed particularly scathing about that.'

'Oh don't mind Andy – he's a big softie when you get to know him.'

Chloe couldn't help the *humph* as they began the walk around the bay. Chloe scanned the shops as they strolled, ticking off a café, a second-hand bookshop, a gift gallery, an ice-cream shop, a grocery store and a chocolatier … this one bore the one sign that seemed to speak directly to her: *"When life gives you lemons, throw them right back and demand chocolate."*

'I have some important shopping to do,' she declared. 'I'll meet you on the beach.'

Chloe exited the shop twenty minutes later with half a dozen twee gift-wrapped packages – they'd be perfect pressies for her London friends. She'd texted them to announce the split with Jonathan on the train ride up here and said she was taking a break with an old friend. Then she'd deactivated her social media accounts so that she couldn't drive herself to despair following Jonathan's every move. She told her friends she needed a digital detox as much as a relationship one and hoped she sounded more in control than she actually felt. She pictured herself meeting them when she got back looking refreshed and recharged, handing them this little gift as a sign that everything was just fine and dandy now.

Chloe popped a chunk of salted caramel crunch in her mouth; it was exceptionally good. With each step and mouthful, her body filled with endorphins so that by the time she reached the bench where Roisin was sitting, Chloe felt quite fired up. She passed a little bag of chocolates to her friend.

'You should try these, they're gorgeous.'

'And seventy percent cocoa – you'll be high as a kite.'

Chloe held out her arms like an aeroplane and they both swooped along the track on the way back to the farmhouse. The warm breeze coming up from the sea brushed her skin and she felt alive. Grumpy surf-dude notwithstanding, this break was doing her the world of good.

Chapter Four

The next day, as they sat in the kitchen taking an afternoon break from decorating, there was a knock at the door which Heather went out to answer. When she returned, she was holding a letter and, at the same time, a gangly teenager with an Xbox complexion popped his head around the kitchen door.

'Oliver is here to see you,' said Heather distractedly ripping open the long white envelope and sitting in her rocking chair by the window.

'Perfect timing,' said Roisin waving him in to join them. 'Chloe, this is Olly. He's building my website. Come on then, show us what you've done.'

The boy sat down, pulled a laptop from his backpack and plonked it on the table.

'I've done exactly what you said.' He switched it on and his fingers flew across the keyboard until a picture of the house came up on the screen.

Chloe's interest was piqued. Roisin would definitely need a website and this was something she actually had some expertise in. She manoeuvred herself to better see the screen; it was a good photograph of the house and far enough away to hide any flaking paint. The image would certainly invite anyone visiting the site to take a closer look. She nodded in approval.

'What are you actually calling this place?' she asked.

'I was just going to keep the name it has – Rothburn House Farm but add Wellness Retreat,' replied Roisin.

'Rothburn House Farm Wellness Retreat,' repeated Chloe. It didn't exactly roll off the tongue and it didn't sound like the kind of place anyone she knew would be queuing up to visit. She needed to think about that one before saying anything and risking offence so asked Olly to show her the rest of the website. He clicked on a tab reading "our ethos".

'I saw that on another website and thought it sounded better than "what we're about",' Olly said proudly. 'I wrote in everything else exactly as you said.'

Chloe scanned what were evidently Roisin's words; they could have come from nowhere but her friend's mouth. Well if the name didn't have any pulling power, the ethos might just have people falling over themselves to find out who on earth had written this. It was hilarious.

"We don't believe you can get well by sitting around on your ass in a fluffy dressing gown and slippers. You get fat that way and don't be listening to anyone who tells you otherwise. Our ethos is that wellness (which is a daft word but we're using it anyway) comes from getting out there in the fresh air, doing a bit of walking and chatting then having a bloody good night's sleep. I don't know why all those people can't sleep or why they measure how long they sleep on their bloody phones but they won't need to do it here. You'll also find out what mindfulness is really about and it certainly isn't about daft internet quotes."

'You really did quote her word for word didn't you?' Chloe wiped tears of laughter from her cheeks and turned to Roisin who had her hand over her mouth in horror. 'Are you sure you want to do this? If you don't believe in what you're doing, it'll be pretty difficult.'

Roisin sighed. 'I do believe though. I really believe this place can make you feel good about yourself; it always did when I came to visit and you have to admit that since you've been here, you're looking a helluva lot better. I just don't believe in half the rubbish people seem to subscribe to. You know what the big thing is for this year?'

Roisin paused dramatically then declared, 'Tongue scraping. Flossing is out so use that string to scrape your tongue. I'm surprised you're not doing it already.'

Chloe resisted telling her that her ex-colleagues were already buying designer scrapers and that she had very nearly bought one in the chemist at the station.

'Who says I'm not?' She laughed. 'What do you think, Heather? Scraping the tongue – is it in or out?'

They turned to the old lady who sat with her head in her hand, the letter lying in her lap.

'What's the matter, Gran?' Roisin rushed over and knelt by her side, pressing the back of her hand to her gran's forehead. 'Are you okay?'

Heather nodded gently and handed her the letter. Roisin's eyes darted across it and she leapt to her feet.

'They can't do that! The bloody cheek of it.'

Chloe quietly thanked Olly and showed him out while Roisin continued to pace the floor, furiously waving the letter and threatening to kill someone. Heather held her hand out and urged her granddaughter to calm down.

'You won't believe what they're doing.' Roisin spoke bitterly to Chloe who had no idea who "they" were so let Roisin continue hoping that she'd work it out. 'Well it's not going to happen. I won't let it!'

Nope, not enough clues in that. Chloe looked over at Heather and held out her palms in question.

'Please sit down, sweetheart,' Heather urged Roisin and gently pulled her to a chair. 'We've had a bit of news,' she told Chloe.

'My delightful cousins,' spat Roisin, 'are trying to get power of attorney over Gran's finances so they can be the ones to sell the place.'

'I don't understand,' replied Chloe. 'Why would they want to do that?'

'Because they're grasping idiots with no sense of history or family or ...'

'Roisin darling, don't upset yourself,' said Heather. 'We have to think this through – they're my grandchildren too and I have to do right by everyone.'

Chloe watched Roisin's chest rise and fall as she worked to contain her emotions. She recognized the blank stare that followed shock. There was no way her friend was in the mood to think anything through logically so she would have to do Roisin's thinking for her right now.

'If you don't mind me asking,' she said to Heather, 'what is it that they want? And who exactly are "they"?'

'I have two other grandchildren – they live in Australia,' replied Heather, reaching out and taking hold of Roisin's hand. 'And I did tell all of you that when the day came, I'd leave this place to you all equally. I never thought anyone would be interested in living here but then when Roisin told me her idea, I thought well why not give it a try.'

'I'm going to buy the house from Gran,' said Roisin. 'As soon as I get paying customers, I'm going to apply for a mortgage. I want our history to live on forever.'

'Alas history won't pay their school fees or buy new cars,' said Heather.

'So your other grandchildren don't want Roisin living here?'

'They just think that because Roisin wants to live here and buy the house, I'll sell it to her at a cheaper price and they'll eventually lose out as their share will be smaller. I wouldn't let that happen but it's only natural that they're anxious.'

'But if they try to sell it to someone else, where do they expect you to live?'

'I imagine they see me in some care home with other biddies my age but if I could, I'd probably travel the world instead, pop my clogs on a cruise ship.' Heather smiled. 'They're not cruel but they want to be sure that they'll get their share I suppose. It's all a bit grubby isn't it? But the young need what the elderly have these days.'

That was certainly true; Chloe had only been able to afford the deposit on the flat because of an inheritance from her grandmother. Suddenly she felt tears prickling her eyes. Her grandmother hadn't been rich and Chloe had used that precious gift to buy a place with that scumbag. How could she have been so stupid? Chloe steadied herself, taking a deep breath.

'They don't need it. They're not even thinking about your needs,' Roisin was saying. 'You're staying right here with me.'

Chloe didn't know these relatives and they might very well be evil money-grabbers but then again, they might be ordinary families who could do with a leg up.

'Okay,' she said as calmly as she could. 'The facts are that Roisin wants to live here with you Heather and buy the farm from you. Your other grandchildren are worried that they'll lose some money if that happens, so maybe the solution is for you both to set a time limit and get proper valuations. You promise that by an agreed date, you'll either buy them out, Roisin – or step aside and let your gran do what she thinks is right.'

The room went silent apart from the deep breathing Roisin was struggling to control. Like a bull facing a matador, her nostrils flared and eyes narrowed. Heather stood up and patted her granddaughter on the back.

'That sounds eminently sensible to me,' she said. 'I'll draft a letter suggesting it and I'll send it second class so you've got more time. I know you can do this.' She planted a kiss on Roisin's head and winked at Chloe before taking back the letter and heading out.

'I think it'll take a little longer than second class postage to get everything up and running.' Chloe sighed. 'Do you think we could persuade her to send it by pigeon?'

Roisin wasn't going to laugh or smile or lighten the mood in any way. And to be honest, Chloe couldn't blame her. This was a serious threat to Roisin's dream and really piled the pressure on.

'I'm not trying to diddle anyone,' Roisin said. 'I would buy them out now if I could but I need time. Mum truly loved this place and it may have taken me until recently to appreciate what she saw in it but I hope it's not too late. Am I mad?'

'Obviously but that's beside the point.'

Roisin pulled a bottle of wine from the fridge. 'Too early?' she asked.

Chloe shook her head and stood to get glasses from the dresser. 'I think we need something for the shock.'

They sat twirling the golden liquid around, each deep in their own thoughts.

'Mum would have told my cousins to take a long jump off a short pier,' Roisin murmured.

'Sounds like the right advice.' Chloe smiled. 'I remember her dropping you off at the start of the second year – what was that thing she used to say?'

'Love many, trust a few ...' said Roisin.

'And always paddle your own canoe,' they said in unison. Roisin was smiling but tears were gently rolling down her cheeks.

'As soon as Mum got the diagnosis she moved back in here with Gran so I came too,' Roisin said. 'They both thought the sea air had healing properties.'

'Did she have chemo?'

Roisin shook her head. 'It was too advanced. I think that's why it's still so unreal. Cancer isn't supposed to be like that. You're supposed to battle bravely, do charity runs and shave your heads together – but she was gone so quickly. It's been nearly two years but I still expect her to walk in and ask me what I'm doing with the place. I feel as if she's here, Chloe, and I just can't let this place go.'

Roisin folded her arms onto the table and lay her head on them, sobbing softly. Chloe stroked her friend's back while the tears flowed. Eventually Roisin sniffed and lifted her head, rubbing the tears away with her sleeve.

'Afterwards, Andy was brilliant. He used to bring us groceries and tidy the garden. Gran used to babysit him when he was a kid – he said it was his turn to look after her.'

'But you left?'

'We both did,' replied Roisin. 'I guess we needed our own space to grieve. I taught English to pay my way in India but spent most of the time learning yoga and meditation.'

'That's why you want to recreate it here? Because it helped you.'

'Do you think I stand a chance?' Roisin asked, looking at her.

Chloe took a sip of wine; her head was telling her that creating a profitable retreat would be far more difficult than her friend could ever imagine but her heart was yelling at her, saying that she had to do everything she could to help make it happen.

Chloe emerged from her thoughts with an absolute clarity: yes. Her own life was a train wreck and she had a load of things that still needed sorting out; she had a flat to sell and a career to get back on track. She'd started applying for things and could keep doing that but she was in marketing after all, so right now the very least she could do while looking – was spend her time building a campaign to help Roisin.

'Of course you stand a chance,' she said, counting out the points on her fingers and making a mental to-do list as she'd always loved to at work. 'Number one, we need customers. Two – to get customers we need to advertise your business. Three, to advertise your business we need to find the USP, your unique selling point, the thing that really tells people – four – what you're about. And five – what to expect when they come here.'

Chloe had said that line or something similar in many a meeting with new clients and was starting to feel a buzz, certain that she could help her friend while keeping her own dreams alive. This was the marketing strategy for a brand new start-up and it would look great on her CV. She could do this and be back in the game.

'Can you help us sort that USP thing then?' Roisin asked.

'I can.' Chloe smiled. 'It's exactly what I do.'

Chapter Five

'So what happens at this festival then?' asked Chloe as she swirled the summer dress that had arrived today. In a pale mint colour that showed off her slight tan, it was slim fitting around the bodice then flared out into a knee-length skirt that brushed gently against her skin as she walked. Thank God for internet shopping. She was starting to at least look like her old self again, even if she wasn't quite feeling that way yet.

'Oh you know, usual stuff,' replied Roisin, looking rather different in her dungaree shorts and camisole top. 'A few stalls, some competitions and far too much eating and drinking.'

'Who organises it?'

'There's a committee but Charlie heads it up.'

'And there'll be lots of visitors?' Chloe was unable to imagine the man she met in the hut doing anything proactive.

'A few – why?'

'It's just a great opportunity to do some research,' said Chloe. 'I can ask people why they chose to come here and what they particularly like about it now they're here. And I could find out about their ideal wellness retreat – everything they tell me then gets built into your marketing campaign.'

'Do you want a clipboard?'

'Oh yes, if you have one. I love clipboards,' replied Chloe before realising that Roisin's shoulders were rocking with laughter. She threw one of her new flip-flops at her and it bounced neatly off her head.

'Good shot. I deserved that,' said Roisin handing it back. 'But I actually do have some somewhere – they might help make us look semi-professional.'

Kyrrby was certainly busier than usual when they arrived; a banner announcing the Midsummer Fayre hung alongside the tattered bunting and most of the shops were setting up outside tables to showcase their goodies and tempt visitors in. There were stalls selling home-made arts and crafts around the tourist information hut and the ice-cream shop had a queue snaking down the promenade. Then there was the square of sand on the beach that was being flattened by a huge roller.

'What's that for?' asked Chloe.

'The games that happen later,' replied Roisin. She flexed her biceps, imitating a strong man in a circus. In a deep voice she added, 'Feats of strength and endurance to find our strongest warrior.'

'I'll look forward to that.' Chloe laughed. 'I might even enter. I must stand a chance after all the work you've had me do.'

The podge that she'd noticed on that first morning here was definitely on its way out. Putting on the dress that morning she knew she was more toned and the fresh air had worked wonders on her complexion.

'With that I wouldn't bother – Andy always wins.'

Chloe found herself making an involuntary sound – he was going to be here? She wasn't quite sure how she felt about that after all Roisin had said.

'It sounds as if he's done a lot for you and Heather.'

'He was a rock when we needed one,' replied Roisin before smiling and adding, 'but don't tell him that – can't have him getting a big head.'

They strolled a little further on in silence.

'Penny for them?' asked Roisin.

'Just thinking about Jonathan,' replied Chloe. 'I used to call him my rock – turned out to be more of a pebble.'

Roisin smiled at her. 'Better to find out now I guess. How did you two meet? It was a work party wasn't it?'

'That's what I told everyone,' snorted Chloe. 'I was too embarrassed to tell the truth – it was online dating.'

'That's nothing to be embarrassed about. Loads of people get together like that.'

'I guess so and I couldn't believe my luck when he turned up – handsome and funny. But then conmen are always charmers aren't they?' replied Chloe, tucking her hair behind her ears and changing the subject. 'So when do these games start?'

'This afternoon, so we can do some of your questionnaires first then grab something to eat while we watch them if you like.'

It was a plan, so taking opposite ends of the promenade they split up to start getting answers to the market research. Everyone Chloe approached seemed to be a local and while their views were interesting, they didn't tell her why anyone would want to come to this village. After an hour or so her feet were aching so she plonked herself down on a bench. Within a few minutes, a woman she hadn't seen before came to sit down beside her and gaze out at the sea. Chloe wasn't going to look a gift horse in the mouth so asked the woman if she would answer a couple of questions about her visit.

'Thank you,' said Chloe when the woman agreed. 'So first of all, could I ask you what made you come here today?'

'Well it's absolutely beautiful isn't it?' replied the woman. 'I mean just look at the place.'

'Anything else?' asked Chloe. 'After all, the whole coastline is stunning so is there anything particular to this village that appeals to you?'

The woman seemed to think hard about the question before replying.

'The people here – they're absolutely lovely. And the pub – that's one of the friendliest places you could ever have a drink.'

Chloe was fervently writing everything down.

'Their ale is well kept and they've a great selection of wines too. The food's fantastic and I hear the landlady makes it all herself. She's apparently a bit of a looker too.'

Chloe stopped writing and looked up at the woman.

'I'm guessing you're the landlady.'

The woman roared with laughter and introduced herself. 'And you'd be guessing right. Maggie Farrell at your service. You're the one from the advertising agency who's helping Roisin aren't you?'

Chloe nodded and wondered how many others in the village Roisin had told.

'Well just make sure those guests of yours work up a thirst will you? There are vitamins in a gin and tonic you know – very few people realise that.'

Having dispensed her completely spurious advice, Maggie leapt up and tottered off across the road singing *A Spoonful of Sugar* – well that was the tune but the words seemed to have changed to being a glass full of gin helping the medicine go down.

'She also tells people crisps are a vegetable.'

Chloe turned to find Andy now standing behind the bench shaking his head as he watched Maggie leave. Boy he looked good in the plain white T-shirt that stretched across his chest and the cut-off jeans that cupped his incredibly cute butt.

'I suppose technically it is,' she replied, pulling herself together and standing up. 'Or was at least.'

She smiled up at him and in that millisecond saw his eyes behind those sunglasses checking her out. She smoothed down her dress, glad that at least today she looked half decent.

'Shouldn't you be oiling yourself up or whatever strong men do?' Roisin's voice interrupted their mutual admiration and lodged a completely inappropriate image in Chloe's mind.

'That'd be right,' said Andy. 'And maybe I'll get myself a pair of those leopard skin undies and a big moustache to twiddle.'

'I might even pay to see that,' added Chloe trying to join in the banter. When they both looked at her with furrowed brows she realised it had sounded more sleazy than funny.

They walked with him to the sand where a group of men were gathering and a loudspeaker announcement told everyone that the Kyrrby Midsummer Games were about to start. The girls watched as ropes were tugged, kayaks filled with sand were carried up and down the beach, press-ups were performed and barrels of beer were hoisted overhead. Andy paddled the ocean every day so it was no surprise that he made most things look easier than anyone else. There was only one event left and it wasn't about strength, but accuracy. At the far end of the games area, a brass bell had been suspended from a pole wedged into the sand. Contestants were given three sand-filled juggling balls and the winner was the one that made the bell ring three times. One by one the men took their shots and everyone hit the bell at least once but no one managed the treble. Chloe handed Roisin her clipboard and ran onto the sand; alongside all the huge muscled men, she felt positively tiny.

'Can I have a go?' she asked the judge.

The crowd whooped and, looking very entertained by her, Andy gathered up balls and put them at her feet. Chloe picked up the first, feeling the weight and balance of it in her hand. She nodded to herself and focusing hard, hurled it at the bell. There was a collective intake of breath from the crowd and then a round of applause as it skimmed the side but still caused the clapper to ring out – it counted. She picked up the second and again it skimmed the bell but counted and the audience started shouting encouragement. It was her third and final shot; she picked up the ball and gave it a kiss for luck. There was a collective intake of breath as she lined it up and hurled it with all her strength. The bell rang alright – she knocked it off the post! When she was declared the winner of that round, the crowd hollered and a contestant on the sand hoisted her up onto his shoulders parading her round. Chloe suddenly felt overwhelmed by all the noise and looked for a way down. As if reading her mind, Andy appeared and reached up to lift her off the man's shoulders and put her feet back on the ground.

'Well done you,' he said. 'You're full of surprises aren't you?'

Chloe thanked him and waving a goodbye to the crowd, grabbed Roisin to make a quick escape. She'd acted on impulse and while it had felt really good – especially that lift down – she really didn't want any more attention.

'I didn't know you were an ace marksman,' said Roisin as they plonked themselves down on a quiet bench. 'How did you learn to do that?'

'Instinct,' replied Chloe. 'It was the same shape and weight as a sourdough roll.'

Roisin frowned quizzically.

'It had already been the most horrendous day.' Chloe took a deep breath guessing it was time to get it all out in the open. 'I'd been "asked to resign", not sacked, that would have been illegal but that's what it really was. My boss made it very clear that my persona was very much non-grata.'

'Why?'

'They were pitching for a new account, a huge conglomerate – it was worth millions. The thing is, I know they're not very ethical – they eat up small businesses, pay peanuts and pump out plastic waste like there's no tomorrow. I asked to be excluded from the pitch team.'

'Sounds reasonable.'

'Not to them – if I wanted to pick and choose clients, I could do it somewhere else apparently. I was asked to leave.'

'So what next?'

'I went home and planned a lovely meal for us so we could talk over what had happened. I went to the deli to get sourdough and cheeses, some wine – you know the kind of thing. When I got back, Jonathan was already there. Standing in our kitchen. *With* his new woman. He told me we had to talk. I hurled the bread at him and got him right on the nose.'

'That would have been worth seeing.'

'It was.'

'So I'm guessing there's no chance of you getting back together after that?'

'None whatsoever,' replied Chloe finally exhaling.

They stood up and walked along the beach, then stood facing it as the sea rolled gently and Chloe closed her eyes, letting that swooshing of waves ebbing and flowing over sand, free her thoughts. In these three weeks she'd gone from hurt, betrayed and humiliated to angry and empty. There was still a big hollow in her chest but it wasn't Jonathan sized. She wouldn't take him back if he begged. Chloe reached down to her side and lightly touched the spot where Andy's hands had been when he lifted her down when she'd needed help. She shook that thought right out of her head and folded her arms.

'But enough about the past,' she said to Roisin, clearing her suddenly dry throat. 'Did you get anything from the research?'

'Nothing we couldn't have guessed.'

'Me neither,' said Chloe. 'There must be something unique about this village. Did anything interesting ever happen here? Is there no history to work with? We don't even have a Wikipedia page.'

'Well it's not official but if you speak to Charlie, he'll tell you that the Vikings actually settled here when they first arrived in Britain,' replied Roisin.

'Really?'

'Well according to him anyway; he says they fought in Bamburgh but those who settled did so here. They called it Kyrr Bay because it was the end of their days at sea. It means serenity or calm I think.'

Chloe swung Roisin round to face her. 'Are you kidding me?'

Roisin looked puzzled.

'You let me parade through town with that stupid clipboard and you called the place The Rothwhatshisname House Farm Wellness Retreat or whatever it was when we are literally standing on a gorgeous beach called *Serenity Bay*? It's a good job you're not in advertising.'

Roisin nodded as the penny dropped. 'The Serenity Farm Wellness Retreat.'

'*Noooooo* – for goodness' sake – simply Serenity Bay.' Chloe picked up a stick and, skipping along the beach, wrote the words in huge letters on the sand. '*Welcome to Serenity Bay* – this whole place is about wellness.'

The girls danced around the words then Roisin lay down next to them making sand angels with her arms. The summer sun glimmered in the background and this was definitely the shot for the home page of their website. They sat down on the sand, bubbling with excitement.

'So tell me what to expect when I visit Serenity Bay,' Chloe asked. 'I'm guessing it's all home-cooking for a start.'

Roisin nodded. 'As much seasonal produce as we can get. It'll be wholesome not fancy. Also I want people to get out in the fresh air, not sit in gyms or lounge around reading magazines. They'll do yoga on the beach, surf the waves or walk the coastal paths. I might need to change the words a bit but the sentiment Olly wrote was exactly right – this place should be about living, talking and laughing.'

'I'm sure we can bring in the Viking heritage somehow. They weren't exactly known for wellness but I'm sure they liked a laugh.' Chloe smiled. 'And there must be ways of getting other people in the village involved – we just have to think.'

Chapter Six

Back in the farmhouse that evening, Roisin dragged an old fashioned blackboard and easel into the kitchen and stood it at one end of the table.

'Where on earth did you dig this up from – the dark ages?' asked Chloe.

Heather wandered over and flicked a duster over the board. 'It was yours wasn't it? From when you used to come here as a little girl. You used to sit in your little chair beside me and draw pictures while I painted. In the cellar was it?'

Roisin nodded. 'Behind a sledge, a bike and dozens of hula hoops – why on earth would we have so many of them?'

'We used them to keep our waists trim,' replied Heather, putting her hands on her hips. Now that she'd dragged in the sides of the loose tunics she constantly wore, the girls could see the remnants of an hourglass figure. 'You couldn't let yourself go, not back then, not if you wanted to wear all the fashions and nab yourself a man.'

'You could teach our feminist module,' said Roisin, heaving the blackboard onto the easel.

'Oh I burned my bras and kept a waistline at the same time.' Heather laughed. 'And anyway, your ways aren't working out that wonderfully are they? Two good-looking girls alone with an old woman in the back end of nowhere.'

'Touché,' replied Chloe, raising a mug of tea to her. 'Now shall we get started?'

She picked up a piece of chalk and wrote some words across the top of the board.

Serenity Bay – restores mind, body and soul.

'It's about having a truly authentic experience in a place with a long history of making people welcome,' she said.

'What does a *truly authentic experience* mean?' asked Heather.

'We need to work out the details but Roisin wants this place to be a wellness retreat based on nature's power rather than machines and lotions,' replied Chloe. 'The food would be as local as possible. For example, I think I heard a cockerel the first morning I got here so for breakfast we could serve our own fresh eggs and more of that gorgeous freshly-baked bread.'

Chloe was hoping to inspire her audience but they both suddenly started laughing, tears in their eyes.

'Are you going to tell the cockerel he has to start laying eggs or shall I?' snorted Roisin.

'You do it,' replied Heather. 'I'll get the milk that came from one of the bulls out there.'

Chloe stood, hands on hips, like a schoolteacher in front of a naughty class.

'Will you two take this seriously?'

Roisin mouthed an apology then sneaked a look at her gran who was focusing on the table but her shoulders were jigging up and down and when she eventually looked up at Chloe, tears of laughter glistened in her eyes.

'Oh my cheeks hurt,' she said wiping the tears away. 'I'm sorry. Oh! I have something you might like.'

She pottered into the pantry where the girls could hear her clattering about. When she re-emerged, her arms were filled with glass jars. Roisin raised a quizzical eyebrow as they were dumped down in front of them.

'They tell me that eating out of jars is a big thing now.' Heather shook her head in bewilderment then walked over to the kettle, picking it up and twisting it around as if it were some foreign object.

'And steaming your downstairs parts,' she continued in earnest bemusement. 'Something I sincerely hope you won't be offering your guests. I mean, how on earth do you do it anyway?'

Chloe and Roisin doubled up. 'We promise, Gran, absolutely no downstairs steaming in the kitchen,' choked Roisin.

'Good,' nodded Heather. 'I'd never be able to look at that kettle the same way again.'

She left the room singing *Polly put the kettle on, Souki sat on top of it ...*

'Credit where it's due, she's been reading up on all the trends in wellness,' said Chloe still laughing. 'The jars are actually perfect. Overnight oats are still in – people will love them and that's breakfast sorted. I guess we just have to agree the other twenty-three hours of the day now.'

They sat for the next couple of hours throwing ideas around. Linking with any sort of Viking heritage was proving difficult.

'We can hardly advertise pillaging as one of our activities,' said Roisin.

'It's more of a Nordic theme, like hygge and campfires.'

The blackboard started to fill up with activities like Roisin's yoga, hiking along the coastal path, stargazing and sea kayaking. The menu would have fresh locally caught fish and they'd also serve local ales, which might not appear in most health retreats but Chloe could imagine sitting on the beach on a clear night enjoying a beer after a day of action.

'So we'll be the antidote to all those really extreme regimes that no one can possibly maintain?' asked Roisin. 'A little of what you fancy does you good.'

'Exactly. Now, guests will probably stay for at least a long weekend so we'll need three or four days of activities covering every hour of the day, menus agreed and some luxuries, like massages or facials. It might be all about nature but if you're stressed out, a massage at the end of the day is just blissful, besides which, people will want to go home looking better.'

Roisin stuck her jaw out and studied the ceiling, deep in thought. 'I think Fiona in the village does facials and maybe Andy could turn his hand to massages.'

'Andy?' exclaimed Chloe. Her thoughts drifted back to the

beauty spa she used to visit in London. Every month she'd go for a full day to have all her maintenance treatments and after the pain of waxing, she'd treat herself to a full-body massage. She remembered how good it felt after a full week at work and then, horrified, realized the massage she was imagining was much better than any she'd ever had in real life and on top of that, the imaginary hands on her skin certainly didn't belong to her old therapist!

She shook her head and forced herself back into the real world. Her next appointment would be coming up soon; she'd have to remember to cancel it. No, not cancel it, postpone it. By the time she'd helped Roisin with the retreat she'd probably be ready to get back to normal – whatever that meant. She knew how it started anyway – facing Jonathan, selling the flat then getting back on track with a new job and a new apartment. She'd be ready when the time came, but meanwhile there was a lot to do here.

'I know he teaches his surf students some stretches when they finish,' Roisin was saying as she drifted back into the conversation. 'And I think he shows them how to massage their shoulders – he's a man of many talents.'

'Hmm, maybe he is but we're probably better off having someone qualified.'

They got back to the brainstorm and Chloe was feeling increasingly positive with each activity that was chalked up. It was starting to sound like the sort of place she'd want to go to. She could picture herself finding the details of somewhere like this and suggesting it for a team retreat. The problem was, she wasn't simply *going* to a place like this, she was helping manage a place like this and she knew as much about stargazing and sea kayaking as she did about nuclear physics. She asked the million dollar question.

'Who can we get to run all these activities?'

'We need to get ourselves down the pub tomorrow morning,' declared Roisin. 'We can see if anyone knows anyone who can do any of it – it would be great to get as many of the locals involved as we can.'

'That helps to advertise the whole village too. Now what else will we need while we're there?'

They finished a potential list of activities then walked around the house and lodges noting what they might expect in a nature-based retreat. Chloe's technique was to walk into a room with her eyes closed and once Roisin told her where she was, she'd open them and say the first thing that came into her head.

'Okay – the sofa room for relaxing, talking, reading.'

'It's cosy.' Chloe nodded. 'But we could make it even more snuggly with some books, new rugs, throws and cushions – cheerful colours, natural fibres.'

'The yoga room.'

They walked into the former dining room which looked out onto the sea through it's enormous floor to ceiling windows. If you only faced in that direction, it was stunning but the rest of the room was quite bland without the souvenirs.

'I'm not surprised your gran held painting classes here with this light. What did she paint?'

'Landscapes mainly,' replied Roisin, gesturing to the view. 'The canvases must be in her cupboard.'

Roisin walked to the back edge of the room and pulled aside a heavy curtain to reveal a set of double doors that Chloe hadn't noticed before. When Roisin opened them, Chloe stood open-mouthed at the stacks of canvases leaning against the walls. They pulled one out.

'Wow, she's really good,' said Chloe, looking at a pastel seascape where a hundred shades of blue from the darkest to the slightest swirled to create a distant storm and peaceful haven simultaneously. 'Does she still paint?'

'Not any more.'

'We should definitely put these up in here and maybe some of the smaller ones in the lodges – they're really calming.'

They took a couple through to the lodges and, as expected, the hand-painted scene which matched the view out of each window was just perfect. Aside from the coat of paint, the rooms needed accessorizing; they needed to feel gentle and welcoming.

'You know those souvenirs you let me keep,' said Roisin. 'I have an idea.'

She suggested placing one of them in each room and putting a little card beside it explaining who had brought it to the house and where they came from.

'We could name each room after the souvenir – the Snowdome Lodge or the Harbour Lodge after the Sydney Harbour Bridge model we found. I think it would mean a lot to Gran.'

'It's a lovely idea,' said Chloe. 'So all we need now is a little scent and something to create ambience.'

'You're going to go all clichéd girlie on me aren't you?' Roisin laughed.

'You cannot have a retreat, not even an authentic all-action retreat without those two things, besides which with our decorating skills we need as much low light as we can muster.'

Chloe looked at Roisin sternly as if she were peering over school ma'am glasses as she wrote at the very top of their list: *Candles! Lots & lots of gorgeous scented candles!*

'You can take the girl out of London ...' mocked Roisin, taking the list and shoving it in her pocket.

Chapter Seven

The next day, with the excitement of the festival over, the village was back to its usual quiet self. An old collie lay outside the pub yawning before deciding whether or not to have a bit of a scratch. In the end it was too much effort so it lay back down again.

'Where to first?' asked Chloe.

'Louise at the gift shop,' replied Roisin. 'She sells those scented candles, so that should keep you off my back.'

They walked along the street that was now becoming very familiar to Chloe. The pretty facades of the shops still created a picture-perfect village scene as they waited expectantly for customers like shy debutantes at a ball waiting for someone to ask them to dance. Roisin and Chloe walked through a bright pink door and although the bell rang announcing their arrival, it took a few moments for someone to appear from the back room. When she did, she took one look at Roisin and trundled up to her, pinching both her cheeks.

'You're the image of your gran,' she said smiling. 'I heard you were both back at the farmhouse for good. So what are you up to?'

She listened as Roisin explained that they were opening up the house as a health retreat and gave her the list of things they needed.

'Oh Lord, this is quite a list.' She whistled. 'I don't keep nearly this amount in stock. I could get them to you in a few weeks if you like.'

Chloe had the word "internet" on her lips and was sure she could get a bulk order of candles by this time tomorrow when Louise continued.

'That's if I start making them this afternoon.'

'You make them here?' asked Chloe, getting an 'of course' in reply. The cogs started whirring. 'Can they be made in a normal kitchen? Like the one at the farm?' She got the same reply.

'Rois, what if we buy up what we can but then have the guests make their own signature candles? Louise, could you teach the guests? Are there kits you could use? Something that would suit novices? And can they be scented?'

Louise nodded enthusiastically at each of the questions fired at her.

Roisin clearly loved the idea and ticked *candles* off her list. 'Next, pub,' she said. 'Let's see if we can find anyone to lead the walks.'

The Fiddler's Arms rang out with song as they walked through the door – and holding the broom like a microphone, the landlady was in full flow.

'... *I dreamed a dream in time gone by* ...'

Roisin coughed loudly and the songstress turned, patting the back of her hair before putting down the broom.

'That Susan Boyle, she's an inspiration isn't she? I always think it could have been me if I'd had the guts. I know all the musicals.'

As she led them back to the bar, Chloe whispered, 'Please do not ask her to run a singing workshop for the guests.'

'Spoilsport,' replied Roisin. 'Maggie, meet Chloe.'

'Oh we're old pals aren't we – now what can I get you ladies?' Maggie asked breathlessly and the girls explained what they were looking for.

'If you want someone who knows this area like the back of his hand, you'll want Mick the Mouth.' The landlady looked at the clock. 'It's only a quarter to one – he'll be in at five to. Will you have a drink while you're waiting?'

They ordered glasses of wine and a couple of sandwiches to tide them over and had barely started when, at five to one precisely, a man in a waxed jacket and tweed cap sauntered in. The landlady had the pint of ale ready. She handed it to him and nodded over to Roisin and Chloe.

'The landlady must be psychic,' said Chloe when Mick came over with his hand outstretched. 'She knew exactly when you'd be in.'

'Either that or I read the bus timetables,' hollered Maggie, repeating the line and laughing at her own witticism.

Mick sat down and took off his cap. Chloe hadn't expected the lake-blue eyes framed by laughter lines; he had to have been quite a looker in his younger days and even now, there'd be many a woman who'd fall for a silver fox like this. She made a mental note to find out his story as the man sitting in front of her couldn't have made it to this age without being pursued. Roisin kicked off with an interview of sorts, explaining that they were expecting some guests over at the farm and they needed someone to take them on a nature walk. Mick nodded and the landlady came over to eavesdrop, without even pretending to have another reason for standing behind him.

'We're told you know all about the bird and wildlife around here,' continued Roisin. Again Mick nodded. 'So would you be interested in doing it?' Another enthusiastic nod but no words.

'Oh, by the way,' explained Maggie seeing the glances between the girls, 'he's called Mick the Mouth because he never says a word.'

Horrified by the lack of political correctness and dismayed by what seemed like a waste of their time, Chloe asked the obvious question.

'If you don't mind me asking, how do you actually tell people what they're seeing?'

Mick winked at her and reached into his pocket. Taking out a dog-eared book, he demonstrated pointing at a flower and then pointing at it in the book, then pointing into the sky and again finding the imaginary bird on the pages.

'So you take this along and show people what they're seeing?'

He nodded.

'Don't forget the whistling,' nudged the landlady and Mick's eyes lit up. He closed his palms together and raised them to his lips. Blowing between his hands he made the sound of a seagull and then pointed said gull out to Chloe. Maggie and Roisin gave him a round of applause as the landlady cried out, 'Would your guests like to learn any tap-dancing? I wasn't half bad at it when I was a girl.'

She proceeded to demonstrate a heel-ball-turn which had Roisin in stitches. Chloe smiled meekly and excused herself.

She locked the door of the ladies cubicle and leant her head against the cool of the tiles. If this retreat was going to be a viable business for her friend, she couldn't let Roisin get distracted by Maggie and her desire to entertain everyone. She had to get back out there, pull Roisin to one side and create a proper recruitment process, a methodical way of finding out what people had to offer, evaluating them carefully and turning them down if they needed to, without causing offence. If this was going to work, they couldn't simply take on anyone who offered – or whistled – for that matter. She washed her hands, splashed her face and smoothed down her shirt ready to tell Mick that they'd be in touch once they'd considered his kind offer. When she walked back into the bar, Roisin greeted her with a huge hug.

'Great news! I've booked Mick, and Maggie has rung round everyone and they're all coming down to tell us what they can do at the retreat. It'll be a gas – our very own Serenity's Got Talent. We'll have a programme up and running before you know it.'

Chapter Eight

'Darling? Where on earth are you?'

Chloe had been putting off the call to her mother and wasn't totally ready for it now if she were honest. 'We're just back from our cruise so I called the apartment and Jonathan tells me you've left him.'

'I left him?'

'But why?' replied her mother completely missing the intonation. 'We thought there might be wedding bells soon. I've even been looking at hats. You won't find anyone better you know.'

Chloe took the phone from her ear, knowing her mother would be spending the next five minutes extolling the virtues of her ex. Her mum absolutely adored Jonathan though Chloe had always suspected it was really just the idea of him. Now as she listened, she wondered whether she was really all that different from her mum. He had been perfect on paper; a handsome guy who wanted to focus on his career before settling down, get on the property ladder and eventually move to the country. She couldn't believe her luck at the time. He was also the dream boyfriend to take home: a doctor training to be a brain surgeon. Once when they'd gone to stay at her family home for a few days, her parents had taken them to their local pub quiz. Her mother had waited until there was a difficult question before speaking out. Loudly.

'Gosh, you'd need to be a brain surgeon to answer that one. Good job we have one in the family.'

Chloe remembered blushing with embarrassment and pride in equal measures but now she recalled that night she could see Jonathan had looked quite happy with the attention.

Tuning back in to the call, Chloe could hear her father

yelling in the background but there was no way he would get control of the phone while her mum was still ranting.

'Are you sure it wasn't just a tiff? He might take you back. You shouldn't stay apart too long. Where are you staying? With someone from work? What about your lovely apartment?

Chloe sighed silently. She actually hated letting her parents down in any way. They'd done so much to help her through university and they simply loved the fact that she lived in London and worked in the glamorous world of advertising. She'd brought them down to a shoot once when one of their favourite TV stars was appearing in an advert for Battersea Dogs & Cats Home. They'd had to stay in a hotel because of the size of the flat but her and Jonathan had taken them out to dinner and for extortionately priced cocktails at the rooftop bar of the OXO Tower. Her parents had taken a million photographs including the exterior door of the hospital where Jonathan was training and had shown them to everyone back in Hexham. Heck, her parents had started showing the photos to complete strangers on the tube. Chloe thought back to that day, the glow of happiness on her parents' faces and the real relief she'd felt. They'd been so proud of her then and this was another reason to make sure she got her life back on track. She decided to keep the second piece of bad news to herself. When she did find that new job, she'd tell her parents that she'd just moved on. They need never know about the sacking.

'I'm pretty sure it's permanent between me and Jonathan but we'll see. And work has let me take some annual leave while I sort things out, so I'm staying with Roisin. I just needed a break.'

Making hopeful noises about distance making the heart grow fonder, her mum said goodbye and, as they were now only an hour away, made her promise to bring Roisin over for dinner one day.

Having got that dreaded conversation out of the way, Chloe opened her laptop; it wasn't that she hadn't been trying to get back on her feet, it was just that she wasn't getting anywhere. Her inbox was littered with rejection after rejection. As it was, this coming Friday would mark a month since it all happened and she knew the longer she was out of work the harder it would be to get a break. She had to keep focused and the one thing that would help her case right now was turning this place into the sort of retreat she could talk about in interviews, somewhere her future employer might be interested in and want to stay. She wanted Serenity to be fabulous so that Jonathan and her hideous ex-boss would look at what she'd achieved here; they'd see she could make it without them and regret letting her go. They'd want her back but she'd refuse and could imagine turning her nose up at their pleas. She wanted her parents to be proud of the boutique resort she'd helped launch and pictured them bringing all their friends. Yes, this place had to be a huge success because her future happiness depended on that just as much as Roisin's did.

On the back of her success creating this retreat, Chloe pictured herself accepting a fabulous new position with a huge salary as she sent her CV off to some new recruitment agencies. Roisin popped her head around the door and Chloe slammed her laptop shut, suddenly feeling a guilty glow in her cheeks.

'Did I catch you watching muscular firemen rescuing kittens then?' Her friend laughed. 'Heather's just said dinner is ready.'

Chloe put her things away and linked arms with Roisin as they headed for the kitchen.

'I was applying for jobs and felt guilty,' murmured Chloe. 'But I did tell you I had to find something didn't I?'

'I know you did,' replied Roisin. 'And when the time comes, I'll wish you the very best of luck and wave you a fond goodbye.'

'Thank you.'

'I just hope that moment takes a *verrrrrry* long time coming.' Roisin smiled.

Chloe squeezed her arm affectionately. She had to stick to her plans but meanwhile was absolutely determined to do everything in her power to make this retreat work for Roisin.

Dinner would be a good time to get a menu agreed. It was nearly time to launch the new website and it had to feature some typical dishes; everyone would want an idea of what they'd be eating when they arrived. They walked into the kitchen where the warmth of the range surrounded them immediately. A pot bubbled gently on the stove, the aroma alone making Chloe's stomach rumble. She opened the lid and inhaled deeply, stirring the casserole and releasing even more gorgeous smells. She picked up a spoon and went to dip it in the casserole hoping for a taste but from nowhere, Heather appeared, grabbed the spoon before she got the chance and tapped her on the fingers with it.

'Do you have an alarm on the pot lid?' asked Roisin.

'I might just get one,' said Heather. 'I hope you've washed your hands – it's almost ready. Now this is one of my specialties and I want you to tell me what you think.'

Chloe sat down while Roisin poured out three glasses of wine then joined her. Heather ladled the casserole into bowls she put in front of them then returned to the aga to pull out a fruit pie, setting it on the windowsill to cool.

'That's for later,' said Heather as she sat down with them.

The Moroccan spices that Heather had used, transformed the vegetables and pulses into something rather wonderful and with only a few mouthfuls, the room fell into quiet contented murmurs and chatter. Chloe listened as Roisin bantered with her gran. For all her friend's plans, she did wonder whether she was really ready to run the farmhouse as a business. Roisin was an intelligent woman but teaching English abroad wasn't really preparation for a career in hospitality. How would her friend cope with paying guests, with their quirks, comments and demands? How would she feel if she saw a bad review? It was bound to happen no matter how hard they worked to please people. This whole project was such a personal quest, Roisin's homage to her mother, and Chloe wondered if her friend would ever forgive herself if she thought she'd let her mum down. This scene in front of her, the cosy kitchen, the delicious food and the genuine friendship was a sanctuary in itself but could they really bring themselves to share it? Then again, if they didn't, it would be sold and a family legacy would be gone. Chloe shook herself from her thoughts to hear Roisin explaining the forthcoming talent competition – and found she had an unexpected ally in Heather.

'Do you think that's a good idea, sweetheart? Watching the locals demonstrating their unique abilities after a few drinks?' Heather smiled. 'Dear Lord, please don't ask me to come with you – I don't think I could stop laughing.'

Chloe realized she was mirroring Heather, with hand over mouth, eyebrows raised, and shaking of head at Roisin.

'You two could be twins.' Her friend laughed. 'And anyway, it'll be fun.'

'But it could be an absolute disaster too. I mean are these people qualified? Will they turn up and do what they've promised? Then there's the whole house to sort out. You seem to be taking on rather a lot and I worry about you.'

Heather held her arms out and Roisin walked in for a hug.

'You don't have to do this you know,' Heather continued.

'I want to,' replied Roisin. 'And I'm not doing it alone anyway – I have you two.'

Heather sighed then sat everyone back down and fetched the fruit pie. Chloe blew out her cheeks as a slice was placed in front of her along with a jug of cream.

'I have no idea how I'm managing to lose weight here,' she

said, pushing her belly out and rubbing it comically. 'Is this the kind of meal you're planning on giving the guests?'

'It's all I know how to cook,' replied Heather. 'That's if you're planning on having me do the cooking.'

Chloe looked across at Roisin who seemed deep in thought.

'I hoped you would but if it's too much for you …' said Roisin.

'Of course I will, at least until you can hire a fancy chef. Now what will our retreat guests want?'

'If they're anything like the London crowd I've just worked with, they'll want to photograph the food then push it around the plate.' Chloe laughed, trying to lighten the mood.

'Oh they are definitely not coming.' Heather smiled, keeping up the banter. 'I'll be feeding them with a spoon until it's eaten.'

'It would never come to that,' continued Roisin. 'One taste of your culinary delights and they'll be scoffing plates full.'

They all finished their plates of fruit pie as if to make the point.

'Seriously, though,' said Chloe, 'as much as I love your cooking, it could be a problem with the food being so good. No one will want to put weight on when they're here – they'd go on an all-inclusive cruise if that's what they were after. And they have to be on a high when they walk out that door – that's when they'll write reviews and tell friends. What we need to do is think about how we want them to feel when they leave and work backwards.'

Roisin and Heather looked at each other as if she were suggesting something ridiculous. Catching their expressions but ignoring them completely, Chloe continued.

'It works, honestly. Close your eyes.' She waited until they'd reluctantly done as they were told. 'Now picture yourself saying goodbye to our first guests. Okay? We're there, waving them off at the front door.'

She started waving her hand and saw Roisin squinting

through one eye to check it wasn't a joke before she eventually joined in.

'Now what do they look like?

'Happy,' replied Roisin. 'They're smiling, relaxed.'

'And how do they feel?' asked Chloe.

'They feel alive, full of fresh air and they're messier then when they first got here,' added Heather. 'I'm picturing ironed shirts arriving and wrinkled ones leaving.'

'Oh, that's a lovely image,' Chloe said. 'And they've achieved something. They're messy because they've been rolling up sleeves and getting their hands dirty somehow.'

'They're surprised that they've actually lost weight because they've taken time to eat slowly rather than wolfing it down,' said Roisin.

'And because no one got fat eating good home-made food,' added Heather. 'They're thanking me for the lovely meals and asking for recipes.'

'Good, that's really good,' said Chloe. 'They want recipes then we can create a pdf or a cookbook of all the recipes and send it to them when they get home. That gives us another opportunity to promote the retreat.'

'Or it could just be a rather lovely thing to do,' said Heather. 'I could teach them how to make the bread they eat.'

'What do you think, Chlo? They're already making candles, do you think it all sounds a bit do-it-yourself?' asked Roisin, opening her eyes.

Chloe knew that it wouldn't be a conventional type of retreat but then again, they had absolutely no chance of recreating one of them.

'Well, it's certainly not your Bhutan hillside luxury spa and it never will be but people want experiences now, to learn things and maybe take that skill home. Your bread is simply delicious, truly the best I've ever tasted and I imagine guests would love to learn how to make it. Besides, you have to be different because you are anyway, but if we're doing this then we have to be very careful about what other activities we offer – it can't descend into farce with the whole village joining in.'

Chloe seemed to be wagging her finger at Roisin an awful lot and was doing it again. 'I'm serious. I know we have to listen to what everyone can offer but you have to promise me we'll be very discerning tomorrow.'

Roisin crossed her heart and poured them another glass of wine.

Chapter Nine

The Fiddler's Arms was heaving with people as they pushed their way through the door at six o'clock. Every table was occupied and even the standing room was sparse; laughter and chatter bounced off the walls – before spookily easing as the girls walked in. A hundred eyes clocked them. Then, from behind the bar, Maggie waved them over, clearing a path with one whistle and directing them to two barstools with beer mats on them. The mats had been scribbled on: *Reserved for tonite's judges.*

'Nice one.' Roisin grinned and nodded as she sat down and Chloe noted the noise had returned to its former level. 'I feel like a VIP,' Roisin said.

Chloe wanted to show everyone that she wasn't here for fun, that she was taking it all very seriously, so had strode in wearing her old work suit. She brushed off her stool before sitting down. It was an automatic gesture but when she looked up from her action she realized both the landlady and her friend were giving her disapproving looks. Neither of them asked whether the barstool was now satisfactory for her ladyship but the question was written across their faces.

'Sorry, it's just a habit. Fabulous turn out tonight,' she said, trying to make the peace. 'Is all this for the talent night?'

'It is,' replied Maggie, nodding her acceptance of the apology while serving them glasses of the same wine they had last time. 'Half the room's raring to go and the other half are dying for a laugh. If I'd known I could pull a crowd like this on a Wednesday night, I'd have put one on years ago.'

'We're glad to be of help,' replied Roisin, raising the glass to her.

The landlady then stood on a chair and yelled at the room

to be quiet. Again, the effect of fifty people stopping talking at precisely the same time was quite eerie.

'Now, I've had a think about this,' she said, 'and you can't all be talking at once.'

She looked at the girls for approval and they waved her on, waiting to see what she had to say.

'If you're here as an entertainer or just watching then go over to the left hand side of the room near the fireplace.'

Several people shuffled, juggling pints with musical instruments.

'And if you're here because you can do something useful like plumbing, then move over to the right by the gents.'

Chloe perked up on hearing this. She hadn't expected any of the talents to be practical. After some murmuring, two or three people reluctantly moved to the right; they'd probably come to watch the show rather than be part of it.

'Fair enough, you lazy beggars,' said Maggie. She turned to the girls and asked them if there was anything specific they were looking for. Chloe stood up and cleared her throat.

'We'd really like to find people who can teach crafts or lead fitness activities, like cycling, pilates or bodyboarding, or something like that.'

She sat down and Maggie took the floor again. 'So if you can do something like that, and you can actually teach it, move over to the right too.'

This time a few people did get up and sit on the right hand side of the room; Chloe couldn't help but note that those on the right were, on the whole, a lot younger, quieter and fitter looking than those standing by the fireplace.

'Okay, ladies,' said Maggie. 'Pick a side and find your talent.'

Favouring the prospect of interviewing the younger, fitter crew, Chloe darted to the right before Roisin was even off her barstool. Her friend glanced at both sides of the room and shook her head, laughing, but Chloe was already sitting down ready to hear from those who claimed to have some talent in activities.

Not quite sure how to manage the group of people looking expectantly at her, Chloe asked them to call out the activities they could lead so she could put together a list. It was evident that some of them (flute and trombone lessons) would never really fit the bill but many others (like Ceroc dancing and fishing) might be interesting to keep up their sleeves so that when they had actual guests in the future, they could tailor breaks that met their needs. As people spoke to her, Chloe started mentally developing active stag and hen weekends, meditation sessions and reunion parties. As the time went on, she found herself surprised by how much the villagers had to offer between them and was sure that just by packaging all their skills together they'd have everything the visitors could wish for. Once her list was compiled, Chloe proposed fifteen minute sessions to hear from each person in more detail. They all seemed happy with this approach and while they waited, they drifted to the bar and ordered themselves another drink. They chatted to each other, comparing the slings and arrows of running a small business. As Chloe eavesdropped, she was reminded how important Roisin's dream was not just to her friend, but to the whole community.

First to sit down in front of her was a man she recognized and who seemed to recognize her. Chloe matched him smile for smile and friendly greeting for friendly greeting, trying desperately to remember where she'd met this person.

'Did you get through that entire salted caramel crunch yourself? It's my favourite.'

That was it; this was Tony from the chocolate shop that she'd practically bought out. Chloe had been in a bit of a heavenly daze but now she thought back, she remembered the dimples in the shop owner's cheeks. At the time, they'd reminded her of Jonathan's smile and she'd felt that gaping hole in her chest all over again. She wondered how he was doing and whether he had moved in with that woman. Since arriving, Chloe had stuck to her self-imposed ban on social media and was feeling calmer for it. Now seeing the shop owner again smiling with those little half-moons either side of his mouth, there was much less of a squeeze on her heart and she knew that the first thing she would do on getting back to her room would be to see what Jonathan was up to. She had no idea how she'd feel seeing his picture again but it was time to test that out.

Getting back to the task in hand, she listened to the shop owner telling her that he ran chocolate workshops where people learnt about the origin of the beans, the process involved in them becoming chocolate and then they were able to create and design their own slabs to take home. He provided the melted chocolate but the guests could add their own touches.

'Then they get a little gift bag with a ribbon. I could make little tags with the name of the retreat on so that they take home their own souvenir. It's all Fairtrade. Obviously I hope they also buy some other bars while they're here,' Tony added almost apologetically.

Chloe nodded along with everything he said. More food but it seemed like a perfect end-of-retreat activity. It couldn't be dressed up as healthy but it was creative and it would give the guests a sense of satisfaction. This was definitely going on the list but Chloe couldn't start selecting and deselecting quite yet so gave a polite thank you and promised to call him when she'd spoken to everyone.

Glancing across the room, Chloe watched Roisin wipe tears of laughter from her eyes as a guy wearing oil-stained overalls attempted to River Dance. Everyone in the group was doubled over with the exception of a bald-headed man in a formal suit. He looked completely out of place and Chloe noticed he was the only one not watching the ridiculous dancing; Mr Bald had his eyes glued to Roisin. He must have felt Chloe's gaze on him as he spun round to catch her staring. He didn't look away or smile rather he just stared at her until she looked away.

'Don't go wishing that evil eye on yourself,' said the person who was approaching her for his fifteen minutes.

Chloe looked up and saw a familiar six foot of handsomeness grinning at her before sitting down.

'You know him?' Chloe squeaked before clearing her throat.

'No, but he doesn't look as if he's up to any good.' He held out his huge hand and shook Chloe's firmly. 'Pleased to meet you again – and very glad to see you're still here.'

'I promised to help Roisin and I will. Now, erm, you said you could take clients sailing and kayaking, is that right?' Chloe was doing her best to sound professional but the memory of that slightly rough but soft skin was lingering.

'That's me, but I do more than that. I'm also a qualified surf instructor and have a seven-seater minibus to carry my own students. So, on a practical level I can collect people from the train or airport – it all helps pay the bills and keep me in this luxurious lifestyle.' He smiled and held his arms out wide, revealing patched-up elbows in his jumper to make his point. 'So, Ms Advertising, let me tell you more about what I have to offer ...'

The man in front of her was evidently very comfortable in his skin (and it had to be said, it did fit that surf-muscled body pretty well). He was also clearly used to making his way through life by spreading a little charm – when he needed to. Chloe knew he was only being nice to her to get work but decided early on in their conversation that being flirted with just to get some surfing clients was better than not being flirted with at all. They were both adults, knew what they were doing and, to be honest, it made the whole conversation a lot more fun. It helped that Andy obviously knew what he was talking about and could offer the guests a full morning of outdoor activity every single day. After their allotted fifteen minutes – which, okay went on for a little longer – Chloe shook his hand again and promised she'd be in touch. Andy held her hand for longer than necessary but then seemed to drop it quite quickly as he said, 'I will look forward to that.'

When Chloe's conversations were over, she escaped to the bathroom. She splashed water on her face before looking at her slightly flushed cheeks in the pub's bathroom mirror; she was almost surprised at the person staring back at her. Outwardly, she saw a fresh face, blushing from the flirtations and doing a very good job of hiding her real feelings of complete and utter confusion.

'You look, dare I say, aroused.' Roisin laughed as she walked into the bathroom and joined her at the sink. 'Been talking to Andy by any chance ?'

Chloe shook her head dismissively, wiped her almost-dry hands on her trousers and together they left the pub.

'Nothing wrong with a bit of flirting,' continued Roisin. 'You can't say you don't deserve it and he's one of the good ones.'

'Hmm and there's nothing like being on the rebound to lead you astray,' replied Chloe as they got into the jeep. Roisin revved the engine and they set off.

'Do you think you're still in rebound territory?' asked Roisin as they drove along.

Chloe was leaning her head on the window. She thought about the question then sat up facing Roisin. 'No. I really don't.' She paused. 'When I think about him, I just feel angry. He didn't just hurt me, he humiliated me. And I don't think I did anything to deserve that. I did everything for him and that bloody company.'

'How dare they dump you!' shouted Roisin.

'HOW DARE THEY!' yelled Chloe.

'HOW BLOODY DARE THEY!' they both roared.

'What was she like?' asked Roisin when they'd got their breath back.

Chloe hadn't been able to bring herself to visualise the woman standing behind Jonathan before but now she did, her impression was that she was older than him.

Chloe shook her head. 'I can't really picture her properly. The thing is you don't fall out of love with one person and into love with another on the same day. With him and her it had to have been going on for a while. I think that's what hurts the most. The fact that it was all going on behind my back makes me furious just thinking about it.'

'You don't know that Chlo – unless you checked his Facebook?'

Chloe shook her head. 'You know the break-up rule.'

'Cold turkey for at least a month,' they recited in unison.

'I bet it's driving you absolutely nuts.' Roisin laughed.

Chapter Ten

'Do you think they actually employ someone to come up with these names?' asked Roisin.

'I know they do,' replied Chloe. 'It's crucial to selling it. You're far more likely to buy ocean breeze than pale blue.'

'But how do they decide? I mean, do they stare at shades of white all day trying to think what it looks like? Did someone stir this pot until the light bulb appeared and they thought, *"I know, it looks like a pebble: pebble white"*.'

'Probably.' Chloe stirred the pot in question. 'They could have said chalk cliffs but that sounds colder doesn't it?'

'Or seagull poo,' continued Roisin. 'But you're right, we wouldn't be painting that on our guests' walls.'

'You'll never get it finished if you spend all day gibbering on like this.'

The girls jumped before turning to see Andy standing there, laughing at them. His arms were folded, his smile wide. Chloe hadn't seen him since the night at the pub nearly a week ago and as she looked up at him, with his wavy hair taking on a life of its own, she thought he was almost the personification of Ocean Breeze.

'I can start that work on the pipes and guttering now if you like? It'll take a few days. A kayak customer's just cancelled on me.'

'That's inconsiderate,' said Roisin. 'Had they paid?'

'Only the deposit and I'd booked the whole day out. I tell you, this place can't get up and running quick enough for me.'

'Oh Andy I thought I heard your voice.' Heather arrived with a tray bearing three glasses of fruit juice and some biscuits. 'Stop and have a snack.'

'I haven't even started yet.' Andy smiled. 'I've got to earn one of your gorgeous cookies first.'

'Oh I think you've earned more than these. How are your boys?' asked Heather, offering to show him the section of guttering that needed emptying. Andy picked up a biscuit and followed her, saying something that made Heather roar with laughter.

'She really loves him doesn't she?' said Chloe. 'Who are his boys?'

'A group of kids he works with; none of them have done well at school so he volunteers for this programme where they try to get them into outdoor jobs. He's been doing it for years now and apparently it works really well,' replied Roisin. 'He says everyone deserves a chance. And yes, Heather adores him – he's the grandson she should have had.'

They went back to their painting and continued for another couple of hours, freshening up the fourth and final of the lodge rooms with pebble white and ethereal sea blue. As the last stroke of paint went on, they sighed and slumped on the room's bed, exhausted.

'I don't think I've ever worked so hard,' said Chloe, rolling her shoulders and stretching her neck.

'It's been a pretty full on few days. Come on, let's do some stretches.'

They washed the paint off their faces then headed out to the garden. Roisin told Chloe to stand straight, reaching her arms above her head as far as they would go. Then they took big deep breaths, exhaled noisily and flopped their arms forwards to touch their toes. Lying on their stomachs on the grass, they grabbed their ankles and pulled their bodies into the bow pose. Although groaning, Chloe could feel every inch of her body letting go.

'Ah, this feels wonderful,' she said when they'd come out of that position and Roisin had shown her how to relax into a child pose, kneeling down then stretching forwards on the ground, reaching out with their arms.

'I'm surprised you didn't learn yoga when you were in London,' said Roisin. 'I know it's very trendy now.'

'It is: hot yoga, beer yoga, cat yoga – everything but normal yoga,' replied Chloe. 'No, that's not true. I could quite easily have found a class but I became that cliché – the workaholic.'

'And you really want to go back to it?'

'I liked it Rois,' said Chloe facing her friend. 'This is fun but I did love being part of the agency, especially on shoots. It was great being with the production team and everyone knowing their role. It gave me a real buzz.'

Roisin gave her a single nod of the head and shrugged.

'Not that this isn't great and I love spending time with you,' continued Chloe. 'It's just I have to earn a living at the very least.'

'I know,' said Roisin, getting up and holding out her hand to pull her friend up. 'And so do I at some point, but I'll miss you. Come on – Olly should be here soon.'

They sat at the kitchen table taking Olly through the ideas they'd developed at the talent evening. Chloe knew that Roisin's outdoor ideal would only appeal in the summer months so together they'd brainstormed programmes, like the crafting sessions, that would keep people coming to the retreat all year round. Now they needed Olly to keep the website updated throughout the year with these seasonal events and activities.

'Think of it like a shop window,' said Chloe. 'You don't see good shops with baubles and gift wrap on display at New Year. They know what people will be looking for and when, so we have to change the offer over the months.'

'So there's no point in us telling everyone to come and enjoy a weekend hiking when it's tipping down,' added Roisin. 'But they might like baking over autumn when the fruit is in season.'

'And the different activities would attract different kinds

of people so we eventually get widespread appeal,' said Chloe.

Olly nodded and joined in. 'So like birdwatching when the chicks have hatched?'

'Precisely,' said Chloe. 'And in the early summer, just before the wedding season, we can advertise active hen and stag parties.'

'So January could be for yoga retreats when everyone is recovering from Christmas,' added Roisin.

They were all in the swing of it now and the ideas flowed. They put together a calendar showing which activities they'd promote when and which local business would be leading it. By early evening they had something they were really pleased with and, importantly, it involved the whole community. They chose some photographs of the bay and the village and Olly worked as they spoke, slotting their words into spaces on the screen. The website was coming to life and it was looking good. Heather walked in to start making dinner and invited Olly to stay.

'I'll just have a wash before I help you with things,' Chloe said, leaping up.

She closed the door to her room and threw herself on the bed for a few moments. It had been a very full-on day but hugely satisfying: physical labour, seeing the final room finished, having the yoga session and then working with her friends to set up the website. It felt like a real day's work but in the most glorious of surroundings and amongst friends. She looked at her phone charging by the bed; it was telling her that she had some missed calls and twenty-four emails. Chloe guffawed a little. Only a few weeks ago there'd have been over *two hundred* and twenty-four emails waiting for her by this time of day. And most of them would be completely irrelevant. However, she'd kept up to date with emails since being here and had noticed the number declining day by day. At first there had been all of the concerned emails from London friends and colleagues, then the official severance negotiations with her old agency but all of that was settled now and the worried friends seemed to have stopped worrying. She skimmed the list of senders, stopping at one that made her body run cold. Jonathan.

It was the first communication from him since that day and she hesitated before clicking it open. It had the title "APARTMENT" and in a completely unemotional tone, told her that the person she'd once shared her life with, had undertaken (and yes, he'd written *undertaken*, as if she were some ex-colleague and they were dissolving a business) three independent valuations of their property – they were attached – and could she let him know whether she wished to buy his share or sell it and split the proceeds. Chloe could feel the blood pumping angrily through her veins. There was no polite, *how are you?* Or a gentle, *I thought it best to get things moving* – nothing to soften this blow. Chloe pictured him showing estate agents around their flat, probably with his new woman in tow. Had he pretended they lived there together? She rubbed her eyes and stretched her hands over her face then through her hair. It was over, she knew that of course, but it was now very definite. An angry tear escaped and she wiped it away roughly; her chest rose and fell with heavy breaths as she thought about all the people he'd betrayed. People she loved. Her grandmother who'd left her that money to enjoy life, her parents who'd welcomed him into their home and she herself who'd believed him every time he'd said he was working a late shift. Was he really? Well at least she could make darned sure that she got her grandmother's money back and she wouldn't make another mistake like that with it.

She put on the caps lock and poked at the keyboard – JUST SELL IT & GET OUT OF MY LIFE YOU LOUSY TWO-TIMING PIG-FACE. Then she deleted all of that and, expressing the same message that she'd just deleted, replied politely but professionally that she wished to sell and asking that she be copied in on all relevant communication and for a date and time when he would be out of the apartment so she could collect her things.

Having done that, Chloe calmly moved his email to her "past-life" folder where all her old work correspondence now sat so she wouldn't have to look at any of it again and skimmed through the other twenty-three. There were fourteen vouchers for eyelash extensions, five job vacancy alerts, a wine club offer and three responses from a headhunter. She opened the first of the three telling her that the ad agency Blue Banana was interested in her CV. The second email said that in fact they were *very* interested and would she please call to arrange an interview. The third email practically shouted that the headhunter had tried calling but she wasn't picking up so could she *please* get in touch. Finally, someone was interested. Chloe checked the missed calls list and saw the London number's eight attempts, each with a message for her to call back. If she'd opened these emails first, would she have told Jonathan to sell the flat? Or would she have bought him out? If she got this job, it would be very easy to step back into her old life with a new company. She didn't have to make that decision yet; right now she just had to arrange an interview date. Chloe emailed the headhunter and gave him some dates for the interview, very aware that she was typing quietly so as not to let the whole house know.

In a clean T-shirt with her hair brushed and her ponytail tightened, Chloe opened the kitchen door and got ready to tell everyone her news. Roisin and Olly were hunched over the laptop so she sat down beside them.

'Shouldn't we put photos of the lodges on?' asked Olly. 'People will want to know where they're sleeping.'

'We will once the paint's dry,' replied Chloe. 'But I think we're nearly there. We have a vision and a programme for the year. The test website is looking fab and you've done a brilliant job with the Facebook page, Olly. We should all put it on LinkedIn when we're ready so maybe we can attract some corporate customers. Do you know anywhere else we could share it, Olly?'

He looked up as if he'd had a great idea and then hunched over the laptop typing away.

'Then your work here is done,' said Roisin, smiling at him and then instantly frowning when she caught Chloe's expression. 'What's up?'

Chloe couldn't look at her as she explained everything that had happened in the past half hour and that she had an interview. She stared at the table as she spoke, only looking up at the end.

'Wow, well done you. I knew you'd get something,' said Roisin. 'Though I have to confess I'm gutted to be losing such a dedicated apprentice.'

'It's only the first stage,' replied Chloe. 'They might not like me and if they do there'll be lots more hoops to jump through before you lose your slave labour.'

Chloe smiled but her insides were churning while a million thoughts whizzed around her brain, colliding and crashing. Getting the interview was exactly what she'd been working towards; it meant she wasn't a failure after all. Someone wanted her. Besides, it didn't have to mean she'd never see Roisin again. She'd never lose touch again and if she got the job, she might be able to persuade her new agency to book company retreats up here. And yet ...

'The selection process usually takes weeks and we should have things up and running in that time,' she continued. 'If I get offered the job then there's usually at least a fortnight before the starting date so we'd have time to get adverts scheduled so they run automatically. I would never leave you in the lurch. It'll all be fine.'

Roisin nodded. 'That would be good,' she said quietly. 'How long do you think it'll take before we get some actual paying customers?'

'I don't know. I suppose there might be something for late summer.'

From his laptop, Olly looked up.

'You'd better be ready before then.' He smiled goofily. 'There's some people booked in already.'

Chloe and Roisin rushed to stand behind him, looking over his shoulder. There on the booking system was a green confirmation light – a party of people was indeed arriving in a mere six days' time.

'How did you do that?' Chloe's voice had stuck in her throat and this came out as a cross between a squeal and a croak.

'I looked up the names of some bigwigs and attached a link to the website on their search results. That lot are always googling themselves and now when they do, we pop up. I saw it on a programme once – neat idea isn't it?'

'Email and tell them we're not ready. Say we're sorry, say ...'

It was Roisin's turn to place her hand on Chloe's back.

'Relax, we can do this, and we'll have to do it on our own when you're gone. It's probably a sign, that it's finally time for us both to stand on our own two feet. Anyway, how hard can it be to look after a few people for a few days? Who is it, Olly?'

Olly pulled up the details of the booking.

'It's a company, someone called MediaFifty.' He laughed. 'Mad name or what?'

Chloe felt her knees buckle and Roisin caught her just in time.

'You've heard of them?'

Chloe nodded. 'They're only one the biggest independent production companies in the country.'

Chapter Eleven

Chloe sat quietly throughout dinner as around her, Roisin and Olly toasted their good news and speculated what the first guests would be like.

'We could do some of those painted stones for them to commemorate their being our first guests, or leave champagne in their rooms. What do you think, Chlo?'

'Yeah,' she murmured, actually thinking both ideas sounded lovely but not having the strength to enter into the conversation.

After dinner, Chloe waited until the others had gone to bed and opened the back door, breathing in the sea air. Night had long fallen but as ever with so many stars and the moon shining through the deep blue, it wasn't dark. She needed to think, to take this all in – so walked the track towards the beach, following the path of the moonbeam. The buildings had been so high in London that even though her office was on the forty-sixth floor, she hadn't seen so much sky for a very long time and it still overwhelmed her. To anyone watching her life, she seemed so far away from where she'd once been – but was she really? One part of her was still standing outside her old office, waiting to be invited back in and the other part was scared to enter.

The great expanse of sky, like a star-spangled velvet throw, seemed to want to wrap her up, comfort her and show her how nothing she'd been through really mattered when you considered your tiny role in this universe. It wasn't working; it did matter and Chloe started tensing up, getting inexplicably angry that it was so difficult to be really angry in such a beautiful place. Why weren't there people nicking your cab or standing on your feet on the tube or jumping the queue here? If there was anything, anything at all to get angry at then she could let it all out, instead her angst and fear was building and festering inside her.

'*Ahhhh* – stop being so bloody gorgeous all the time! Stupid sea, ugly stars, pathetic moon. I've seen far better beaches than this – you're nothing!'

She bent over and picked up handfuls of dampish sand, throwing them out at the waves. The breeze caught a throw and threw it back at her. Spitting sand out of her mouth, Chloe kicked at that beneath her feet, only for her toe to find a rock buried beneath.

'Jeez, anything else to throw at me?' she yelled out, hopping her way to a piece of driftwood to sit. 'Well done, universe! You gave me something to get worked up about.'

Calming herself down, she noticed a torchlight heading down the path towards her; Roisin was calling out for her so she put on her phone light to guide her in.

'I heard you talking to yourself,' said Roisin, plonking herself on the driftwood and taking off a backpack. 'Did you have anything interesting to say?'

Chloe shook her head. She wasn't in the mood for banter, even with Roisin. Her friend unpacked the bag, pulling out a down jacket which she wrapped around Chloe's shoulders, two cups, which balanced on their makeshift seat, and a thermos flask. She shook the flask gently then poured out something hot and steamy. Now that she'd stopped thrashing about, Chloe felt the chill in the air and was enormously grateful for the rescue package. She held the cup in her hands for a moment, enjoying the warmth radiating from it, then held it to her face to defrost her nose. Chloe could smell hot chocolate and, on taking the first sip, realized it had been fortified with a little something.

'A bit of brandy,' said Roisin noting the quizzical look. 'Part celebration for actually getting a booking, part "oh heck, what do we do now?"'

Chloe snorted. 'You can say that again.'

They sat silently sipping their drinks; the sea swept in and out, in and out, almost hypnotically. Roisin broke the silence.

'I really do appreciate everything you've done for me you know. I wasn't sure how I'd feel being back here but you've made it fun. I haven't laughed so much in a long time.'

Chloe leant over and put her head on Roisin's shoulder.

'And as much as I would like to lock you up and never let you leave,' Roisin continued, 'I know you have your dreams as much as I have mine, and you deserve yours to come true.'

Chloe lifted her mug and they toasted. *'To dreams'*.

'So an interview with Moldy Banana.' Roisin nudged Chloe playfully. 'That paint colour wouldn't sell would it?'

'Certainly wouldn't,' Chloe replied. 'And they're called Blue Banana – not that it would sell any better.'

'Do you want me to come down with you and lend some moral support?'

'It's just a first stage – they'll do it via Skype.'

'So you might not even get it?' chirped Roisin, getting a jab in the ribs. She linked her arm into Chloe's.

More silence was broken, again, by Roisin. 'Do you think you're ready to go back?'

'I'm scared but guess it's time to find out,' replied Chloe. 'I don't want them to think they've won.'

'Are you kidding?' said Roisin. 'Look at this place – you're the one that won.'

Chloe smiled at her. 'You're right and I've loved being here. I just want to show them, that's all.'

'Promise me you won't do anything just to prove a point – do it because you alone really want to.'

'I promise,' replied Chloe. 'MediaFifty are pretty well known,' she continued. 'They're big on social, they have huge influence and loads of followers around the world. They're trendsetters so they could be really good for you.'

'Or a disaster if we don't get this right,' said Roisin. 'What on earth are we like? Here we are terrified because we've got exactly what we've both been hankering after – what's that saying? *Be careful what you wish for?*'

'*Lest it come true,*' added Chloe. 'It's just nerves isn't it? What we're feeling? Normal nerves and if we just put one foot in front of the other and get on with it then there's nothing to be scared about.'

'Well there's one thing that we should definitely be scared of,' replied Roisin.

'What?'

'That tide – it's coming in a bit too fast.'

As she spoke a foamy wave splashed their feet and soaked them. The girls leapt up, quickly re-packing the bag, before linking arms to walk back up the path.

'You'll do brilliantly at the interview and I won't let this place fail,' said Roisin after a few moments of silence. 'I can't afford to.'

'The cousins?' asked Chloe.

'Not really, they're just the cattle prod. Mum couldn't be cured but she said just being here made her feel better. I'm convinced this place can help people and I don't want to lose it.'

'It's still a big ask. I'm sure she wouldn't want it to become a burden to you.'

'I know that, but giving up without even trying …?'

'How long do you have?'

'The cousins want us to meet their representative and talk about "the options" as they call them.' Roisin sighed. 'I'm glad I can show them one booking but it's not enough. I just want to earn enough to get a mortgage and buy out everyone else. They're circling like vultures waiting for me to fail.'

Chloe instantly had the image of a man's head on a vulture's body in her mind; he was sitting on a tree like they do in apocalyptic zombie movies, just waiting to feast on the spoils.

'So I was really pleased to have a paying client so quickly,' continued Roisin. 'Although I would rather have you around when they're here.'

'I will be,' Chloe replied. 'There'll be at least two interview stages and I promise not to arrange any when they're here. We'll do this together.'

It felt to Chloe like the beginning of the end. She'd come here to escape Jonathan, look for a job and help her friend while she did so. Now that it was all coming together, there was a very definite sadness in the air – like the end of a really good holiday when you promise to stay in touch but know that your old life will swallow you whole as soon as it can.

'Now shall we get back before we freeze our butts off?'

'Roger that.' Roisin saluted. 'Race you!'

She darted off screaming and Chloe took off after her, catching her up as they reached the yard. Laughing and breathless, they opened the kitchen door to find Heather in her dressing gown talking to the house plants. She looked up startled as they walked in.

'They're good listeners.' She smiled. 'Just in case you ever need them. Night, night.'

She kissed both Chloe and Roisin on the cheek and locked the door. The girls watched her head to bed as they made cups of chamomile tea to take up, then pushed each other up the stairs to their bedrooms. Having said goodnight, Chloe lay back in the soft bed with heavy blankets and stared up at the ceiling.

Her earlier angst wasn't quite gone but it did feel as if it had been wrapped up in tissue and hidden in a box under the bed. She was scared but that was only natural; everyone got nervous before interviews so why would she be any different? And that's all it was – wasn't it? Roisin had been right. She had to be sure of her next steps. Chloe knew for certain she didn't want Jonathan back and didn't want to live in that flat with the memories it held. She said those things over and over to herself and listened to her body. There were no jitters, no gripping sensation around her heart, the type that would tell her she was kidding herself when she thought about her ex.

'And I can't wait to get back into advertising and being creative,' she murmured, picturing the busy streets and the buzz of an office.

She'd tried to be as upbeat as possible but it was definitely there, those telltale jitters.

Chapter Twelve

'I spritzed your suit with some of my favourite perfume,' said Heather. 'It's white heather so it might just bring you luck.'

'It's on Skype, Gran – no one will know,' said Roisin. 'She could wear her jammies and get away with it.'

'Chloe will know and it will boost her spirits.'

Chloe thanked her, took the jacket and went back to her room to shower and dress. Standing tall, she swept up her hair and looked at herself in the mirror, twirling from side to side; putting on the suit felt odd but quite good and, to her surprise, very natural. She had the glow of a person who'd spent a lot of time outdoors; her skin was looking the best it had done in ages and she'd lost a little weight.

'We should have done a before and after photo of me,' she said to Roisin as they walked into the yoga room where the laptop was set up. 'What a month at Serenity can do for you.'

'Well that is the point of the place,' said Roisin. 'Just remember to tell everyone in the Bruised Banana about us – get them up here.'

'I know you're getting the name wrong deliberately,' replied Chloe, shaking her head at her friend. 'But I *will* tell them. By the way, is there something wrong with your gran? She seems a bit melancholy today.'

'I noticed that,' replied Roisin. 'Maybe it's knowing you might be going soon.'

'Oh don't say that, I feel guilty enough. You don't hate me for going for this interview do you?'

'Of course not! This is my dream and you have to follow yours. I won't lie, it has been fabulous having you here but I wouldn't want to stop anyone following their heart.'

Roisin gave her a peck on the cheek for luck and closed the door as she left the room. Chloe had a few minutes before the start of the interview so read through her notes. Blue Banana was a new and very trendy agency focusing on what they called *social-experiential fusion* marketing. Chloe laughed to herself on reading that again. If she'd mentioned that phrase to Roisin or even worse – to Andy, they would have simply despaired. Despite the ridiculous name, it simply meant building experiences and events for brands that people would want to share on social media. If she got this position, there would definitely be opportunities to feature Serenity Bay. Chloe took out a notepad and started jotting down some ideas for Blue Banana's existing clients and some further ideas about other brands the agency could approach. As she wrote and the cogs started whirring again, Chloe realized that she had actually missed this part of her life; she enjoyed marketing, developing ideas and making a success of brands.

That familiar Skype ring tone started chiming. Chloe sat up straight and smoothed down her hair then pressed the "accept call" button. Two people appeared on the screen. From the background, their offices were obviously in a converted church building and it looked simply beautiful. Light streamed through the arches in the background and almost gave her interviewers a halo. The old parquet floor they'd found in the farmhouse would probably be perfect there, mused Chloe. 'Your offices look simply amazing,' she enthused.

'Thank you,' said the obvious top dog, a handsome forty-something man, dressed head-to-toe in black, who introduced himself as Gareth. 'We wanted to show people that just being in a different space can make people feel different about a brand.'

'It works,' replied Chloe, looking around the airy yoga studio and understanding exactly what he meant.

They talked through her CV and when Chloe was honest about the reasons for leaving her old job, they simply nodded and said they could understand her position.

'I think you were right to follow your instincts,' said Gareth. 'It takes a lot of guts to do that.'

It was music to Chloe's ears and before long they were discussing the ideas she had for their brands.

'TruNorth aftershave and men's cosmetics,' said Chloe, 'have a very outdoors, rugged brand image. The sailing experiences used now make complete sense – but they're not very accessible for many people. Also, we need to attract a younger audience so need something they might do. Surfing and sea kayaking happens all around the coast and is very easy to arrange. I can access a fabulous training centre in Serenity Bay which would be perfect.'

The interviewers nodded along and took notes as Chloe spoke. She continued without taking a breath, the ideas flowing one after the other.

'I also read that Medus Olive Oil are looking for a new agency. I think that there's something missing from their strategy. They don't have the Italian heritage that other brands do, so they should avoid that area. They could be talking about slowing down, baking bread, taking your time and enjoying each moment, each mouthful. I know a woman in Serenity Bay who has the most wonderful bread recipes and could also do YouTube videos to teach people to bake. The flavours remind you what food should taste like and would be a perfect match for Medus.'

'Maybe we should have Serenity Bay as a client.' Gareth laughed as they concluded the interview. They promised to be in touch soon and Chloe practically skipped out of the room. She knew she'd done a good job ... but equally knew something else.

She opened the French windows and walked around the house; her thoughts were so far away that she walked into the ladder before noticing it.

'Look out!' came a cry from above her.

Andy was at the top continuing the guttering job and in the

struggle to steady himself had dropped the bucket of gutter-grunge which predictably went all over Chloe. He hurried down, leaping off the final six steps and holding her by the shoulders.

'Are you okay? Did it hit you?' She looked up to see the deep concern in his eyes. He looked so worried.

Chloe pulled a clod of soggy wet moss out of her hair. 'I'm fine.' She shook her head. 'Really. The bucket didn't get me – but I caught the aftermath.'

Together they picked bits of leaves and twigs out of her hair and then Andy held the back of her jacket whilst she slid out of it, careful not to get any of the grunge down her shirt.

'I'm guessing the suit was for the interview,' said Andy, brushing the jacket down with his hand before hanging it over a rung of the ladder.

'Roisin told you about it?'

Andy nodded. 'So did you get it? Are you leaving us?'

'Would it matter if I was?'

'Of course it would,' said Andy, gently brushing some moss from her cheekbone. 'Roisin would really miss you.'

There'd been a slight pause between the two halves of his sentence. He was toying with her she suspected.

'Well I don't know if I have it yet, that was just the first stage. The next stage would be a presentation in London and then a chemistry meeting with the other executives. They need to get the right fit.'

'Sounds a load of baloney to me,' said Andy looking directly at her – and holding her gaze. 'You don't need all of those stages. You know straight away if there's chemistry.'

Chemistry? Chloe could have been sitting on a Bunsen burner for all the heat that was radiating through her at that moment. She was sure her clothes would have spontaneously combusted there and then if her phone hadn't started buzzing. She snatched herself away from Andy's gaze and slipped back into the yoga studio.

"Call me – agency very keen – will arrange second interview asap. Well done" read the message from the headhunter. Chloe was delighted to know she'd done herself proud but thinking back to Roisin's words, she knew exactly what she had to do next. She sat calmly and dialed her parents' number.

'Sit down, Mum. I need to tell you something. I'm not on leave from the agency. I was sacked.' Confused noises came down the line but Chloe continued. 'They wanted me to create an advertising campaign for a huge conglomerate but I just couldn't. I didn't approve of their ethics and I had to say something. They told me to leave and I didn't want to let you down so I didn't tell you I was basically unemployed.'

'Oh,' said her mum, 'but you'll get another job won't you? You don't want to throw your career away and everyone pollutes something. I even forgot to recycle the egg carton yesterday.'

Chloe sighed; this wasn't going the way she'd planned.

'You've always done so much to get me through university,' she continued. 'I know you were really proud of my job.'

She heard her mother hand the phone over to her dad and ask him to talk some sense into her. 'Don't listen to her. We're proud of you, not your job,' he said. 'You could do anything and we'd still be proud of you.'

Chloe could feel a weight lifting from her shoulders. 'Anything?' she asked.

'Why?'

'Well I have been invited back for a second interview at one of the trendiest new agencies in London.'

'Don't say you're not going to take it!' yelled her mum, obviously still listening to every word. 'I sense a *but* coming on.'

'There is,' replied Chloe, her whole face smiling with what she'd decided. 'In my heart, I know it's not really what I want to do. I'm turning it down and staying here at Roisin's – at Serenity. I have no idea whether this will work but I'm going to set up a marketing company to promote the whole village, to get more visitors and to show people how fabulous it is. Is that a mad idea?'

'Dear Lord,' her mother exclaimed. 'Don't they have tourist boards for that kind of thing?'

'You go for it, Chlo,' her father said. 'I'm over the moon to have you so close to home and if this is going to make you as happy as you sound right now, then just do it – I'll sort her out.'

She smiled even more at the thought of her dad trying to convince her mum that all of this was a good idea. 'Thanks, Dad! Love you.'

Tingling with excitement, she made her next call. Chloe told the recruitment agency she had decided to set up on her own but also said she'd personally call Blue Banana to thank them for their time and explain her rationale. The headhunter, having lost the promise of his fee, was not best pleased but wished her luck.

Chloe hadn't felt so alive in eons so walked back out into the grounds with the widest smile on her face.

'You got the job didn't you?' said Roisin, standing beside Andy.

'Maybe I would have.' Chloe pulled the band out of her hair and let it fall loose around her shoulders. 'But I'm not going to take it. I'm staying in Serenity.'

'Are you serious?' Roisin gawped. 'Please tell me this isn't a wind-up.'

Chloe shook her head and opened her arms as wide as the smile on her face.

'Oh my God!' exclaimed Roisin, rushing in to hug her. Over Roisin's shoulder Chloe met Andy's smile. She smiled broadly back. Chloe couldn't remember a time she'd been happier.

At Andy's suggestion they all celebrated with a barbecue on the beach. Heather brought down a bottle of fizz and they toasted new beginnings from paper cups. The summer sky was only just darkening when Chloe let out a huge yawn and knew she had to call it a day. She felt the deep tiredness that only ever happens when you've done the right thing. She'd sleep well tonight.

Lying in bed, she wanted to do one more thing – announce to the world that she was back. She logged into her Facebook account, finally feeling calm and collected enough for this moment. Like many people she knew, Chloe had spent so long posting happy photos of her seemingly wonderful life that when the time came, she just couldn't bring herself to post that it had all collapsed around her. Now, having made a decision she was truly happy with, she logged in.

She clicked on Jonathan's profile and took a deep breath. There it was, the thing she was looking for and dreading in equal measure: a picture of Jonathan and the new woman. She was older than him and handsome rather than pretty with a sleek chestnut bob and incredible cheekbones above perfect lips. She had that perfectly groomed look of someone very wealthy and was apparently called Courtney. Chloe gasped on seeing the name and remembered a morning, a few months ago, when Jonathan had accidently called her by that name. He'd said it was the name of a woman in the office. Just how long had it been going on for? She scrolled through Jonathan's timeline and while she'd been eradicated from his virtual life, Courtney was everywhere and they weren't just recent pictures. There was one that had to have been taken just before Christmas where Jonathan and Courtney were sitting side by side at a long table in an expensive looking restaurant with lots of beautiful people she didn't recognize; she guessed they were Courtney's friends. Were they together then or is this where it started? She clicked on Courtney's profile.

Talk about overkill. Her profile picture was of her and Jonathan, her cover photo was of her and Jonathan and her pinned post was ... yep another one of her and Jonathan.

'Okay, we get it,' Chloe whisper-yelled at the screen.

In a few moments she learned that she was a partner in a law firm and they'd met at a fundraiser. Courtney had also posted the pictures of a Christmas party where she and Jonathan were kissing under mistletoe, entwining glasses and wearing *hilarious* Santa hats – or you'd have thought they were hilarious the way the two of them were laughing. These pictures were taken over six months ago and the final nail in the dignity coffin was Courtney's posting of the gift Jonathan bought her for Christmas. Teasing a tiny corner of pastel coloured silk, wrapped in tissue from a Jean Yu lingerie box, Courtney told the world that this gift was for Jonathan's eyes only. Chloe stopped breathing and nearly choked when she had to exhale – Jonathan buying expensive lingerie? How did he even know about that brand? He had to have been guided very closely. Chloe thought back to the gift she'd opened on Christmas morning: a Victoria's Secret kimono which she'd been delighted with and planned to wear that fateful night. That seemed to sum up their relationship now. Chloe had been his polyester while Courtney got silk.

With added resolve and perspective, Chloe deleted every photograph of Jonathan on her account. It left her life looking empty on screen so she changed her personal status to "happy", listed her profession as Ambassador for Serenity Bay and started creating posts with the hundreds of pictures that she'd taken since she arrived here. The endless skies, golden beaches and white-horse waves were picture postcard scenes but Chloe also posted photographs of the house; really seeing it's homeliness and history for almost the first time. She ran her finger over a picture of the smooth wooden kitchen table and wondered how many women had sat around it over the years sharing tales of woe about their men, or even laughter at their antics. How many tears had fallen on it, how many parties had been held and how many glasses of wine or whiskey had been drank? She recalled Roisin's face beaming when she'd told her she was staying in Serenity, then Heather's embrace of both girls together and knew she was part of this story now.

Chloe was about to close the screen when the little notification bell told her that someone had sent a direct message. Dreading that it might be Jonathan, she tried to ignore it but curiosity was always going to get the better of her – she clicked on her messages and lit up with delight at what she saw.

"Yo, Double-Shot, you're back! Wondered why you'd taken off without saying goodbye but new place looks amazing. Tell me more x".

She hugged the screen, letting out a tiny squeal, then bit the edge of the blanket to stop herself waking the whole house.

Chapter Thirteen

'So who is this guy?' asked Roisin, looking over Chloe's shoulder at the picture of Lloyd as they sat down to breakfast.

'Just the nicest person you could ever meet,' replied Chloe. 'He ran the coffee shop I went to every day and was actually the first person I told after I'd been sacked. I wish I could have told him about Jonathan too.'

She recalled that day, standing on the busy London street outside her former office. She'd noticed a passerby giving her a look of sympathy and realized she was clutching a box which told everyone what had happened. Thanks to the news reports of all those bankers being thrown out of the Square Mile after the financial crash, everyone knew what a loner with a box of personal belongings on the street at this hour meant. And no matter how sorry she felt for herself at that time, Chloe had not wanted her situation signposted or complete strangers pitying her. She snorted as she remembered taking only one thing from that box – a photograph of herself and Jonathan on top of the Empire State Building. If she'd known what was coming next she would have left it where it was and rammed it with the rest of the box into the nearest bin. She remembered being completely lost, not knowing what to do or where to go and then seeing the Red Roaster beckoning from across the street.

'Yo, Double-Shot, what you doing back in here? Can't resist me?'

'I've just been sacked.'

Saying the words out loud had hurt more than she'd expected them to; she put her hand up to her throat, remembering the lump that she'd felt. She'd been blinking back tears when Lloyd had rushed from behind the counter and sat her at a table then brought her a glass of water.

'Tell me about it,' he'd said.

And she had. Chloe told him the whole sorry story, relieved to be able to practice saying it out loud before having to tell the rest of her friends and family.

'So who sacked you?' he asked. 'The espresso or the decaff soya latte with hazelnut syrup?'

Chloe recalled his disdain at that order. 'The latte.'

'Couldn't work for a guy with such bad taste anyway – you're better off without him.'

With a small act of kindness he'd given her the strength to face the world and she was so pleased he was still in her life. One day she'd see him again and repay that kindness.

'Earth calling Chloe, Earth calling Chloe.' Roisin was tapping her on the side of the head. That irritated!

'Sorry, I was miles away,' she said, shaking her head rapidly to get away from Roisin's taps.

'I could see that. I was asking what's on the agenda today?'

'I'm going to contact the guests who are coming and see if there's anything they specifically want to do when they're here,' Chloe said, heading over to the sink to wash up her breakfast things – an action that seemed to astonish Heather who stood by her side itching to wrestle them from her and do them properly.

'After all,' continued Chloe, 'there's no point in us organizing lots of activities if all they want is a peaceful place for brainstorming.'

Roisin nodded her agreement and after breakfast they went their separate ways. Chloe took the laptop to the yoga studio and her friend went glossing the exterior doors of the lodges.

Chloe looked up the names of the people who'd booked in. She was half-relieved and half-disappointed to see that they weren't the top guys: a production manager, a production co-ordinator and an account manager. They could have been up here shooting an ad so perhaps this was a wrap party? Chloe made the call and established that her guesses were correct. They were filming nearby and their visitors had simply wanted to see more of the coastline before heading back.

'It's been a pretty hardcore schedule,' the production manager said to her, 'but we've been blown away by how gorgeous this place is. So fresh air, good food and a bit of a laugh would be nice.'

'We can certainly deliver all of that,' Chloe reassured him.

They would arrive on the Friday evening and leave first thing Monday. Chloe mentally noted three breakfasts and three dinners plus two full days of activities. They could be flexible depending on the weather but surfing lessons would be perfect for one day, yoga and a hike or bike ride would be great for another; the chocolate workshop would be a more relaxing activity and of course they'd have a night of music at the pub. She had started to see each activity as a little snapshot and if she gave their visitors enough variety, both the guests and Olly could share everything on social media and awareness of the retreat and it's range of activities would spread. It wouldn't be enough to get Roisin the steady stream of customers she needed but they had to start somewhere. Chloe had found out all she could so slapped shut the laptop and joined Roisin at the lodges.

'Wow that makes such a difference,' she declared on seeing the shiny glossy turquoise doors. 'They all look brand new now, almost Mediterranean.'

Chloe took some pictures of the buildings being painted and of Roisin standing smiling, her face speckled with paint. She'd give them to Olly for posting later and thought up a joke about the cakes being handmade and lodges being hand-painted to go alongside.

'Well don't just stand there like my executive assistant,' Roisin said, flicking paint at her from the brush. Chloe looked down at herself, splattered with gloss, relieved she was still wearing one of Roisin's old tie-dyes. 'Get a brush and get painting.'

Chloe did as she was told and joined her friend, brush in hand, carefully giving the buildings their finishing touches. She gathered paint on the brush and applied it to the knots and gnarls of the old doors; the strokes went up and down, and carefully from left to right until the tired became fresh again. Stretching high on her tiptoes and then bending to the ground, Chloe couldn't remember a time when her whole body had been worked like this; she was feeling muscles she'd forgotten she had coming back to life. Her breathing also fell into rhythm with her arms, inhaling up and exhaling down. Despite the effort, it was calming – as if they were nurturing themselves and the farmhouse at the same time.

'I thought you might like something to drink.' Heather appeared behind them with a tray of homemade lemonade and flapjacks. Seeing them was enough to make her stomach rumble and as hers started groaning, Roisin's joined in.

'It's good to see the place being looked after again,' said Heather, looking up at their efforts as they finished the plate of food. 'You girls are making an old woman very happy.' And with that she picked up the empty plate and headed back to the kitchen.

'Neither of you ever mention a grandad,' said Chloe as they watched the farmhouse door close.

'I guess that's because I never knew him,' replied Roisin. 'It's always been just Gran. I think he died not long after Mum was born.'

'That's so sad. Was there ever anyone else? I can't imagine her living here all alone for all that time – she seems too amiable for that.'

'She didn't remarry, I know that but she was never alone because of all the art retreats she ran. I do remember there being an artist who she seemed quite sweet on. He used to come and stay every now and then. He had a big beard and Gran used to tell me there were birds nesting in it. I actually looked for them.'

'Do you think he was the one that got away?'

'Or maybe he did her wrong too and he's under the floorboards.' Roisin laughed.

'Oh for goodness' sake, if I wanted to do anyone in I'd use arsenic and feed them to the fishes.' The girls jumped at the sound of Heather returning with another plate of flapjacks. 'It smells just like the almonds I've put in these so they'd never know until it was too late.'

She handed Chloe the plate and headed back to the kitchen, turning round to face them before disappearing inside. 'Enjoy.' She grinned mischievously.

Chloe looked down at the plate while Roisin picked up a flapjack and took a sniff.

'It's cinnamon not almond.' She smiled and took a huge bite.

'We'll have to put your gran in charge of Halloween ghost stories when the time comes,' said Chloe following suit. 'I'm still shaking.'

With the doors complete and needing to dry, they decided to take a walk down to the sea. It was yet another glorious day and that cornflower canopy of a sky was barely disturbed by cloud, while down past the golden sand, the sun glistened on the wave tops. A seagull cried out overhead.

'We should make a video,' declared Chloe taking out her phone and narrating as she did.

'Here I am, in a stunning corner of the world – blue skies, birds and endless ocean.' She pointed the phone at Roisin. 'And this is the yoga guru who'll be looking after you when you arrive.'

She panned the sea and zoomed in as she spotted a black object bobbing around.

'Oh my God, is that a sea lion?'

In the background Roisin laughed. 'You're not exactly Dr Doolittle are you? We get seals around here, not sea lions – they're the ones with the flippers that go ORrk-OrRk.'

Roisin was doing sea lion impressions as Chloe turned the camera back on her and their joint laughter filled the background.

'Sun, sea, sand and animal impressions, what more could anyone want? Come and see us at Serenity Bay.'

As soon as the video was posted, Chloe got several replies saying it looked stunning and telling her how amazingly lucky she was to have escaped the city. She used every comment to suggest that people come up and see it for themselves, hoping they didn't think it was a free invitation. Nearer the shoreline, the black bob came into focus; it was a head not a seal and the head belonged to a surfer in a wetsuit. Not any old surfer, but, as he rode back onto the sand: Andy. Chloe had to admit, he wore that wetsuit well.

'You two down to check me out?' he yelled. 'To check I actually know what I'm doing and won't drown your customers?'

Chloe was glad he'd qualified his first question as she realized she had been staring at him for more than would have been considered polite. They were now stood by the rock where he'd evidently dumped his clothes and towel, and as he approached them Roisin automatically held out the towel for him and he used it to rub his shaggy hair.

'Nice day for it,' was all Chloe could think to say.

'It's always nice when the waves call,' he replied, unzipping the back of the suit and unrolling the top half. 'I've got a flask in that bag over there if you fancy a coffee.'

Relieved to have something to do other than watch him get changed, Chloe hotfooted it over to a bag on the sand where she spent far too long retrieving the flask, just to give him enough time to pull off the rest of the suit. Roisin didn't move and if Chloe had known anything about surfing, she'd have realized there was no need to try and respect his modesty as surfers were adept at changing anywhere and at any time. As she walked back towards him, she couldn't help but think that if she could get a picture of herself and Andy onto her social media accounts, it would certainly let the world (and yes, by world she meant the man who'd dumped her) know she was having a very good time indeed.

'Can we get some pictures?' she asked. 'To advertise the retreat? Maybe you and Rois then all of us together? They'll be on social media if you don't mind that.'

'It's a necessary evil,' he replied. 'Just as long as you're not one of those oversharers. You know, here's my dinner, here's my toenails, here's my latest bowel movement.'

'I'm sure no one actually does that.' Chloe grimaced.

'I bet you they do somewhere,' replied Andy handing her a coffee. 'The great irony of it all is that everyone is trying to be mindful while they're doing all this social media. People spend good money to get away from it all so they can focus on the here and now. Then they can't wait to get back onto their damn phones to tell complete strangers how mindful they were. I tell you the world is mad.'

'Well we're here to try and make it a little more sane aren't we?' said Roisin.

'Doing what we can.' Andy high-fived Roisin. 'So where do you want me?'

They took action shots, laughter close-ups, staring into the distance shots, arty wave and surfboard shots and pretty much everything else they could think of. As Chloe swiped through the images they'd captured, Andy nodded, impressed.

'Looks like a surf catalogue,' he said. 'I could use some of them myself if you send me them.'

He said his goodbyes and packed up his things, leaving Chloe and Roisin watching his muscular frame heading towards his van.

'I imagine we're going to have a few of our female guests falling head over heels with him,' said Chloe. 'They'll be staring into his baby blues as he tells them how to stand straight.'

'They're hazel,' replied Roisin although Chloe had actually spotted that for herself. 'Apparently a rare combo, blonde hair and hazel eyes.'

Chloe held back a pang of anxious jealousy and gave her

friend a friendly punch on the arm. 'Roisin Norton. Here I was thinking you were doing all this for the health of the nation and it's all just lust. You've got the hots for the surf instructor!'

Roisin shook her head. 'Absolutely not. We've known each other for decades – one of his exes told me about the colour of his eyes while she was mooning over him in the bar.'

'Has lots of exes does he?' asked Chloe, relieved that her friend was genuinely not interested.

'No, he's not like that actually. Just as well. He knows that Gran and I have to approve any woman he goes out with and we have very high standards,' said Roisin with a sly smile on her face. 'But you'll be pleased to hear you've passed our test.'

'What do you mean?'

'Always happens in films – city girl heads to the country and falls in love with the gorgeous local, ends up living there and making a living baking cupcakes or whatever. So you've done the living here part, and I saw the way he looked at you – it could be your happy ever after.'

Was he? Looking at her in that way? 'I very much doubt it,' she mumbled. 'I can't bake for a start.'

They sat down on the sand looking out at the sea, saying nothing more but listening to the hypnotic sound of the rolling waves over the sand. Chloe lay back and closed her eyes, letting her entire being just drift and shortly afterwards she felt Roisin lying down beside her.

'What are you thinking about now?' asked Roisin.

What else could she be thinking about after that conversation? She'd been recalling every time she'd bumped into Andy trying to picture the look he'd given her. Had it meant anything? It felt as if fate was playing a very big part in her life right now. She pushed herself up onto her elbows and looked across at her friend.

'I've got this feeling that anything could happen here. You're going to make it, Roisin.'

'I feel that too.' Her friend smiled. 'It's a magical place.'

Chapter Fourteen

When Chloe walked into the yoga studio after a long morning's walk, the first thing she saw was Roisin's backside pointing into the air.

'Downward dog?' she said to the rear end of her friend.

'I don't want to be rusty when they get here,' said Roisin. 'Come and join in.'

Chloe stood alongside Roisin and followed her instructions through a Sun Salutation, jumping her legs forward to a half fold, then full fold and eventually ending up in Mountain pose with her hands in a prayer position. They repeated the sequence three times and by the end of it, Chloe was feeling alert and six inches taller.

'That was incredible,' she said. 'They're going to feel fabulous after a session with you.'

'I think we're ready,' replied Roisin without acknowledging the compliment. 'But we should check everything is set before they get here. You said they sounded fairly relaxed on the phone but you never know. We'll have a run through with Gran and then you can text them to see if their ETA is still the same while I air the rooms.'

They walked towards the kitchen together and Chloe put her hand gently on Roisin's back.

'I know we'll be very busy today,' she said softly, 'but I haven't forgotten the date.'

Roisin shook her head and waved away the comment.

'So if you don't feel like facing anyone,' continued Chloe, 'just let me know. I know it's our first guests but we have a full schedule in place and I could probably manage getting them to where they have to be.'

'Thank you,' replied Roisin. 'But I'm good, honestly. Now, shall we see what's on the menu?'

They walked into a wave of heat and a frenzy of flour.

'You'll have to get yourselves something, I'm busy,' said Heather without looking up from her mixing bowl. 'When they walk in here tonight, there'll be fresh scones, cakes, bread and pies all waiting for them.'

'*Ohhh*,' groaned Chloe just imagining it. 'The aroma will be fabulous. I can just picture it like a cloud of gorgeousness wafting from here to the bay – they'll be like Bisto gravy kids following it, their noses in the air.'

'How do you know about that?' asked Heather. 'Those ads were from before my era, never mind yours.'

'An advertising classic. I also know about the Shake n' Vac adverts and could probably even sing the song.'

Heather smiled at the memory and continued whisking the life into some butter and sugar while the girls helped themselves to toast then cleaned up everything, including the bowls the housekeeper was still attempting to use.

'As much as I appreciate your help,' she said as she yanked the spatula out of Roisin's hand, 'do you two think you could keep busy somewhere else?'

It was an affectionate reprimand and the three of them had a group hug before leaving Heather to her domain. They had two hours to kill but had checked everything so many times over the past couple of days that there really was nothing left to check. They were as ready as they could be.

'So tell me again what all of these people do?'

'Well they're the ones who actually film the ads and do the photography,' Chloe explained. 'An ad agency comes up with the idea but they hire a production company like this one to actually make the ad. The production manager and co-ordinator will make sure that the filming is on schedule, that it goes smoothly and comes in on budget. If anything goes wrong, for example if it rains when they're due to do an outside shot, they'll re-work things to find an indoor venue or change the schedule around so it doesn't cost more. They're very practical people.'

'And the other one?'

'The account manager looks after the client so if the company whose ad it is wants to watch the filming, then they'll make sure they're taken care of,' continued Chloe. 'They'll also answer any questions that might come up. It sounds as if they just want some time to relax. Shoots can be pretty demanding, especially if you need night scenes – you can be working eighteen hours a day.'

'Sounds horrendous.'

'It's not, it's actually really exciting.' Chloe had a sparkle in her voice. 'You're a team working together to get a job done and everyone knows their role. And it's creative. You might not be the director but you see the magic come together before your eyes.'

'And now you can witness the magic of our project,' said Roisin. 'You can watch as stressed out advertising executives become relaxed human beings again in just forty-eight hours.'

'Now that is what you call a miracle.' Chloe smiled as her phone beeped a text. She checked her phone and took a really deep breath. 'And you better be ready to make it happen because they're half an hour away.'

Screaming with excitement, they ran back to the house yelling, 'They're on their way!' They stopped dead as they walked into a baking equivalent of Willy Wonka's Chocolate Factory. As Heather had promised, the work surfaces were piled with fresh, warm goodies and she was still putting a final tray into the oven.

'Don't touch a thing,' she said waving a finger and leaving them in a room full of temptation.

'It's not exactly a health retreat is it?' said Chloe looking round at a year's worth of calories cooling on racks.

'Here's hoping they're starving when they get here. Come on, quick spruce up.'

By the time the knock on the door came, Heather had a new apron on, Roisin had new harem pants and enormous feather earrings in, Chloe's neat dark ponytail was bound with a new scrunchie and there were fresh roses cut from the garden in a vase on the table. The final batch of scones had emerged piping hot and smelling fabulous and the blackboard had its first slogan written:

'Laughter is brightest where the food is the best.'

When two men and a woman walked through the door, Chloe felt a shiver of delight; okay so they'd arrived before they'd had the chance to get the place really up to scratch but whether they were ready or not, Serenity Bay was officially up and running. Now all they had to do was make sure these three people had a lovely time. They were currently looking around the kitchen with eyes like dinner plates.

'Wow,' said the production manager she'd spoken to on the phone. He introduced himself as Kareem. 'This looks amazing. Are you expecting a hundred other people?'

Heather accepted all their compliments with grace and soon had them sitting down for a welcoming slice of cake. Roisin talked them through the schedule for their stay and then Chloe took them to their rooms in the lodges. Throughout this first hour, Chloe was relieved to note the atmosphere was friendly and relaxed. Their guests looked exhausted and she was absolutely sure that by the end of their stay, they'd feel a whole lot better. There would undoubtedly be a moment when the conversation turned to how this place had been set up and Chloe was hoping that, when the time came, she'd be able to casually mention that she had a background in the ad industry and was happy to talk to them about hosting film shoots here.

Having had a short rest and unpacked, the guests re-emerged in the kitchen. Kareem, along with Will the account manager and Jemima the production co-ordinator, said they wanted to be outdoors. They'd spent several days indoors filming a medieval banquet scene in one of the Northumbrian castles and said they were simply craving some fresh air.

'So what was it for?' asked Roisin. 'Some historical drama?'

'Wild boar flavoured crisps, but don't worry, no animals were injured in either the filming or the actual manufacture,' replied Kareem, raising his eyebrows at the ludicrousness of the situation.

'That's a relief,' said Roisin. 'You don't half have to do some weird things in your line of work.'

Chloe looked to give Will and Jemima a knowing glance but of course they didn't realise she was one of them and were sharing that look between themselves.

I know what it's like! Chloe wanted to shout but couldn't. It wasn't time yet.

Later that afternoon she led them down to the coastal path where five bicycles were waiting for them.

'We're going to start the weekend with a cycle along the coastline to get that heart pumping and those lungs full of fabulous fresh air. It's quite flat and not hard to navigate – basically keep the sea to the right.'

They laughed in the right places and picked out the right-sized bikes and helmets then, wobbling at first, set off along the cliff edge. Predictably, the guys started racing each other then collapsed out of breath after less than ten minutes.

'There's something about bikes isn't there?' said Jemima as she cycled alongside Chloe. 'They make you feel as if you're in some sort of adventure book.'

'It's like being a child again,' replied Chloe, meaning it. 'I don't know what it is, maybe the wind in your face, the sense of freedom?'

'And the basket on the front. I feel like one of the Famous Five.' Jemima laughed. They reached a steep downhill slope and both took their feet off the pedals, freewheeling and shouting '*Wheeee*' as they went. Roisin stopped the group every now and then to point out the islands that lay off the coast and tell them snippets of history. Both Chloe and Roisin had crammed some knowledge of the early Christian settlements and Viking invasions but they would never be able to answer every question so had decided simply to note anything they were asked and google it when they got back.

'That was brilliant but it's going to be a tough cycle back,' puffed Will after they'd cycled for a couple of hours and had come to the end of the path. 'The wind direction's moved – it'll be in our faces all the way.'

Chloe smiled and, holding her hand over her eyes to shelter them from the sunlight, looked over the fields that led from the cliffs towards a small road. On cue, a van was driving towards them.

'We're not cycling back,' she said like a magician about to pull a bunny from a hat. 'The wind always moves this time in the afternoon, so we're leaving the bikes here but keep hold of the helmets as we're taking a different mode of transport home.'

Andy pulled up and gave the group a little salute before taking the bikes from everyone and loading them into the van. He'd told Chloe about the change in the wind direction and she guessed correctly that, although their visitors wanted exercise, on the first day there, they didn't want to be completely worn out.

'So how are we getting back then?' asked Kareem.

'By yachts,' declared Chloe. 'More specifically: land yacht.'

There were murmurs of excitement and nervousness all round and Roisin led the group down the cliff path onto the vast open beach.

'This sand is amazing,' said Will, reaching down to let the grains run through his hands. 'It's so soft, almost like moss or velvet.'

Roisin beamed with pride and walked everyone over to a firmer stretch of sand where what looked like go-karts with sails stood waiting for them. A friend of Andy's strapped them all in and gave them their instructions before letting them loose to whizz along the sand, back towards home. Chloe had never done anything like this before and while it had looked easy when it had been demonstrated to her a couple of days ago, now she was in the driving seat, it was both terrifying and exhilarating. The speed of these tiny carts was incredible and if you tried to turn too quickly, the wheels lifted off the ground. It was like being on the dodgems but strapped to a kite. Screams of delight and laughter accompanied their return journey as each of them flew along the beach in less than a quarter of the time it had taken them to cycle the distance. The banter continued as their guests mocked each other's efforts and recounted tales of personal speed and courage throughout the evening.

When their guests finally went to bed that night with rosy cheeks and full bellies, Roisin opened a bottle of wine and poured glasses for Chloe and Heather.

'I think our very first day went well,' she said as they clinked glasses. They all sighed together.

Chapter Fifteen

'Woah – this is stunning,' said Kareem as they walked towards the bay. Ahead of them, the sun lay low and mellow in the morning sky and the glistening waves rolled gently beneath it. 'It must be an incredible place to live.'

Chloe had deliberately walked alongside Kareem and kept the pace slow, hoping for the ideal opening in the conversation and there it was.

'It's stunning isn't it? But I don't really live here – the retreat belongs to Roisin.'

'So you're just helping out?'

'For now. I used to work in advertising as well.' Chloe told him the name of the company and he whistled.

'Big guns eh? Bet you're finding all this a bit different from London.'

Chloe nodded and was about to sandwich in the fact that she was hoping to continue using her advertising skills up here when the rest of the party yelled at them from the beach to hurry up. Kareem whooped at them and started leaping down the sand until he barrelled into his colleagues and, wrapping his arms around Will, rolled him onto the sand. Jemima raised her eyebrows.

'I've been a gooseberry all week,' she told Roisin and Chloe as they walked towards the stack of surfboards waiting for them. 'It's great to finally have some other company.'

'Nothing worse than being the spare wheel is there?' replied Roisin jokingly. 'Chloe knows all about that.'

'You might just be the world's worst best friend you know,' said Chloe, then yanked her friend's sunhat off her head and, pulling Jemima with her, started running down the beach with it.

They soon reached Andy who shook his head at the group chasing each other and rolling around.

'You look as if you have a lot of energy to burn so let's get moving. Wetsuits are over there. I'll help you find the right size and then we'll get moving.'

Both Chloe and Roisin noted that Jemima was checking Andy out and heading towards the wetsuits first.

'That man could probably have a different woman every night,' said Chloe.

'Don't worry yourself,' replied Roisin. 'It'll be your turn soon enough.'

They exchanged a few more friendly jabs as their guests were fitted out. They all looked pretty good in their gear so Chloe walked around the beach taking lots of photos; the windswept hair, sunglasses and smiles were simply the perfect images for the retreat.

'Come on you two!' shouted Andy. 'You're not getting out of this.'

Reluctantly, Chloe allowed herself to be squeezed into a wetsuit and led towards a board lying on the sand. Andy started off with exercises to limber them up then moved onto how to stand on a board, giving them balance exercises which he explained were simply to give them confidence. With her years of yoga practice, Roisin was soon doing a tree pose – standing on one leg with the other folded and resting on her thigh – *on* the surfboard. Chloe tried to copy and wobbled over.

'Roisin's a natural,' said Andy as he held Chloe by the waist to steady her. She hoped her cheeks weren't glowing as much as the rest of her body seemed to be. 'Now let's practice popping up.'

Andy got everyone to lie down on the ground as if they were swimming out on the surfboard and then led the group through a series of movements to get them standing. Even on the ground Chloe couldn't get into position so when, after half an hour of practice, Andy suggested moving onto the wobbly training board, she politely declined.

'I'll take the pictures,' she told Andy. 'I think I'm meant for more stable activities.'

Chloe sat down on the sand and watched their guests relaxing. She and Roisin had joked about turning advertising executives into normal human beings in only forty-eight hours, but here they were, focusing so intently on standing up on a piece of foam board that Chloe knew they wouldn't be worrying about the last shoot or even the next. If she could get this group to spread the word amongst other ad agencies, then Roisin could have a lucrative income stream. Chloe recorded a note for herself to develop some short weekend breaks to be marketed as de-stress packages and got back to taking pictures.

Out on the sea, everyone was managing to stand on the surfboards so Chloe waded in thigh deep to get the pictures of each of them surfing. Okay, so they were only in two feet of water and the waves were gentle and rolling, but with a bit of cropping and editing, these pictures would look very impressive and Chloe knew they'd be delighted to show them off. She posted a couple of pictures of Roisin on their social media pages telling the world that the owner was having as good a time as the guests. Zooming in on the big smiles she'd captured, Chloe realised she was as relaxed as the rest of the group. It was going well. Their first guests were happy and enjoying themselves. This might not be a conventional wellness retreat but it certainly seemed to be making everyone feel better.

When Heather appeared on the sands with a basket of food, Chloe checked the time – it had been five hours since they last ate and even though she hadn't done much of the exercise this morning, she suddenly felt hungry.

'What's in the basket?' she asked, trying not to lick her lips as they spread out a checked picnic rug and she eagerly helped decant the goods in the basket. It was yet another picture perfect image and Chloe managed another couple of snaps before Heather shooed her out of the way.

'Pasties, easy to eat with your fingers.'

More carbohydrates, Chloe mused. That was one aspect of this retreat that really needed to be addressed if the guests weren't going to go home pounds heavier. Heather called out for everyone and left them to the food, making Chloe promise to bring the picnic basket back. Will, Kareem and Jemima were soon tucking in, seeming to have no concerns about the carbs.

'This is definitely what you need after all that isn't it?' enthused Will. 'So what's next?'

Roisin explained that no matter how good they felt right now, all that leaping about in the sea would have exercised muscles that hadn't been worked in ages – even at the gym. This afternoon was dedicated to stretching and meditation in one of her yoga classes. They had a little over an hour to shower and change into gym clothes while Roisin and Chloe helped Andy to gather up the equipment before meeting in the yoga studio for the session. As they watched the guests make their way back to the house, Roisin wrapped her arms around Chloe and hugged her.

'It's going well isn't it?'

'It really is,' replied Chloe, returning the hug.

Despite all being adamant that they had the energy to do the surfing session all over again, there was definitely snoring going on in the meditation session. Roisin had guided them through a series of very deep stretches and ended with everyone lying on their backs with their palms upright by their sides, eyes closed in corpse pose. Chloe tried to join in but realized that although she wanted to relax, she couldn't. From out of nowhere there was a tension holding on to her. She pictured Jonathan and the last time she saw him in the apartment; that wasn't the source of the tension she was feeling – in fact it felt as if she was remembering a scene from a movie rather than her own life. The emotions had gone, or at least the love had. Roisin was asking everyone to mentally scan their bodies to see if there were any pockets of stress hiding away and as Chloe scanned hers, she tried to work out what she was feeling. There was something there but she couldn't quite name it.

'You're welcome to lie here for as long as you like.' Chloe tuned in to hear Roisin calling the session to a close. 'Or you could have a power nap before tonight which will be another active session that I'm sure you'll all enjoy.'

Chloe was relieved to be able to get up as her tension was turning to anxiety and her body began to twitch. She felt as if she could only relax when she was active and, fortunately, the final night was going to be an evening of local music and dance at The Fiddler's Arms. Again it wasn't a traditional retreat activity but Maggie had been determined to be part of the schedule ever since holding the talent evening. Chloe had a couple of hours to herself before being back on duty and wanted to post the pictures she'd taken today. She retreated to her room and propped herself up on pillows with the laptop balanced on another. Will, Jemima and Kareem had all given permission for the shots to be shared and tagged; they'd even complimented her on making them look so proficient on the surfboard. She sent the pictures to Olly to upload onto all the social media sites he'd created for them. Then, thinking it would be a good idea to promote this place as a de-stress retreat for the advertising industry, Chloe drafted an idea for a small article in the industry trade mag, *Advertising Weekly*. It focused on her career change but predominantly sold the bay.

"Serenity Bay has a unique vibe that simply melts stress and nurtures harmony," she wrote. *"When I was first asked to build a marketing strategy for this place, I just knew it was the perfect place for the ad world. Here you escape the hype and get back in touch with what matters."*

She added a glorious photo and pressed send; who knew, it might be different enough for them to feature. The whole proposal had all the buzz words anyone looking for a company awayday would want to hear and she'd got her own name and role in the piece too. Her plans for making a living here were developing and if they ran it, she could forward the piece to the Tourist Board or local council and might be able to persuade them to create a paid role marketing this stretch of the coast.

The sound of seagulls fighting over something made her look up; she went to the window and breathed in that ubiquitous blue sky. The gulls were fighting over some scraps that Heather had thrown out and Chloe smiled as one of the seabirds plodded off with a crust of Mediterranean Vegetable Quiche in it's beak.

'I remember the day when you lot ate bread crusts,' she said to it. 'Honestly, these days even the gulls have hipster taste buds.'

Chloe closed the window and changed into some cropped jeans and a jumper for the evening. Whatever it was she'd been feeling while lying on the floor in the yoga class, it hadn't been regret about Jonathan, nor her decision not to return to London – but neither was it peace or relaxation. It felt as if she'd been climbing a mountain and could see the peak; but when she got there, she realized it was only a small peak and the real climb was just behind it, coming into vision. Roisin now had her first guests and it was going well but Chloe couldn't get sucked into running the retreat – this wasn't her goal. To fulfil her own dreams, she had to find a way of marketing the whole of Serenity – and get paid doing it.

Chapter Sixteen

In fairness to Maggie, she'd really pulled out the stops in decorating the pub for the guests. The brass was sparkling, the wooden handles of the pumps shining and the fire was roaring away. Chloe gave her a discreet thumbs-up as they were led through a crowded room towards a table especially reserved for them.

'We've got live music tonight so this is close to the action and not too far from the fire. It might be summer but being cosy works all year round in my book,' said Maggie to the group. 'Now what can I get you all?'

The publican highlighted an extensive range of craft gins and local ales which Chloe was pretty certain hadn't been offered to them when she'd first arrived. Kareem, Will and Jemima delighted Maggie by each choosing something from her new range, leaving Chloe and Roisin thinking it would be rude not to do the same. In the corner of the room, a four-piece folk band started setting up and tuning their instruments.

'Oh God, I hope they're good,' whispered Roisin.

'My thoughts exactly,' replied Chloe, clenching her teeth at the screech of a bow being pulled painfully across a fiddle. 'It's been such a brilliant day – we can't leave them with an awful final night.'

The whole group jumped as the drummer knocked over a cymbal stand and then, as the singer staggered up with a bottle of beer in her hand, the room went quiet, shifting awkwardly in chairs wondering what on earth was happening and whether they should do anything. Chloe could feel her heart thumping and looked over at Maggie to see how she was reacting to the band she'd booked. Maggie looked quite relaxed and smiled back at her. The fiddler stood at the centre of the room and started playing. Chloe thought it sounded okay but then she knew she hadn't a clue what constituted good folk music. Then the singer joined him and started singing into the beer bottle, then realizing it wasn't the microphone, she put it down and picked up the mike with an exaggerated sway before winking at the audience. The room breathed a collective sigh of relief and the band started up with their first song.

'*A seagull stole my sandwich, I was saving it for you. Then you left me for my sister, I guess that seagull knew ...*'

The lyrics and the performance were hilarious and soon had the whole room laughing and clapping along. They were all really good musicians and mixed the funny songs with some regional sea shanties which had everyone singing and a few old guys dancing. Jemima was dragged up from her seat and swirled around the floor so the guys got up too and performed something that looked like a cross between an Irish jig and a Morris dance. The night ended with one of the locals teaching everyone how to do an extremely energetic dance called Stripping the Willow. It left the entire retreat group completely exhausted and queuing for liquid refreshment.

'Well this isn't what I expected from a health retreat,' said Will, taking a sip of amber ale. 'But there should certainly be more like this.'

'Health is all about wellbeing,' replied Roisin. 'And happiness is the key ingredient to wellbeing. As long as you don't overdo anything, it's like my gran always says – *a little bit of what you fancy does you good.*'

'And she's a wise woman but still, can you imagine the *Turning Back the Clock* crew agreeing to this?' said Kareem.

'What's that?' asked Chloe.

'It's a brand new reality show we're shooting in a few weeks. Celebrities stay in one of the top health resorts in the world and get all these treatments. They have their biological age checked at the beginning and then again at the end to see if the health treatments have made them turn back the clock.'

The cogs were whirring as Chloe tuned out of the conversation. This was what Roisin needed – something big to make the place famous. As the group left the pub and headed back to the retreat, Chloe hung at the back and cornered Kareem.

'That programme you were talking about,' she said. 'What are the chances of making Serenity one of the retreats featured?'

Kareem shook his head. 'Probably pretty minimal I'm afraid. I've loved these last few days but the celebs want all the high-tech stuff. They go on so they can get fat sucked out, have fillers pumped in and the years burned off with acid peels.'

Chloe grimaced.

'I know, sounds gross doesn't it but they come out thin and with fewer wrinkles so they're happy.'

They strolled along in silence as Chloe wracked her brain for possible angles; this just seemed too good an opportunity to lose and she couldn't let it go without giving it another shot. 'You said they have their biological age checked? Is that heart rate, blood pressure and stuff like that?'

Kareem nodded.

'Well we could probably hold our own with those measurements; tell me you don't feel less stressed than when you arrived.'

'I feel fabulous,' replied Kareem. 'But I'm really not sure the executives or the network would go for it.'

A frenzy of adrenaline was rushing through Chloe and she got the feeling she always used to when pitching for a new client or brainstorming an idea. This wouldn't just be good for Roisin – but for the whole village!

'Let me put together a proposal,' she said, swinging round to face him. 'All that high-end stuff is all very well if you're a celebrity but the bulk of your viewers won't be able to afford it. We'd be showing what can be achieved with fresh air, laughter and exercise. It'd be a bit of what you fancy versus technology; Grannies' advice versus the scientists'. This could work, you know it could.'

'You're persistent, I'll give you that.' Kareem laughed.

Chloe raised her eyebrows at him.

'Okay, okay. I cannot promise anything but if you put something together I'll put it forward to the network.'

'That's all I ask.' Chloe hugged him and planted a big kiss on his cheek. They strolled back, linking arms and, as they walked, Chloe gathered as much information as she could for her proposal. Ahead of them on the road, a set of headlights appeared and Andy's van came to a stop. He poked his head out of the window as they got closer and offered them a lift.

'Thanks, but we're fine,' said Chloe abruptly, before Kareem had the chance to accept. She needed to keep him talking for as long as possible and tightened her grip on his arm.

'Okay, didn't mean to disturb you both,' replied Andy, equally abruptly. His tyres screeched as he drove off immediately.

'I hope he didn't think …' Kareem sounded apologetic. 'Are you two an item?'

Chloe shook her head but realized that she was walking arm in arm with a handsome guy from out of town and that could certainly be misconstrued. Damn. She hoped Andy hadn't put two and two together getting five. How could she slip it into the conversation with Andy that nothing was going on? The tension she'd felt during yoga reared its head and she knew why. It hadn't just been about carving out her role in this retreat but importantly she also needed to know what Andy thought of her or whether Roisin was actually barking up the wrong tree? Whatever, she really didn't want him to think … She shook her head at herself. She simply didn't have the time to worry about all that right now. First things first.

'No ... we're not,' she replied. 'Now, what do you think I need to put in this proposal?'

That night, after the guests had retired, Chloe started drafting a document for Kareem. Her nature versus science idea was the central theme of the pitch but beyond getting outdoors for exercise which any country or coastal town could propose, what could she actually include? Chloe googled Viking health myths to tie-in with the heritage of Serenity but couldn't find anything beyond learning that the Norsemen had a fish-based diet and cured many illnesses with onion soup. There had to be something she could use.

Chloe forced herself to stop thinking about it in the hope that her unconscious mind would have a revelation. Instead, she mentally worked her way around the village thinking of the different ways each business could play a role in the proposal. The chocolate shop was surprisingly easy to include; there were actual studies which proved the benefits of dark chocolate in lowering blood pressure. Beyond eating the stuff and getting your antioxidants that way, Chloe read all about creating chocolate face masks. This was a great angle: Botox versus cocoa – which could rid the guests of their wrinkles better? The recipe she found for a rejuvenating chocolate mask also included honey which would be a fabulous way of including stories about the monks over on Holy Island and the honey they used in making mead.

Chloe worked until her weary eyes told her it was time to stop. She had sections on home-made food and diet to lower cholesterol, mindfulness through baking and aromatherapy, exercising made pleasurable outdoors, laughter and dancing to get the heart pumping and daily yoga to stretch and recuperate. There wasn't a thing in the programme that couldn't be continued at home – this was a retreat that everyone could recreate. If they could prove health benefits on TV, she was sure it would boost bookings and get them on the roster of locations for future ad shoots. She just needed a finale to hook the production company and the viewers, something very visual that said success. Like a runner at the Olympics climbing onto the podium getting a medal – something that said the celebrities who'd stayed at Serenity had achieved their goals. It would come to her but right now, she had to get some sleep. Chloe put her laptop down by the side of the bed and stretched her arms above her head before snuggling down and feeling each vertebra sink into the mattress. She closed her eyes, happy that it had been a good day and the proposal was practically ready to send. Sleep came quickly and she dreamed of that Olympic runner, rising to the podium. Then she suddenly woke up with eyes wide.

'That's it!' she exclaimed, picking up the laptop and writing up the idea that had just come to her in her dream. She knew exactly what the final activity of the retreat would be. And it was absolutely perfect.

Chapter Seventeen

As they said goodbye to their first ever guests, Chloe had to hold Roisin back from actually hugging them. Instead, affectionately appropriate hand-shakes and air-kisses were exchanged as all three visitors promised to spread the word about the fabulous time they'd had there.

'That would be very helpful,' said Chloe in professional mode, 'and I've emailed a pdf of our proposal. So when you get the chance to look through it, just call me if there are any questions. I'm sure we can accommodate amends if the network needs them.'

Kareem raised his eyebrows in surprise. 'You must have been up all night – that's keen.'

Chloe resisted replying *'desperate, if the truth were known'*. She simply smiled at him. With their arms wrapped around each other, the girls waved them off and then retreated back to the kitchen. Heather had large mugs of coffee ready as they both slumped into chairs around the table, the relief of the success finally taking hold of them.

'I'm exhausted but elated at the same time,' said Roisin. 'Does that make sense?'

Chloe nodded and said she felt the same. She then explained what she'd put in the proposal and Roisin agreed that it all sounded feasible if they could get the village to pull together. They sat drinking their coffees in silence, each deep in their own thoughts and relaxing for the first time in days. Chloe eventually broke the contemplations.

'I thought I'd go into the tourist information hut today and see if Charlie can help me with some more history of the place just in case the TV company want to progress things. Do you want to come?'

Roisin shook her head. 'Heather and I are going to see Mum.'

Chloe reached out and squeezed her friend's hand. The anniversary of her death had happened during the retreat but Roisin had kept going although Chloe knew she'd been thinking about her mum throughout the day. Her friend had scattered her mother's ashes at sea, near a large rock only visible when the tide was out.

'*It's to show that although I can't always see her, I know she is always there*,' Roisin had explained once.

'It's a low tide this afternoon,' she continued.

After finishing their coffees, Chloe went into the garden and picked a bunch of wildflowers for Roisin to take with her. They hugged and went their separate ways.

Charlie was snoozing in his armchair with his chin dropped down on his chest, a magazine on his lap and his glasses precariously close to falling off the end of his nose. Chloe walked over the threshold of the hut but still he didn't budge. She walked back out again and this time pretended to trip over the doormat, yelling an exaggerated, '*Whoops!*' Charlie was startled out of his slumber and caught his glasses just before they hit the floor.

'I was just reading about the food festival happening in Craster over the weekend,' Charlie stuttered, obviously still half asleep and wondering what he'd missed. 'Do you think we should have one of them?'

'Possibly,' replied Chloe, 'but we did struggle to get people here at midsummer so I'm not sure how much of a draw they are any more. I could look into it.' Then, thinking she might be stepping on Charlie's toes, added, 'Or I could help if you're already doing that?'

'I wouldn't know where to start. Tea?'

Chloe accepted the offer and sat down on the foldaway chair offered to her while Charlie took out a flask and poured the milky-looking drink into a plastic beaker for her. Chloe looked around the hut.

'Is there no electricity in this place?'

'There's generally no need. We only open in the summer and there's enough light. I have these battery operated fairy lights and a head torch if it clouds over; then again, when it clouds over, any people who've accidentally found themselves here go home so I might as well shut up shop anyway.'

Chloe sipped her tea, sighed inwardly and wondered where to start with tackling this litany of defeatism.

'Is this a part-time job then?' she asked as an opener.

'It's not even a job – it's voluntary,' replied Charlie. 'There were two of us offered to do a couple of shifts each but then Sheila's daughter had kids and she gave it up to look after them when the daughter went back to work.'

'So it's just you now? Won't the council get someone in to help you?'

'No money they said. It's all about return on investment for them. R – O – I they call it.' Charlie practically spelled each letter out for her but he needn't have bothered because all marketing was about ROI and a cash-strapped council would most certainly have to make sure every penny they spent was accounted for.

'I'd love to give this up now,' Charlie continued. 'The other lads my age have started up a rambling group but I can't get away. I don't want to let anyone down.'

It was the opening she'd been looking for.

'I'm at a loose end you know,' she said gently as if the idea had just come to her. 'I wanted to do some research on the area so I could man the hut for a day or two if you want to go rambling ... but you'd have to show me the ropes first.'

If she'd expected a slight bristle of affront then it didn't happen. Charlie couldn't get out of there fast enough. He'd thrown the remainder of his tea onto the sand outside the hut, screwed the lid back onto the flask, wedged it into his rucksack, and picked up his own foldaway chair and left with it before she could finish the sentence.

'Nowt to it, lass,' he said, handing her the keys. 'Open the door, put the leaflets out and sit on your backside for the day.'

Chloe stood shocked and motionless as he shook her hand, wished her luck and whistled his way down the street. What had just happened?

'He played a blinder there.' Chloe tuned back in to her surroundings and saw Andy approaching, wiping tears of laughter from his eyes. 'He's been dying to get out of running this place for ages but didn't want to lose face with the community.'

'There I was thinking I'd be doing a devoted local servant out of a much-loved position,' replied Chloe, joining in the laughter as it eventually hit her how wily Charlie had been.

'Welcome to my new abode,' she continued, holding her arms out wide and touching both sides of the hut at once. 'Not enough room to swing a cat but enough to do a twirl.'

'Suits you,' replied Andy, still smiling right the way to his eyes. Chloe looked again into those hazel eyes with their flecks of amber that seemed to glimmer in the sunshine; whoever his ex had been, she'd been right – they were quite exceptional.

'I'd offer you coffee but apparently we don't have electricity.'

'That's no problem to sort out. I could hook you up in a few hours,' said Andy, starting to look critically at the hut. 'What are you planning to do with the place? Aren't you supposed to be working with Roisin?'

With the only chair now being the one Chloe was sitting in, Andy sat cross-legged on the floor beside her. He was very supple and beneath the baggy jeans and thrown-on T-shirt, he was muscled from torso to toe. She had to pull her eyes away from the long line of lean thigh – and when she did, she noticed that he'd been looking her up and down too. She quickly composed herself and answered his question.

'I am but I can't do anything like you two can – run activities or workshops – so I'm doing the marketing. But to make the retreat work, we have to make the village work, bring more customers to everyone. Roisin can't advertise an outdoor activity retreat if you go bust and can't offer any surfing or kayaking.'

Andy nodded along as she spoke, adding, 'And they won't come to a village that only has tumbleweed in the high street. So what's the plan? How is the city girl going to save we country bumpkins?' There was a slight edge to his voice which surprised Chloe – that's not how she saw her new role at all.

'Is that still how you see me?' she asked.

'I was only kidding – no need to be touchy.' Andy added a very awkward sounding laugh. 'Go on, tell me the plan.'

Chloe decided to give him the benefit of the doubt although that was the second time he'd implied she was the city interloper. She knew it took some time to be accepted into small communities but she'd just given up the opportunity of a new job to do this. She had to make it work – and she'd need the community to support her while she did.

'We have to find our own niche,' she said in an amicable and steady way which bore no relation to how she felt. 'I need to explore the Viking heritage more to see if we can exploit it in any way. Did you know the Norse translation of Kyrrby is Serenity Bay? How many more customers would you get if we were allowed to rename it?'

Andy nodded and looked thoughtful.

Happy that he hadn't ridiculed the idea, Chloe continued. 'Then I want to try and encourage more photo shoots up here. I'm hoping that the production team who just visited will help us get a place on TV.'

'So the handsome bloke you looked very cosy with will be back?'

'Kareem? Erm, yes, I suppose so.'

'No ulterior motive then.' Andy smirked. 'Just the welfare of the village.'

'Hang on a minute,' said Chloe. 'I seem to remember you getting on very well with Jemima. I'm sure you wouldn't object to seeing her again, adding her to the notches on your surfboard.'

'Well you seem to know my sort.' Andy sounded to be fuming. 'Just a beach bum with a new tourist every week.'

He promptly got up and walked off without saying goodbye as Chloe watched, wondering whether this hut had some magical power that made men walk away from both her and it. The person she'd been worried about offending had practically danced away and the guy she had no intention of hurting had taken a pop at her and then looked as if she'd stabbed him through the heart. What a bizarre half hour.

'I'm pretty sure Kareem and Will are an item anyway,' she murmured in Andy's direction. Then she shouted at him, 'You won't forget my electrics hook-up will you?'

He had heard that as he shook his head, without turning round. Chloe guessed she'd probably kissed goodbye to the idea of Andy as the hut's handyman, without even getting the kiss.

Chapter Eighteen

'We've got another booking,' cried Roisin the following day, dancing around the kitchen, waving her phone in the air.

'Let me see.' Chloe took the phone being held out to her and read that a party of three was coming for a yoga retreat the coming weekend. 'That's brilliant news. Have the production crew put up a rating on TripAdvisor yet?' She checked the website and saw that they hadn't. 'I'll give them a call later on today. It's a good excuse to find out what they thought of the proposal anyway.'

'I'll freshen up the bedrooms and yoga studio,' said Roisin. 'Are you at the hut?'

Chloe nodded and couldn't help but smile that they'd both found their rhythm working together.

'Well have a good day then,' continued Roisin.

'You too.'

The likelihood of having a good day was extremely high, even the tiff with Andy couldn't dampen her mood these days; the sun was shining, her office was a beach hut and strolling along the promenade sure beat cramming into the tube. Chloe practically skipped to the hut and, having opened it up, took some pictures and posted them on every social media site she could.

"Another day at the office – life's a beach" she wrote, knowing it was a well-worn pun but loving it this morning.

Chloe started by sorting out the piles of leaflets stacked everywhere; many of them were years out of date but rather than being thrown out they'd just been hidden at the back of the hut. She'd never be able to carry this lot to the recycling bins in one trip. She needed a wheelbarrow or ... brainwave: her wheeled suitcase would do it. She'd pop back to the house for it at lunchtime. For now, she piled the leaflets up out of sight and put some rocks on top so they wouldn't blow all over the sand. Once she'd tidied up the remaining leaflets, there was a surprising amount of space in the little hut. She switched the fairy lights on just to make it look more welcoming and set up her laptop on a small table at the front. It was time to get to work.

'Knock, knock.'

Chloe was startled from her research by a couple tapping on her table to attract her attention – some tourist guide she was if she didn't even notice the customers loitering.

'I'm so sorry,' she said with a big smile. 'I was completely engrossed there.'

'We didn't like to disturb you. It must be very interesting,' said the woman.

'Actually,' Chloe stood up and showed them the screen of her laptop, 'it really is. Did you know that this village was a Viking settlement and the name means Serenity Bay?'

The visitors looked extremely interested. 'What a lovely name for a place,' they both said.

'I thought so too,' replied Chloe. 'I was just researching how to get the name changed.'

'It would be a lot easier to say than Kyrrby. I wasn't sure how it was pronounced.' The man laughed.

'Oh,' replied Chloe. She hadn't considered that before. 'It's Kee – Er – Be.'

It was well known in wine marketing that if customers couldn't pronounce the name then the brand didn't sell as well. It was one of the reasons that Australian wines with names like Madison Creek were outselling the big French vineyards; customers simply didn't know how to ask for *Macon-Lugny* or *Pouilly Fume*. It was an argument she could add to the name change application.

The couple wanted a recommendation on where to go for coffee. Chloe was about to send them to the coffee shop when she looked up and could see there was a "closed" sign on the door. That wasn't much help to her quest for more visitors. 'I recommend The Fiddler's Arms,' she said. 'And they do a great sandwich if you're peckish. Just tell them I sent you over. And while you're here, that chocolate shop is fabulous – they have things for children and adults so if you want to take something back or just eat it yourself, honestly, it is to die for.'

The couple thanked her and headed towards the pub. Chloe watched them go in and let out a little sigh of relief; maybe she'd helped someone today.

Her research into changing the name of the village hadn't been altogether successful. A quick google search had left her completely bamboozled as all of the links were about changing the name of a village within a computer game. She needed to talk to someone about the process involved and wondered who she could ask. As she was thinking about it, her phone rang. It was Roisin.

'Just wondered if you wanted me to bring you down some lunch? If you can't get away from the crowds that is.'

Chloe laughed and although there weren't any other visitors waiting for her pearls of wisdom, she realized she couldn't really abandon her post at lunchtime so gratefully accepted Roisin's offer and asked if she'd bring the suitcase down with her.

Roisin arrived with her case, and boxes of freshly made quiche and salad, displaying Heather's unmistakable magic touch.

'Does she ever make a bad meal?' asked Chloe, moaning with delight at each mouthful.

'Not even an average one,' replied Roisin, putting the lids on the boxes and looking at the hut. 'This place looks bigger.'

Chloe explained the clear-out and her morning's research. 'Who should I talk to about the name?' she asked.

'Louise,' replied Roisin. 'She used to work at the council before opening up the store. In fact everyone had a past life, even our favourite surfer.'

Chloe expressed surprise. 'Oh yes,' continued Roisin. 'He hasn't always been this beach dude you know. For years he was a lowly schoolteacher. Well not exactly a lowly one. He was a head of some department or other. Wore shirt and tie, combed his hair, and went to meetings – the whole shebang.'

'I can't imagine any of that,' replied Chloe. 'Just as well it's not him I have to quiz. The last time we spoke wasn't exactly amiable.'

'I wouldn't worry,' replied Roisin. 'He doesn't bear grudges for long and besides, I told you, he likes you.'

Chloe snorted. There she was saying that again. Well he had a very funny way of showing it. It felt like he'd been antagonistic with her since day one. It was ironic that despite that little fact she *could* picture him surrounded by children and guessed that's why he had been so good at teaching the agency people. He had patience with everyone but her it seemed.

When Roisin had said her goodbyes and started off home, Chloe got back to work. She called Kareem's number and got through straight away – he was very pleased to hear from her.

'I still have this enormous smile on my face when I think about the weekend,' he said – and she could hear from his voice that he had that smile on now.

'That's what I wanted to hear,' Chloe replied. 'Did you get the chance to put up a review for us?'

She knew he hadn't yet but was relieved to hear that he'd earmarked some time this afternoon to do just that.

'I'm doing it before I take the network chiefs through your proposal,' he said. 'The first pass with the junior staff went well – they really like the nature versus science angle.'

'Wow, that's brilliant news. When do you think we would hear?' Chloe was trying to hide the excitement in her voice.

'As soon as I know, then you will, but these things can take a few weeks. The network have commissioned two series so I'll be proposing Serenity for the second. But don't raise your hopes too much at this stage because we have a number of retreats to consider.'

'None as good as us surely.'

'That's what I'll tell them.'

They ended the conversation with promises to keep in touch no matter what. Almost as soon as she'd ended that call, her phone rang and she could see it was a London number.

'Hello, Chloe Walsh speaking.' She answered tentatively, not knowing who it could be.

The voice on the other end was equally hesitant. 'Hello there, I hope you remember me. It's Gareth – I interviewed you for the role at Blue Banana?'

Chloe was surprised and curious to hear from him but nonetheless expressed delight; after all, it might be another corporate booking. Gareth told her that they were sorry she had decided not to join them but they'd loved her ideas and had pitched them to their client. They'd jumped at them and now Gareth wanted to set up a photo shoot in Serenity.

'I know we could do this much closer to London but it was your idea and it seemed only fair to give you the option.'

Chloe was jumping up and down, silently screaming with joy. She had to contain it all as she calmly replied that they'd be delighted to host the shoot. 'Which idea was it that you pitched?' she remembered to ask.

'Oh, that might have been helpful to mention wouldn't it?' Gareth laughed. 'It's the TruNorth campaign, with sea kayaking to get the younger guys. They loved it.'

Chloe could have laughed out loud but managed to stay professional until all the details were taken. After the call she let the laugh out. 'Ha, Mr Teacher-cum-surf-dude, let's hear what you have to say to the city girl when she tells you about the business she's just landed you.'

The couple who had been directed to the pub reappeared to tell her the recommendation had been fabulous and also that they'd discussed the whole idea of changing the name to Serenity Bay with the pub landlady. 'She thought it was a lovely idea too.' The woman smiled. 'She said someone called Louise might know how to do it.'

'Louise,' replied Chloe. 'Yes, that's what I've been told too. I was just off to try and catch her!'

Chapter Nineteen

At the end of the afternoon, when it really did look as if no one else would be asking for her help, Chloe packed her suitcase full of the old leaflets, locked the hut doors and wheeled the bag towards the recycling bins behind the pub. The sun was still shining and a light breeze was blowing across the bay; who wouldn't want to live in a place like this? It had been a good day: Roisin had a yoga booking, Chloe had helped some visitors, her TV proposal was still being considered, she'd actually secured a photo shoot – *and* she was being paid a fee for the idea. It felt as if, step by step, things were coming together. A little more of this and she'd be a whole lot more relaxed about her decision to go it alone.

'A suitcase? Novelty of living here worn off already has it?'

She brought the trundling wheels to a sharp halt and looked over the street to see Andy with his arms folded and scorn oozing from every inch of him.

'And there was I thinking you were different. Well you lasted longer than most of them anyway.'

Chloe opened her mouth to protest but then shook her head and walked on; she was trying to appear calm but the little wheels of her case gave the game away, whizzing faster and rattling more loudly ... then tripping her as she tried to pick up the pace. Out of the corner of her eye she could see Andy striding purposefully towards her so she tried to speed up but the case skipped over a loose paving stone and bounced bang-smack into her heel, leaving it with a bloody gash. It really hurt and she couldn't pretend otherwise. Chloe kicked the case then hopped around on one leg, holding her foot up.

'Let me look at it,' said Andy, now dashing across the road and putting his hand under her elbow to steady her.

She thought twice about letting him help but this really hurt!

'Sit here. I've got a first aid kit down at the shack.' He led her to a bench on the seafront before running to the Surfshack and back. He held her foot gently, cleaned up the blood with an antiseptic wipe and then put a small plaster on the wound. She hoped it might have needed a slightly bigger one.

'Do you think I'll live?' said Chloe as he slipped her flip-flop back over her toes. Her anger had abated some.

'It's touch and go,' he replied, putting on the earnest air of a TV doctor.

They both laughed and Andy sat down on the bench alongside her, staring out to sea.

'Are you leaving?' he eventually asked.

'And why is that any of your business?' replied Chloe. Despite his medical assistance, she wouldn't have needed it if she weren't trying to outrun him and she wouldn't be doing that if he hadn't insulted her the last time they'd met. She was going to make him work for it before revealing that she had a big new booking for him. Gosh he did rile her!

'You said you'd stay – for Roisin,' Andy replied. 'And I told you, she's a good friend.'

He was evidently going for the couldn't-care-less approach, thought Chloe, but from the way his hands were tapping incessantly on his thighs as he sat, he wasn't feeling as cool as he was acting.

'I'd never let her down,' Chloe eventually replied. 'And no, after I turned my back on the Blue Banana job, I did say I was staying – that hasn't changed. I was actually trawling all the old leaflets to the recycling bin because Charlie never threw a thing out.'

'That would have meant getting off his backside.' Andy laughed. Seeing that the bag was still full of the old leaflets, he wheeled it across to the bin and emptied it while Chloe rested her foot.

Watching that broad shouldered colossus of a man wheeling a cabin-sized pale blue suitcase entertained her greatly. 'That suits you,' she said when he returned. 'I just need to get you a matching vanity case and you're all set.'

He helped her up and suggested that they go to the pub 'to get a quick drink for the shock' before heading home. Chloe accepted and although she could have coped perfectly well on her injured foot, accepted his offer to link arms and steady herself.

Maggie said nothing as she poured drinks for them both but gave Chloe a knowing look and a wink.

'Oh! Louise!' said Chloe, turning and seeing the shopkeeper sitting at one of the tables. 'Would you mind if we joined you? I need to pick your brains. Roisin said you used to work for the council.'

Louise said she'd be delighted to have company and pulled out a chair. Andy helped her into it and they both sat down. Chloe explained the idea of applying for a name change and the rationale behind it. Louise listened and asked the type of questions she might expect from the council and outlined the steps she'd have to take.

'First of all,' she told her, 'you'll have to ensure that the villagers actually want to change the name. Have a meeting and get them to sign up to it before you even approach the council.'

That was a pretty essential suggestion and she knew Maggie would help with sorting the meeting if she asked. Louise outlined the forms they'd have to complete and issues the council would consider, then offered to help with it all.

'Thank you,' said Chloe. 'That would be brilliant.'

Louise finished her drink and left them to it.

'It's funny isn't it,' said Chloe, smiling. 'Everyone in this village has a former life, even you.'

'What's so funny? Were you surprised that a surfer might have a brain?'

Chloe put her glass down and held her palms up. '*Whoa*, let's start again. That is not what I meant at all.' She was getting a bit peeved with walking on eggshells every time they spoke and if she didn't have to talk to him about the Blue Banana job she'd have told him so. For now, the calm, collected approach seemed the best option.

Andy focused on his own drink and said nothing.

'I was surprised when I heard because you seem so at home on the beach, like you've always been there, that's all.'

'I've been running the shack for three years now,' Andy replied quietly. 'But yes, before that I was Head of Geography. I didn't hate it, but didn't love it either.'

Chloe nodded her understanding. 'I feel the same,' she said. 'I liked most of my job but not all of it and if I could bring the parts I liked up here, things would be pretty perfect.'

Rather than agree, Andy snorted and shook his head.

'What's wrong with that?' asked Chloe.

'You bringing your old job here,' replied Andy. 'Everyone thinks that they can improve the place by showing us their big city ways – we're not yokels you know. Maggie, me, Roisin, we're business owners and it's a tough environment but we make a living.'

'I'm not saying that you don't.'

'That would make a change.'

'That's really unfair! I am not like that,' Chloe couldn't help but snap. She took a sip of her cool drink and looked over at him. He looked rather sheepish as if he knew he'd offended her. She sighed and braced herself to tell him about the job. She was thinking he'd either be extremely happy that she was bringing him some business or furious that she'd interfered. Chloe calmly explained it all and held her breath, waiting for his response.

'What would it involve?' Andy wasn't giving away his emotions.

'Taking a model and photographer out for a few days.

They need to get exactly the right shot so it would depend on the weather and sea conditions. They usually send us a storyboard – that's a ...'

'I do know what a storyboard is. Our school did offer media studies.' He gave her a warning look.

She took another deep breath. 'Sorry, I don't know whether I'm talking jargon or not, so tell me if I am.' Her palms were raised once again. 'But anyway, that will say what kind of shot they want: dawn, waves, cliff edges – that kind of thing.'

'Wouldn't it be better if they knew what we could offer first? Why don't I take you out on the sea and show you around – it's easier than surfing so you'll be okay. Take some snaps and let them know what you think. It was your campaign idea in the first place.'

'So you'll do it?'

'Of course. I did say I was a businessman didn't I?'

Maggie came out from behind the bar and started writing up the evening's specials on the board.

'Can I buy you dinner?' asked Andy. 'To celebrate the booking.'

Chloe could almost feel the eyes popping out of her head. It had been the last thing she was expecting but she recognized an apology when she saw one. After calling Roisin to let her know she wouldn't be back for dinner, they looked through the menu together then Andy went up to the bar and ordered them a bottle of wine and the seafood platter.

'Is he going to do that advertising thing?' asked Maggie. She'd appeared by the table with their cutlery the moment Andy had gone into the Gents.

Chloe realized nothing got past the landlady. She nodded. 'I think so, but he keeps turning hot and cold so I'll believe it when I see it. Half the time, he seems to have a problem with me just being here.'

'It's not his fault. He's been burned before,' replied Maggie. Then leaning in as if they were conspiring, added, 'He got close to a customer of his a couple of years ago and they ended up getting engaged. She worked in a big consultancy firm in Edinburgh but came down for the weekends and was always going on about how wonderful the place was. She used to love showing him off to her friends, then after a while she started buying clothes for him and telling him how to dress, started complaining that he wasn't earning enough to take her out and whining that there was nothing to do around here.'

'And she left him, I'm guessing.'

Maggie nodded. 'Not before he tried everything to keep her happy. She was gorgeous, I remember that much.'

Chloe pumped the landlady for as many details as she could remember before he got back and established that Andy's gorgeous ex had tried to persuade him to borrow money and acquire other surf and kayaking schools all along the coast.

'She wanted him to be an entrepreneur but eventually realized he wasn't cut out for it and that was that.'

'Kind of explains why he's suspicious of people coming along trying to change things,' said Chloe. And no wonder he was so incredibly prickly with her. She knew that she'd have to tread gently to keep him onboard. And it was pretty clear that he would always stay at arms' length from her because of his past experience. This last realization saddened her more than she would have thought. She attempted to shrug it off – plenty more fish in the sea and all that – and they were right next to a harbour. It's not as if she'd even been looking for romance!

Andy re-appeared and Maggie left quickly.

'She looked as if she was spreading mischief,' said Andy as he poured the wine. 'Anything interesting?'

'Just some local history,' replied Chloe. 'All old news. What shall we toast?'

Andy held up his glass and they clinked. 'To starting over,' he said. 'And by the way, I'm glad you're not leaving.'

Chapter Twenty

'You'll want to capture the dawn light,' he'd said. 'I can't imagine a campaign for something called TruNorth without it.'

And to be fair, thought Chloe as she wiped the sleep from her eyes, it *was* spectacular. But it was also 5 a.m. in the morning! It was a major nuisance that dawn happened so early in the day. She told Andy this when she met him at the Surfshack.

'Dawn happens too early.' He laughed as he unlocked the door and they headed inside. 'That's a good one. I'll have a word with Mother Nature, see if she can do something about it. Would noon suit madam?'

'You know what I mean.' Chloe smiled back. 'In the summer, you've barely been to bed before it's time to get up.'

It was the first time she'd actually been inside the shack and although she didn't know what she was expecting to see, the set-up was impressive. From the old photographs on the walls, Chloe could see that it had once been a lifeboat station. The walls which ran lengthways had metal racks from floor to ceiling and on each rack lay a bright yellow kayak. Stacked up alongside them were paddles while the surfboards took up the whole of the back wall. From rows of clothes rails hung black wetsuits of various sizes, looking like space suits or alien beings from a science fiction film. This would certainly be a very creepy place to visit at night. Andy's desk, with his highly efficient-looking bookings calendar, was crammed into a corner and then through a door were the changing rooms and toilets. Chloe vanished inside the ladies to change and when she reappeared, Andy had taken down a kayak for her which they dragged to the edge of the sea together and lay it next to his.

'Gorgeous time of day though isn't it?' he said.

Chloe put down the paddle she was carrying and stood alongside him. 'It certainly is. No one here but us and the seagulls.'

They stood watching the tide as it ebbed and flowed. With only a very gentle breeze, the white horses were tamed and the morning light was stretching gently towards them. Chloe took some photographs and a small clip of video but they wouldn't capture the real glory of how this felt. She took a deep breath and held it for a few seconds, hoping the magic it seemed to carry would rush around her body and invigorate every cell. The air seemed lighter, like a tiny feather being brushed along her skin. The hairs on her arms shivered and her hand felt like reaching out and holding Andy's. She looked across at him and he turned to meet her gaze. Then he reached out towards her and ... rubbed her arms briskly.

'Getting a bit brass monkeys now though, all this standing around. Come on.'

Chloe snorted with laughter as the moment was broken. What was she doing thinking she was having a moment with Andy anyway? He would obviously take some convincing that she should even be here, never mind anything else.

Their two kayaks and paddles lay waiting at the water's edge. They both wriggled their arms into the wetsuits and pulled them up properly, helping each other with the long zips on the back. Having ensured their buoyancy aids were on tightly, and that the waterproof camera was stored in a safe but accessible spot just between her knees, they pushed off and started the journey. They paddled slowly to begin with and the water seemed to curve over the paddles as they dipped in and out, pushing further towards the horizon. Chloe could imagine the oars of the longships calming as they reached this point; the Viking settlers exhausted from days of travel. She asked Andy to paddle towards her and tried to capture the movement; a professional camera crew would have so much to work with here.

They paddled further out from the bay, hugging the coastline and the cliffs with their families of gulls nestling amongst the tiny pink wildflowers that decorated the rock. A cormorant standing alone on a rock stretched its wings out to dry while another swooped down into the water in front of her and emerged with its breakfast. The place was teeming with life, just going about its day.

'Chloe look!' She looked in the direction of Andy's urgent whisper. Her heart could have burst with pure joy as she saw it – a small pod of dolphins leaping through the waves. They were heading away from them but close enough to see the sun glinting off their shiny grey skin, turning it silver.

'Did you get the shot?' asked Andy and Chloe nodded. She was too dumbstruck to speak. The whole experience was more beautiful than she could ever have imagined. TruNorth would be absolutely delighted with this and Blue Banana might even give her more jobs when they saw this place. Andy checked that she had what she needed and then led her back to dry land. As they climbed out of their wetsuits, the café was just opening up – it felt rather bizarre to have had so much of an adventure before anyone else had even stirred.

'It's as if we've been in a parallel universe,' said Chloe.

'The world is always beautiful just before everyone else gets up,' replied Andy. 'Although when they do get up it means we can have a full English.'

After putting everything back in its place and dressing, they took seats in the café and sighed with delight as they took their first sips of hot tea. Chloe suddenly realized that she was absolutely ravenous; when the bacon butty she ordered arrived, it was demolished within minutes. Andy looked suitably impressed as he started on his full English.

'I was half expecting you to be an avocado on toast kind of girl,' he said over a forkful of hashbrowns.

'I am sometimes,' Chloe replied. 'You can be a decent person and still eat vegetables you know.'

'Very true,' replied Andy. 'And I shouldn't be jumping to conclusions with anyone, especially when I hate that so many people think they know me with one look.'

'To defying your stereotype,' said Chloe, raising her mug of tea.

Andy smiled at her and continued tucking into his own breakfast. 'So what's next?' he asked when the café owner had cleared away the plates.

Chloe blew out her cheeks and started counting off the things she had on her mental list. 'Send these pictures off, check how the TV proposal is going, speak to someone at the council, get the forms I need for the name change, ask Maggie if she'll organize a meeting, then ring the tourist board. I want to see if they'll give us any funding to man the beach hut or at least do it up. See if Roisin needs any help on the yoga weekend, try and get the shops on the high street to have consistent opening hours ...'

She'd reached her eighth finger and paused before continuing. 'Check when the TruNorth people are arriving and invoice Blue Banana so we both get paid on time. There you go, that's ten things I'll do today.'

Andy nodded, impressed. 'I'm very pleased you could fit me in.'

After breakfast, Chloe decided to start with the shops and cafes; she couldn't really direct visitors to them if they weren't open so wanted to try and get them to agree to stay open all day, every day. She was aware that the visitor numbers now didn't really justify opening on some days but believed in that old adage *"build it and they will come"*.

'If people are passing through and nothing is open, they'll just keep driving,' she said to everyone.

They agreed to the sentiment and although Chloe found it a very hard sell, she eventually won everyone over. The gift shop proved a very interesting visit; as she walked in she noted the typical seaside crafts on display, models of wooden beach huts and lighthouses, photographs of the coast and castles, seagulls and puffins on lampshades, paintings and ceramics – then on the wall, a very familiar style of seascape amongst all the others. Chloe leaned in to read the artist's name and confirmed what she'd thought: it was painted by Heather. Louise walked up to her and stood alongside, gazing at it.

'I could sell that ten times over but it's the only one I have so I don't.'

'But there are so many of them up at the house,' replied Chloe remembering the canvases they'd found in the cupboard.

'Well if you can persuade Heather to part with them, I have a huge space in the back. I'll even put on an exhibition for our local artist, though I very much doubt you'll convince her.'

'Why not?'

Louise shrugged and said that she'd have to ask Heather herself. Chloe left thinking that there did seem to be some sort of mystery around Heather's work. It was entirely possible that she simply didn't think they were good enough to exhibit. Many artists doubted their talents. But they were beautiful, atmospheric pieces. Chloe put this mystery in her mental back pocket for later; she had her list for the day and the next stops were the tourist board and local councils. As expected, there was no money to do any maintenance on the hut but if Chloe attracted any funding locally, they'd match it. Chloe had no intention of asking any local business for money so matching nothing wasn't going to be much help – she'd have to find another way of doing the place up. The council were non-committal when it came to the name change but emailed her the right forms and, as Louise had said, told her that they needed to see written agreement from the majority of villagers before considering her request.

'How long does the whole process normally take?' she asked.

'If everything is in place and we have no objections when the application is made, then it can be approved within the year,' came the reply.

Although it was completely unreasonable of her to expect anything else, the timescale seemed far too long and besides which, she'd really played on the fact the bay was called Serenity in her TV proposal.

'Good news,' said Kareem when she called him from the beach hut. 'The network execs love the idea and you're in the very shortlist for series two. They just love the name Serenity Bay.'

'Fabulous,' replied Chloe through gritted teeth. She was glad they weren't Skyping and he was thus denied seeing the manic expression on her face. She couldn't imagine how she would ever get either the council to speed up or the TV company to slow down. 'When do you think it'll all be confirmed?'

'If they don't find any issues when they're ironing out the details, we should get the green light within the next month.'

Chapter Twenty-One

Maggie had wanted to fill the pub again and had hoped the village meeting would be held there but sensibly it was agreed the debate should be held somewhere without alcohol. Therefore at six o'clock on Monday evening, the entire population of Kyrrby were scraping the chairs of the school assembly hall and sitting down ready to listen to Chloe's proposal. Roisin had her nose in the air, sniffing.

'What is it that schools smell of? It's exactly the same in every part of the country.'

'Gym shoes, chewing gum and carefree days,' replied Chloe, biting her fingernails as the crowd looked expectantly towards the small stage they were both sat on.

'Maybe,' said Roisin sniffing harder. 'But I'm sure there's a bit of pee in there too. I'll ask Andy later.'

Chloe snorted and relaxed slightly. It was time to get things started. Maggie and the man himself had been manning the door and now that everyone was in, they took seats on the front row alongside Heather. They nodded supportively to her.

'*Knock 'em dead*,' mouthed Maggie, or at least that's what it looked like.

Roisin kicked off, explaining how she'd invited Chloe up to help her with the wellness retreat and how her friend had come across the Norse translation of the village name. Chloe took over.

'When I heard the translation,' she said, 'I was blown away. I mean who wouldn't want to come to holiday in a place called Serenity? How wonderful does the Serenity Bay Wellness Retreat sound? Or The Fiddler's Arms at Serenity Bay? This is such a beautiful place and having a beautiful name to match can only help us get our share of visitors.'

'*Us?* Since when were you an "us",' shouted someone from the back of the room. 'You've only been here two minutes and already you're trying to change things.'

The incomer argument was one Chloe had been anticipating and because of that she'd also prepared for it.

'You're absolutely right,' she replied. 'I've been here two minutes and in that very short space of time I've fallen in love with the place.'

'Well get us all together when you've been through a winter,' shouted the voice but this time the rest of the villagers started shushing him and another voice called out, 'Let her speak, you oaf.'

Chloe was very used to making presentations to large audiences and although she always got nervous before speaking, those nerves helped her and she knew to wait until the room was silent. When it was, she started to tell them about the first visitors to the retreat.

'They were the production crew for a TV company, shooting an advert down in the next village and I thought, why aren't they shooting their ad here? Our, sorry, *your* coastline is just as beautiful and we, sorry, *you* have plenty of places for them to stay so they should be shooting here.'

'It's more beautiful than anywhere else if you ask me,' called Maggie, getting vociferous agreement from the room.

'So I've made some suggestions for advertisements to be made here,' continued Chloe. 'The first one is actually happening soon and Andy is going to be taking a crew out kayaking, making an ad for TruNorth.'

Andy stood up and got a round of applause as if he'd won an award. 'I've got a week of business I wouldn't have, thanks to Chloe,' he said to everyone before sitting down again. 'And the day rates are better than I'd normally get.'

'So I'd like your permission to keep working with the advertising agencies and production companies to get more shoots in the village. I will try my best to involve as many businesses as I can but make no mistake, shoots involve far more people than you would imagine and they will be buying things, having a drink in the pub and telling people about the place. It would be disruptive but it could be good for everyone.'

Heather stood up and spoke quietly so that the whole hall had to hold their breath and lean in, just to hear her. 'I do love how you've supported Roisin, of course I do and I know that your heart has been captured by this beautiful place – but I have to ask you, how much would all of this change our village? By becoming Serenity Bay would we actually become less serene?'

Heather pressed her palms together and bowed as she sat down. It was a very valid question, asked with grace. Chloe opened her mouth to speak but Roisin tugged her arm so she moved aside for her friend.

'For me, serenity means calmness of mind,' said Roisin. 'And calmness comes from knowing that I can stay here, in a place I love, because I can afford to and I can make a living. We don't want to become another Blackpool but equally we don't want to disappear. We'd have to manage this carefully but Chloe cares and she can do that. We have to let her try, don't we, Gran?'

'Yes, I really think we do,' replied Heather smiling and giving her a thumbs up.

'Tell everyone about the TV programme they want to shoot,' shouted Andy.

There was a murmur around the room. Chloe tried to gauge whether it was excitement, anxiety or plain old curiosity – in her experience, whenever the word TV was mentioned, any and all of those emotions were roused. She decided to play it calmly and walk the line between all three; after all, nothing was confirmed anyway.

'Well,' she began, 'the company behind *Whose House Is This?* are launching a new reality show called *Turning Back the Clock*. It basically puts celebrities in two completely different wellness retreats and sees which one can improve their health most.'

She paused, listening to the murmur of excitement around the room.

'And though it's not one hundred per cent certain yet, we're on the shortlist.'

There were gasps of delight. 'Can we be in it? I could do with losing a few pounds.'

'A few?'

'Cheeky blighter.'

Banter carried on across the hall and Chloe had to calm them down so she could continue. 'It really isn't confirmed yet so please don't raise your hopes. But the thing is that they're very excited about the name Serenity and want to feature that in the series – it's one of the reasons why I want to apply to the council to formally change the name as quickly as we can.'

She explained the process and the need for a majority agreement before their application could be considered.

'In the meanwhile,' asked Maggie, 'is there anything to stop us just calling ourselves Serenity? Like maybe putting the translation on the tourist information hut or on the pub sign?'

Louise replied that they'd have to register name changes but they could each call their businesses whatever they like and they could certainly use the name online or in leaflets. The conversation in the audience now seemed to be about what could be changed anyway and Chloe was in danger of losing their attention. She called the room to order.

'I know it's time to call the meeting to a close so can I just see a show of hands – how many of you would be in favour of making this application?'

The majority of hands went up, but not all.

'That does look like most people but I can see that there are still reservations. My suggestion is this: if you are in favour then please do sign the paper as you leave the hall; if you're not, then please leave your name or come and see me in the tourist hut over the next few days and tell me about your concerns so that we can find a solution that suits everyone. Is that okay?'

There was a collective yes and more scraping of chairs; the meeting was over and it was time for everyone to get back to sport or soap operas having had their hour or so of debate and excitement.

Chloe let out a huge sigh of relief as the room emptied. Maggie gave her an enormous hug and congratulated her on the evening while Andy left with a little salute. Along with Heather and Roisin, Chloe stayed to tidy the room and leave it ready for the morning assembly. As they worked, a man approached, stealth-like, and made them all jump. Chloe recognized him as Mr Bald from the talent evening and thought it strange that he was so distinct looking yet she hadn't seen him around the village at any other time.

'Sorry, I didn't mean to startle you all,' he said in a way that suggested that was exactly what he wanted to do. 'I'm Jeremy Lindell of Lindell and Partners.'

The name meant nothing to any of them but the card he handed out said he was a solicitor. 'I represent Kelvin and Angus Harris,' he continued.

Chloe saw Roisin's body stiffen and her throat gulp. 'My cousins,' she whispered and Chloe felt a chill run through the hairs on her neck. This couldn't be good news.

'Can we go somewhere to talk?' said Mr Bald. 'Perhaps the house?'

'We'll talk here,' replied Roisin.

Heather put her hand on her niece's arm to calm her and started pulling out the chairs that they'd just stacked away. 'The house is a bit of a walk so perhaps here would be best.'

They sat down and Mr Bald (the name seemed to suit him more than Jeremy) pulled some papers out of a briefcase and addressed Heather.

'My clients had a concern, as I think you know, that Ms Norton would seek to assert a right of ownership over the property at the time of your death if the conditions of the sale are not agreed beforehand.'

Roisin threw her arms in the air in anger. 'That's all they can bloody think about. Gran has years and years left – how can they even talk about that?'

Heather again reached out to hold Roisin's hand and nodded for the solicitor to continue.

'They were happy to receive your proposal and agree to it, provided that the property has an independent evaluation as a residential space and as a business. In the event that you decide to sell the property to Ms Norton before your death, they have instructed me to inform you that they are prepared to accept that decision but would wish to be compensated to the full market value.'

Chloe was following the conversation which seemed to be saying that the cousins didn't want the house, just a share of its value and if they could have it pronto, they'd get out of the way.

'That seems fair,' said Heather quietly. 'It's tough for young people to get on the property ladder now and I don't want my family struggling while I sit here with more space than I need.'

'What about the retreat?' said Roisin. 'You can't sell now. I couldn't afford it.'

'The retreat is a lovely idea and it's your dream, I know that,' Heather replied assertively and calmly. 'I will help you get it off the ground but I cannot deny the others their dream. We'll find a way of keeping everyone happy.'

Chloe put her arm around Roisin who looked utterly defeated. 'I'll help too, Rois,' said Chloe. 'What's the next step?'

'We appoint two independent surveyors to undertake separate valuations. They will need complete access to the house,' replied Mr Bald.

Heather nodded her agreement and gave him her number to arrange the visits. Roisin was silent for the entire walk home and as they turned into the drive she stopped and looked at Heather.

'You can't seriously be thinking of selling your house?'

'This situation won't go away,' replied Heather. 'And I'd rather help you find a way through rather than leave you to deal with it when I'm gone.'

Roisin opened her mouth to protest.

'Even if that is many, many years hence,' Heather interrupted. 'And there are lots of ways that you could still have your retreat, sweetheart.'

Chloe knew that Heather was acting sensibly because Roisin had too much emotional investment in the retreat to be able to deal with her cousins in a rational way. It was the right thing to do. She'd support her friend as much as she possibly could too. But the fact of it was, she had a TV proposal in second stage consideration – and both the town name and the actual retreat itself were not at all settled.

Chapter Twenty-Two

Over the following days, surveyors and estate agents held the hearts of all three women in their hands. Mr Bald wasted no time in getting people out to value the farm and as the companies each walked through the newly restored and painted building, Chloe couldn't help but wish they could have seen it as it was before because right now, the house looked like a home. Roisin had followed the first surveyor each step of the way and tried to imply that there was damp and dry rot everywhere; this was evidently pure torture to her so Chloe suggested that Roisin take Heather out for a walk when the second arrived and she showed him round instead.

'Can you show me around the land, too,' he asked. 'We have to decide whether to package the place with it or sell it off separately.'

Chloe felt a lump rise in her own throat so couldn't imagine how those words would have hit her friend; she was relieved she was completely out of earshot. He was probably only in the house for forty minutes but every moment seemed like a lifetime. Eventually it was over and both companies had promised to send their reports in very soon but both implied that they should get a very good price for the place. They all smiled as they left as if the women should be pleased to hear that.

Her next dalliance with an estate agent came via email. At the sight of the words "Confirmed Offer", Chloe's emotions lurched all over the place – from panic, to sadness through regret and curiosity, eventually arriving at hope. Yes, it did mean that both the relationship and her former life were now officially over but they had been long before she'd even known it. And let's face it, some money would be helpful right now. In her fantasy world, she would open this email and the offer it contained would be way above her expectations; their apartment would have increased so much in value that she could afford to both help Roisin fend off her cousins, and to start to live independently. As much as Chloe loved living with her friend right now, she knew she wasn't really moving on as long as she sponged off her and Heather. Tentatively she opened the email and then clicked on the attachment.

Blah, blah lots of gumph and disclaimers – where was the number? She scrolled to the bottom of the page and then onto the next one. Who on earth puts the only interesting fact on page two? There they were; the six important figures in bold print. Chloe's hope dipped as she ran through the figures in her head: the mortgage that had to be paid off; there were fees for selling and moving out; she'd get back the deposit she'd put down and finally the remainder would be divided in half. At just over the asking price, it was an outstandingly good offer. The apartment had increased a great deal in value in a very short space of time and if she mentioned the price she was getting for a small one bedroomed apartment up here, they'd all be horrified. It was certainly good enough to accept but would it be enough to fulfil her dreams? Chloe looked out the window over the fields to that endless sea and wondered what price would be put on this view. She doubted that she'd have enough left to invest in the retreat *and* live independently with the money she'd be getting; it would probably have to be one or the other. Oh well, she'd have to wait and see. She emailed Jonathan saying that she was happy to accept the offer if he was. To her surprise, he was obviously online and emailed back immediately telling her that he would be instructing the estate agent to go ahead so that they could both *move on with their lives.*

'I think you moved on months ago,' she murmured to herself, closing the laptop on her ex.

Despite the uncertainty, the girls had to push on with their plans as if everything would eventually work itself out.

Roisin had her yoga retreat to focus on and for Chloe, the application for the name change needed completing and submitting – but first she had to talk to those villagers who had a concern or objection. She looked at the names of the people she needed to meet with and saw Tony on the list. Excellent! Chocolate would be the perfect accompaniment to a business discussion so Chloe packed her notebook into her bag and, yelling out to tell Roisin and Heather where she was off to, began the walk to the high street. As she strode along, Maggie was watering the hanging baskets outside the pub and waved at her. Then she bumped into Peter from the corner shop who was putting out the papers; he asked her if she wanted some paint to spruce up the tourist information hut. Chloe looked across at it and thought it could probably do with a freshen up.

'What colour paint is it?'

'There's Seaspray, which is a kind of bluey-green and some white. It'll fit right in,' replied Peter. 'I've got those big fat brushes for woodwork too if you need them.'

Chloe thanked him and he said he'd drop everything off at the hut; a bit more manual work would certainly take her mind off all the uncertainties surrounding her. After chatting a bit more with him about the meeting and the likelihood of landing the TV series, which Chloe played down just in case, she said her goodbyes and walked on with a little spring in her step. She felt like a local or at least someone who was welcome here and having had at least one home stripped from her this morning that was very reassuring. She reached Tony's shop and walked in, the little bell on the door chimed and Tony appeared from his workshop at the back.

'Come through.' He signalled Chloe to follow him and as she was being led towards the most delicious aroma of warm chocolate – Chloe didn't need asking twice.

'How do you resist eating all of this?' Chloe asked, practically salivating at the trays of chocolate cooling, ready to be cut into slabs. 'I'd have nothing left to sell to customers if I worked here.'

'Will power.' Tony laughed, seeming to pour out coffee as they sat down at the table. 'Developed over a number of years.'

Chloe took a sip from her cup and her eyes popped open in delight. 'What is this heavenly brew?'

'My very own version of mocha. Isn't it gorgeous?'

'It could keep Sleepy awake but oh my God, it is divine.' Chloe was scooping out the foam from the bottom of the cup. 'Maybe we should just forget the whole Serenity thing and just tell the world about this – it would have the tourists queuing up. Honestly, it's delicious.'

'Thank you, that's very kind of you,' replied Tony. 'And I actually think your ideas are good but I just wanted to put a view forward, away from the crowds.'

His tone was quiet and considered, making Chloe think that he had taken time to work out how best to express himself. She put aside her cup and gave Tony her full attention.

'I was just wondering,' continued the chocolatier, 'if it might be more useful for us to keep the Norse name as it's part of our heritage. We could tell visitors what it means without losing it – like the road signs they have in Wales and Cornwall.'

It was a valid point and one that Chloe had considered; she had weighed it up against the fact that the Norse name looked difficult to pronounce and that alone might put some people off visiting. She explained this to Tony.

'But let me look into it,' said Chloe. 'I do think Serenity would attract more people but you're right, we wouldn't want to lose our place in Northumberland's history.'

Chloe promised to give it more consideration and Tony added that, given the time everything took, he was happy for the application to be submitted while they thought about the idea. 'Do you have time for another mocha?' asked Tony. 'And maybe a slice of cake?'

'Even if I didn't, I'd make time,' replied Chloe.

Leaving the chocolate shop after that second sweetness overdose, Chloe understood how Tony managed to resist scoffing everything – it was actually too much; something she never thought she'd say about chocolate. It was a good job she had some physical work ahead of her to burn off all the calories.

Peter had left the paint and brushes at the hut door as he'd promised. Chloe opened the lid of the paint tin and saw that he'd been right: this was the perfect colour for a beach hut. She was wearing her semi-respectable cropped jeans and a T-shirt rather than decorating clothes but it wasn't a big hut and she really couldn't be bothered to walk back to the house to change. If she was careful, her clothes would be just fine. Chloe took the hard brush from the dustpan and brush in the hut, and swept the stray cobwebs and sand granules off the surfaces before beginning to paint. The big brush that Peter had donated was fabulous, layering on the new colour quickly and evenly so only a couple of hours later, she was standing back, admiring her handiwork.

'Impressive,' said that voice that always seemed to be sneaking up on her. She turned and shook her head at Andy.

'Were you just passing or did you specifically wait until all the work was done?'

He smiled and took the brush out of her hand. Stretching up to the top of the gable he dabbed a bit of paint onto a spot she hadn't been able to reach. 'There you go,' he said. 'I arrived just in time to finish the job.'

Chloe had been temporarily distracted by the small glimpse of his smooth lightly-tanned back as he'd reached up with the brush and now as he turned round to face her, she was sure he had caught her looking. She blushed and tried to hide it by tidying up the brushes.

'All it needs now is a sign,' continued Andy, picking up a piece of driftwood and painting it white and handing it to her. 'When it dries you can write Serenity across it.'

'And decorate it with shells,' added Chloe, getting a bit of the white paint on her hands so resting the driftwood on some paper inside the hut so it wouldn't drip anywhere.

'Lift home?' asked Andy and Chloe agreed. They walked towards his van discussing the likely timescales for the TruNorth campaign and as they did, Chloe noticed quite a few of the villagers smiling in their direction. Some were even laughing.

'I hope they haven't got the wrong end of the stick,' said Chloe as she climbed into the passenger seat. 'At least we've given them something to talk about.'

'Well you have.' Andy laughed, pulling down the vanity mirror in front of her.

Puzzled, Chloe looked into the mirror and saw her whole face speckled in Seaspray paint, except for her eyebrows which she'd rubbed while her hands were covered in the white. She looked like a Farrow and Ball panda.

'You let me walk through the village looking like this?'

'I thought the blue suited you.' Andy smiled as he started up the engine. 'You always look so spick and span, and besides, it matches your eyes.'

Chloe gave him a friendly thump but couldn't help but laugh at how ridiculous she looked. And he'd noticed the colour of her eyes.

Chapter Twenty-Three

'What does it say?'

Roisin and Chloe gathered closely around Heather as she stood poised with a letter from the first surveyor. Heather swallowed and tore it open. Chloe watched as her eyes scanned the first page of the document and then turned over to the second. Again, she thought, does every estate agent put the only piece of information you're interested in on the second page? Heather's eyebrows rose and, as she handed the letter to Roisin, Chloe scanned the critical page for the number.

'That's not too bad,' she blurted before she had the chance to stop herself.

'Maybe not by London standards,' sighed Roisin. 'But I've as much chance of raising that as I have of getting to the moon.'

Heather took the letter from her and they all sat down at the kitchen table.

'Let's think this through,' she said. 'I want to do right by everyone and although I'm far from dead yet, this piece of paper tells me what it would take to do that. Chloe, have you got a calculator on you?'

Chloe took her phone from her back pocket and followed Heather's instructions: divide the sum by four, Roisin, the two cousins and Heather herself – that's the amount each cousin would get if they sold the house right now. Heather and Roisin had no intention of leaving so if they could raise only half of the valuation, they could pay off the cousins.

'That should keep them quiet till I pop my clogs.'

'Will they go for that?' asked Chloe. 'I hate to say this as they're your family but it sounds as if they might want your share too.'

'They might, but I'm entitled to live somewhere aren't I? My share pays for my board and lodgings for the rest of my life.'

'You would never have to pay a thing to stay with me,' said Roisin, her face looking slightly brighter at the potential solution. 'But it's still a huge amount.'

'I have some savings,' said Heather, 'and you might be able to get a small mortgage.'

'And I will have something from the sale of the flat,' added Chloe, unable to hold back. 'I accepted an offer on it yesterday.'

Roisin squeezed her friend's arm. 'That's really kind of you, but that's your money – I couldn't take that. Unless ... you wanted to be a partner in the retreat?'

Chloe was taken aback slightly. What a wonderful offer to share in her friend's dream – wonderful but not right for her. She paused, considering how she'd respond. 'Wow, thank you. This place is going to be amazing and I will help you in every way I can but it's yours, Roisin. Your family history and your dream. I want us to be able to go down to the pub at the end of the day and swap stories about our days, not squabble over guests or accounts.'

Roisin nodded her understanding.

'But I meant what I said,' Chloe continued. 'If the money from the flat can tide you over – take it, see it as my rent for these past months.'

'I'd never charge you rent,' replied Roisin, squeezing Chloe's hand. 'Not when I can have you work for your supper.'

Heather put her arm on Chloe's back giving it an affectionate rub. Smiling, she thanked her with a slight nod of her head. Roisin was off again, racing through options. 'What about the TV show?' she asked. 'Have we heard anything yet? Do we know what the likely fee will be? And do they pay it in advance? And what about ...?'

Chloe held her palms up to slow her friend down. '*Woah*,

I haven't heard anything recently but I'll give them a call this morning.'

Relieved to have done the right thing and not to have offended her friend, Chloe left them making plans to put the offer to Mr Bald and then finding ways to raise the money. Their conversation faded as she quietly closed the heavy wooden door of the kitchen and walked into the yoga studio to make her calls, but was still audible.

'Well I have a couple of thousand in the post office.'

'And perhaps they'd take it in instalments.'

In the calm of that space, the reality of the situation suddenly hit Chloe. She would soon have enough money to pay her own rent but she had no real job, and if her friend lost the retreat, where would they go? Would Roisin go back to India? Would she stay here and advertise Serenity without Roisin in it? All of a sudden her carefree life seemed as if it was built on a cloud. Her mother couldn't have picked a worse time to check in.

'Just wondering how that new business of yours is going?' she shouted down the phone. Chloe could hear that she was on Bluetooth in the car. 'Only I'm off to tennis and I know the girls will be interested to hear about your adventures over there.'

Translation: *I need to have something to boast about and quickly.*

'Marjorie's daughter is now the senior stylist at the salon and got engaged in the same week. I just know she won't shut up about it, so I'd love to blow your trumpet, darling. Is there any news on the romance front? You'd be Managing Director of this company if you set it up wouldn't you?'

Translation: *It's going to be top trumps on that tennis court. My hand looks decidedly shaky right now and it's all your fault.*

Only a few weeks ago, Chloe would have rattled through the list of things she was trying to land, hoping to impress her mother and making it sound far more substantial than it was. And although she was in the running for a TV show and had landed an advertisement shoot, she'd rather have her mother's help than spend this call pretending all was well. She held the phone at arm's length and let her mother continue her questions while she took a long breath of sea air, truly tasting it for what seemed like the first time. She had the answers to the questions she'd just asked herself. Yes she would stay here; she couldn't imagine living anywhere else right now, and Roisin wouldn't have to either. They'd find a way.

'Do your tennis ladies ever do yoga retreats? You know to help with strength and flexibility for the game?' She completely ignored her mother's questions.

'I don't know, I suppose they might.'

'Then rather than tell you what I'm doing, why don't I show you all. Book a week at Serenity and we'll give you a family discount.'

'You mean we'll have to pay?'

'It's a small business, Mum and I doubt Marjorie's daughter would do your hair for free. Anyway ask them and come up to see it. You'll be impressed, I promise.'

Chloe said goodbye and strode out through the French windows to walk to the beach hut, opening it up with renewed purpose. She laid out some leaflets on a fold-up table on the beach then propped her laptop on the small desk and emailed Kareem for an update. Then she filled out some forms to register herself as a proper business, and, yes, as the managing director. That should keep her mother happy for a while. Although she'd sold the virtues of the retreat on all her social media pages, Chloe had fallen shy of actually asking anyone she knew or had worked with to host their shoots here. Selling the big agency and it's world-class reputation at a major pitch was one thing, convincing these big brands to trust little old her was very different. But it had to be done. She'd taken so many pictures for the TruNorth campaign and could offer a rugged sea, a calm bay, blue skies, flower filled meadows, endless expanse, quaint shops – whatever the advert needed, she was sure she could find it.

Her heart was thumping as she picked up her phone and called an ex-colleague who was now working at a new agency. She told him she was now arranging shoots in a great location and asked to be put on their roster. After the call she followed up with her photographs and ideas for the clients they handled. Chloe added some day rates and said they'd be open to negotiation for new business. The call went well and although no promises were made, it gave her the courage to make the next call and the call after that. By the time she'd called her top twenty contacts, she noticed the beach hut was getting dark and over the sea, clouds were gathering and the wind was picking up. Chloe gathered up all the leaflets and folded the table before they could be scattered across the sand.

The grey clouds hovered like an alien space ship above the sea and you could imagine what it would have been like hundreds of years ago, standing on the sand watching longboats, their oars thrashing, trying to make it to Serenity before they perished. It was perfect; Chloe took out her phone and started snapping. She'd only been able to take cheerful pictures up until now but this, this was powerful and brooding, like, well like a 4-wheel drive car that could negotiate any terrain, or a clothing range designed for the outdoors or even a battle scene in a period drama. She was thinking like a location scout and having taken the pictures, she could draft another proposal and email them to the agencies responsible for brands like that too. Surely, just one of the arrows she was throwing would hit the target. Her phone rang: bingo! It was Kareem.

'Do you want the good news or bad news?' he said but the tone in his voice was so upbeat, Chloe could feel the excitement rising through her body.

'Both?' she ventured.

'You're pretty much there, and the final hurdle is meeting you so you'll need to come down, do some mingling and answer some questions. If everything is okay after that, then we're good to go.'

Chloe screamed and jumped around holding the phone in the air and wishing she had someone to hug right now. Calming herself she leapt back into the beach hut and picked up a pen.

'Okay, tell me where, when and what I have to explain.'

Kareem ran through the list of questions the TV company had and, to her relief, there was nothing that she couldn't answer. She knew there'd be confidentiality agreements to sign and a press release schedule to adhere to so that wasn't a problem. Chloe continued listening as Kareem told her who would be at the meeting. He promised to email everything he'd said to her and then asked if she had any questions. She wracked her brain and then asked, 'You said there was good and bad news, what's the bad – that I have to come down for a final pitch?'

She heard Kareem take a deep breath. 'Err, not quite,' he replied tentatively. 'You remember how I said we'd propose Serenity for next season's show?'

'Yes.'

'Well, things kind of ran away with us. The other retreat is a state of the art facility in Geneva and the network thought the whole nature versus science angle would be brilliant to kick off the show. They're calling it Switzerland v. Serenity. They just love that name so if you get through the pitch, you're kind of on this season.'

'What?'

'Yeah, I presumed you'd want the business sooner rather than later so I promised them you could cope. Shooting would start next month.'

Chapter Twenty-Four

'And what's the fee again?' Chloe had told her friend several times but she repeated it and everyone around the table whistled appreciatively.

'It counts as an income though so there'll be tax to pay and insurance to buy.'

Roisin waved away her practicalities.

'But we're on our way aren't we? I mean this show will put us on the map quickly and it has to result in more bookings doesn't it?'

Chloe was working hard to contain her friend's excitement but the truth was that she was feeling it too. Sometimes good things did happen to good people. She had gathered together everyone she needed to work on the meeting with the TV company; Maggie had brought some ideas for social evenings, Andy provided all the information on accessibility and safety on the sea while Olly showed how they'd keep the show trending on social media.

'Will they ask you all this stuff?' asked Roisin.

'Maybe, maybe not but we have to be prepared,' replied Chloe. 'Think of it like an interview panel. They want to be sure we're the very best people they could hire and that their celebrities will be in safe hands.'

'Now, do we have everything?' continued Chloe.

'Health and Safety, Fire, Qualified Instructor, Food Hygiene and German Measles,' replied Roisin, slapping each one down on the table as if she were dealing cards. 'I was lying about the last one – it's my cycling proficiency which they're also very welcome to.'

Chloe ignored what she knew was nervous jollity and gathered them all up into a portfolio; she was leaving nothing to chance.

'What time are you leaving?' asked Heather.

'It'll take six hours in a fair wind so we'll set off at around eight and get there before the afternoon commuters start hitting the M25,' replied Andy.

Chloe had been mightily relieved when he offered to drive her down and attend the pitch to answer any questions about the outdoor activities. She knew he'd look good in front of any panel and also worked out that if he took his van, they could go to her old place and clear out any of her possessions from the apartment before the sale went through. Chloe was nervously excited and although she wasn't sure what they'd have to talk about for twelve hours of driving, or how they'd cope in each other's company overnight, the unknowns were outweighed by the possibility of a strong shoulder to lean on.

'I could have come with you,' said Roisin.

Chloe shook her head a bit too vigorously and quickly corrected it to an appreciative but clear glance; her friend was a fabulous yoga teacher and advocate for the bay but could probably not stick to a script when it came to the presentation.

'You have to make sure this place is completely ready. The crew will get here before the participants and they'll want to set up shots. HDTVs show every detail – it needs to be immaculate.'

Roisin saluted. 'Message understood, over and out.'

With everyone knowing what they had to do next, it was time for an early night. Chloe walked Andy to the door.

'Thank you for coming with me,' she said. 'I'd have dreaded doing this on my own.'

'The pitch or picking up all your old stuff?'

'Both,' she answered truthfully.

At eight o'clock on the dot, Chloe climbed into the passenger seat having hung up her pitch clothes on a hook in the back. She was impressed to see Andy had cleaned the whole van up. She sniffed the air. 'Is that perfume?'

'TruNorth for women.' Andy laughed. 'Your mate sent me some samples. I thought you'd rather your clothes smelled of that than brine.'

Chloe's nose wrinkled as the full impact hit her. 'It's not that different is it?' She smiled back at him.

The hours passed quickly and amiably with no awkward gaps as they filled the time eating sweets and asking each other random facts.

'Favourite film?' asked Chloe.

'What do you think it would be?' asked Andy.

'Hmm, the obvious thing to say would be some adrenaline junky thing like *Point Break* so I'm guessing it's not that.'

'You're right, it's not. Actually, I prefer some of the classics like *The Godfather*.'

'I love the classics too, but more classics like *The Sound of Music*.'

Andy grimaced so she launched into the chorus of *The Hills Are Alive*. He threw a sweet at her which she caught and ate.

'Don't worry, I only know the chorus.'

He reached over to the sweet packet for himself and his arm brushed hers. He didn't pull it away and neither did Chloe; the warmth and softness of his skin lay against hers making every hair on her neck stand to attention. When he eventually had to move it to change gear, she let out a little sigh of relief – it would have been very bad form to accost the driver when he was concentrating.

As the road signs showed they were getting close to London, Andy asked, 'So what was he like then?'

Chloe thought about having to face Jonathan again and she wasn't looking forward to it. 'You'll see for yourself soon – he'll be at the flat.'

'You never said.'

'I've been trying not to think about it. I really didn't want him to be there but he has the papers I need to sign,' Chloe replied. 'The last time I saw him he was ditching me for a wealthier model.'

'I know that feeling but don't worry, I'll be there every step of the way.' He reached out and squeezed her hand, then smiled. 'Tell you what, I'll pretend to be an eccentric billionaire if you like – make him think that you've already gone on to better things.'

Chloe thought about all she had heard and seen, the way he'd helped Heather and how much of his time he gave away for free. He would certainly be richer if he didn't do that but it's who he was and Chloe could see why Heather and Roisin loved him so much. He didn't need the billions, he was already better than Jonathan and she was really enjoying his company. Of course, she didn't say any of this, and instead she smiled and asked, 'So if you were an eccentric billionaire, would you buy a ticket to the moon or the lost city of Atlantis?'

'Atlantis definitely, what about you?'

'I'd wave at you from the moon and keep the tides safe.'

'I'd like that.'

Those three words, ending a very silly conversation, were so softly spoken that Chloe had to stop herself from reaching out to Andy. Was he remembering the woman who'd ditched him? She'd felt so happy in his company but was he feeling the same or was he just being kind because of what she still had to face?

They were both pretty quiet as they negotiated the streets of London. Chloe knew the tube system like the back of her hand but had never really driven in the city when she lived here so the one way systems and bus lanes were as unfamiliar to her as they were to Andy. He had no satnav in the van so they worked together as a team with her using the map on her phone and guiding him through. They eventually pulled up at the block of flats and found a space to park not too far away.

'Are you sure you're ready for this?' he asked her. She nodded and they leapt out of the van together.

Taking the stairs slowly to mentally prepare herself, they eventually reached the front door and as she opened it, she heard two people speaking; her head went dizzy recalling the last time she heard those voices. She froze unable to go in. He'd brought her?! Andy squeezed her shoulder and went in first, holding out his hand to her and taking it seemed to inject her with courage. They walked towards the voices and there they were: Jonathan and Courtney. To her delight they seemed to be rowing about something but stopped the second they noticed them. As she let go of Andy's hand, Jonathan had the audacity to step forward and try to air-kiss her. Chloe swerved to make sure he knew that a polite greeting was not an option nowadays. She noticed the designer-clad Courtney step in a very proprietary way and take hold of his arm.

'The papers I need to sign?' prompted Chloe, taking a pen out of her bag and clicking it loudly as if ready for action.

Jonathan was looking at Andy and then stumbled a bit over gathering them together. Chloe sat at their breakfast bar and took her time, reading through each and then swirling her signature at the bottom. The room was silent as she worked; at one point Jonathan tried to fill the void by holding out his hand to introduce himself to Andy. Chloe watched out of the corner of her eye and to her delight, Andy pretended not to notice, keeping his arms firmly crossed.

'There you go.' Chloe handed the pile back to him. 'Get the solicitor to keep me updated and if you need anything else from me, I'd rather you communicate through him.'

Jonathan swallowed but nodded.

'As I said in my email, we're going to be staying here tonight,' continued Chloe. 'We have a meeting in the morning nearby so thought we'd combine that with clearing out my things. I take it you don't object to that?'

Jonathan looked to Courtney first and then shook his head. Chloe watched the dynamics of their relationship and couldn't imagine it ending happily for either of them, but that wasn't her problem.

'There is just one thing,' said Courtney. 'Will you be taking any of the furniture with you?'

'No, you can have everything here,' replied Chloe, not wanting a single piece to remind her of her time with Jonathan.

'Hmm, well do you think you could use your van to take it to the tip or a charity shop before you leave? It really isn't my style.'

Courtney looked as if she had a very sour taste in her mouth as she picked up a cushion and then dropped it. She looked towards Andy. 'It's just that, unlike you, I don't know any tradesmen I could ask to help me.'

Chloe could hear Andy snorting but she wasn't going to have that woman insult him. She moved to stand beside him, mirroring his arms-crossed stance and his calm demeanour. If she hadn't, she wasn't sure what would have come out of her mouth – a roar of laughter or a torrent of expletives. Really this woman was just a bit too full of herself.

Showing a complete lack of awareness of the effect her request was having, Courtney continued. 'And obviously we don't really have similar tastes and I simply can't imagine anything second hand in the penthouse.'

Chloe couldn't hold back her gasp of incredulity. Had she really said that? Oh well, expletives it was then.

'You go, girl,' she heard Andy murmur. So she did.

'Bloody hell, woman, get over yourself! You were happy enough with my taste in men so my bloody cushions shouldn't be a problem – and by the way, the guy you're screwing? He's second hand too. I had him first and threw him in the charity bin where you seem to have been foraging. Just get out now and the whole lot will be waiting for you in the morning when you can take your pick.'

Courtney looked horrified and would probably have

retaliated if Jonathan hadn't done the only assertive thing he'd managed all evening and rapidly urged her towards the door.

'And your sort knows hundreds of tradesmen,' shouted Chloe, throwing the offensive cushion after them. 'And the back of their vans!'

Okay, so the last bit had been totally unnecessary but she felt completely invigorated. Chloe turned to face Andy who was doubled up with laughter.

'Glad to see you won't be holding back tomorrow,' he said, high-fiving her.

'You know what? I most certainly won't,' she replied, feeling ready to take on the world.

Chapter Twenty-Five

After the encounter, Chloe packed only the rest of her clothes and a few of her more personal belongings and called a charity to clear the rest of the flat. She really didn't want any of it now. After loading a relatively small number of boxes into the back of the van, they headed to a local pub for dinner.

'So,' said Andy as they walked back to the flat later. 'Is Jonathan the type you usually go for? Successful, doctor ...'

'Liar, cheat.' Chloe finished off his sentence. 'Call me old fashioned but I kinda want to be the only one.'

'Not into polygamy then.' Andy laughed. 'Me neither.'

'And as for the doctor part,' continued Chloe, 'my parents were more impressed by that than me – Mum especially. Although I like people who're passionate about what they do – because I am.'

Andy simply nodded. They reached the flat and Chloe realized they hadn't discussed the sleeping arrangements. Andy disappeared into the bathroom and emerged wearing his boxers and a T-shirt.

'Where do you want me?' he asked.

Chloe gulped and managed to croak, 'You take the bed. You're too tall to get a decent night's sleep on the sofa.'

He thanked her and saying goodnight headed into the bedroom. Chloe noticed that he didn't close the door fully and, as she tucked herself up in blankets on the sofa, she whispered a little 'sleep tight'.

'You too,' came the quiet reply. Chloe smiled and snuggled down further .

Despite thinking she'd probably spend all night awake listening to his breathing, Chloe had fallen quickly into a deep sleep and was now wide awake and fully refreshed. She showered and scrunched her hair dry then pulled it back into a neat ponytail and unzipped her pitch clothes from the suit hanger she'd hung on the back of the bathroom door. She wasn't wearing a suit today because she needed to represent Serenity which was all about the outdoors, relaxation and nature. Navy cropped trousers that were just a bit smarter than her usual jeans and a crisp white shirt which showed off the slight tan she'd picked up over the past few months were therefore donned. Very natural looking make-up and subtle drop earrings added to the look which said professional but relaxed. She left the bathroom and started pulling together her papers for the meeting. Andy soon emerged from the bedroom and Chloe couldn't help but burst out laughing – he'd gone for a very similar look.

'We could be auditioning for a boy band looking like this.' She smiled. 'It really suits you. You scrub up well as they say.'

And he really did. Instead of a white shirt he'd gone for the palest blue which brought out his windswept complexion and hair to perfection. The light, fitted cotton also showed the muscled tone of his arms and chest. He was the personification of health and outdoors. Rather guiltily, Chloe hoped there was at least one woman or man on the panel who wouldn't be able to take their eyes off him.

'Why thank you and may I return the compliment,' he said giving a theatrical bow.

Neither of them could face breakfast – the adrenaline was too high to be able to stomach anything so they decided to get there early and plan on having a celebratory feast afterwards.

And so they arrived at the TV studios full of jitters; they accepted the water offered but turned down coffee just in case of any clean-shirt mishaps. They sat back to watch the hubbub of a busy reception playing out. Chloe felt Andy watching her and turned to face him.

'I was just thinking that I'm not sure I can picture you as

part of all this. Do you miss it?' he asked in response to her questioning frown.

Chloe considered the question and tried to work out what she was feeling. 'Well, I was part of this, and I enjoyed it although I don't miss being indoors for all hours,' she said. 'I really can't believe that I spent all my time on the tube or in an office but it didn't worry me at the time. It was a shock to the system to begin with but I got used to it and just accepted it.' She watched a group of women cross the reception deep in conversation. 'I loved the camaraderie of the good times and the buzz of coming up with a great idea, then landing the business. It gives you an absolute high and I do miss that.'

'And you think you can recreate the parts you do like in Serenity?'

Chloe nodded just as they were called into the boardroom. 'I hope so, but let's land this one to start with.'

Kareem stood up to greet them both, pumping Andy's hand and kissing Chloe affectionately on each cheek. He introduced them to the rest of the panel which comprised Jemima and three people Chloe didn't recognize. As each of them shook her hand she learned that they were from the TV network and therefore would make the final decision. Happily she noted one of them taking more than a second glance at Andy. It wouldn't do their pitch any harm at all; although their case had to be watertight, it was a simple fact of human nature that chemistry often sealed the deal.

Chloe took a seat at the head of the table and plugged a memory stick into the laptop set up for her. She had a formal presentation full of stunning photography to enable her to adlib as required. When Kareem nodded at her to begin, she stood and began the speech she'd practiced so many times. Andy told the group about the activities he could run, the safety of the guests and the health benefits associated with simply being outdoors.

'Because this isn't just an entertainment show,' said the TV

Executive who'd taken a particular interest in Andy, 'we want to show people at home how they can improve their own health – we want to inspire them.'

'Which is exactly why you need Serenity,' Andy said. 'How many times have you heard about some weird diet or obscure fitness regime? Maybe you've even done them yourself – I know I have.'

Chloe picked up the thread. 'Me too. There was the time I ate only white meat and the time everyone was glugging only vegetable smoothies but you always crave what you can't have and that's completely unsustainable. Our programme can be followed by anyone, wherever they are.'

'And the one nutrient that no one gets enough of in the UK is vitamin D because we're all indoors all the time,' continued Andy. 'You'd be able to change that and make a real difference to the health of the nation.'

'Plus,' said Chloe flicking through the pictures of Kareem and Jemima smiling and laughing as they played in the surf. 'It's fun. Life shouldn't be a struggle to keep fit. Eat well, have a laugh being active and get more sleep – it's the Serenity formula.'

There was a spontaneous round of applause and Chloe handed round the formal proposal containing the various certificates, arrangements for housing and feeding the crew and the location fee. They were asked to sit outside while the proposal was considered so, after another round of handshakes, they found themselves back in reception.

'I get what you mean about the buzz of pitching for business,' said Andy with a high flush in his cheeks. 'That was amazing.'

Chloe smiled, itching to give him a huge hug. 'You were brilliant in there – we're a pretty good team.'

'We certainly are. Do you think we got it?'

'Let's just wait and see,' she replied and they squeezed each others hands before sitting down quietly, each lost in their own thoughts.

The wait seemed to last an interminable length of time and with each minute that clicked over on the clock that sat taunting them from the wall opposite, Chloe doubted their performance just a little more. Finally, after forty minutes of pacing the floor and assuring the receptionist that they still didn't want any coffee, Kareem finally put his head around the door and invited them back in.

'They're not going to tell us we haven't got it to our face are they?' asked Andy, looking more spooked than she felt.

'If they do, smile politely,' she told him. 'Wish them the very best of luck with the show and remember to invite them up. If it's a no this time, we have to start working for the next show now.'

'God, you're tough,' murmured Andy as they entered the room.

The expressions on the faces on the panel gave nothing away but Chloe knew this was the norm; everyone liked to hold the cards for as long as they could. Then she spotted Jemima take a surreptitious glance at Andy and give him a tiny smile. Her head went a little light – that had to mean they'd won it but she held her composure until the words were uttered.

'Congratulations! We'd like Serenity Bay to take part in the very first series of *Turning Back the Clock*.'

As they were leaving after the back-slapping and contract signing, Kareem rushed out after them and told Chloe he was really looking forward to working with her. His parting hug was particularly enthusiastic.

'You have a fan there,' said Andy as they walked towards their late breakfast.

'You can talk.' Chloe laughed. 'Jemima looked as if she wanted to eat you whole.'

There was only one place Chloe wanted to visit for breakfast. 'Come on,' she said, grabbing his hand and pulling him along the pavement. 'I'm taking you to my favourite coffee shop. I used to go here every morning.'

They arrived at the Red Roaster and Chloe pushed open the door, hoping Lloyd would be in. He was.

'Double-Shot, you came back to me!'

He ran out from behind the counter and picked her up, swirling her around. The other customers in the café might have been intently focused on their phones before this but they now looked up and cheered. Andy shook Lloyd's hand as Chloe introduced them to each other briefly, then he ordered at the counter and took a seat in the corner while Chloe and Lloyd chatted excitedly.

'So what are you doing here?' Lloyd asked. 'Tell me everything.'

Chloe explained the whole day and Lloyd enthused about it all before telling her that he was starting up a new business of his own.

'A coffee place?' asked Chloe.

'No, this place pays the bills but I've just qualified as a personal trainer. What you've been saying about getting people healthy is music to my ears.'

'Wow, then you definitely have to come up to Serenity some time – you'd love it.'

There was a queue forming at the counter so Lloyd promised that he would visit before getting back to help serve customers. Chloe joined Andy; in the time she'd been chatting to Lloyd he'd eaten the two bacon sandwiches he ordered.

'It would have gone cold if I hadn't,' he said as she sipped the cold cappuccino that he had left for her.

She got up and ordered a blueberry muffin and fresh coffee. Andy was silent as she ate and bubbled over about the day and about meeting up with Kareem and Lloyd again.

'What a fabulous day,' she chirped happily. 'Won't it be brilliant to have them all in Serenity – maybe even together? I don't think Jemima would be able to resist you this time. All my favourite people in Serenity – what a lovely thought.'

'And here I was thinking we were all there already,' said Andy, leaving a tip on the table and walking out.

'You know that's not what I meant,' said Chloe picking up the muffin and running after him. 'I meant even more of my favourite people.'

'Just teasing.' Andy laughed. 'We made quite a team in that pitch didn't we? My brains and your brawn.'

'Absolutely,' replied Chloe. 'So if you ever need to call on my expertise to bag yourself a huge kayaking deal then count me in.'

Chloe smiled then jokingly thrust out her hand to shake on it but Andy didn't take it. And when she looked up into those hazel eyes, there was a hint of pain.

'Why would I need a big kayaking deal? Am I not enough as I am? Would I not impress your mother?'

'That's not what I meant,' replied Chloe remembering what Maggie had told her and wishing she hadn't opened her mouth. 'Come off it, Andy – it was just a joke.'

'Let's get this joke back where he belongs then shall we?'

Chloe shook her head, and followed him to the van. They buckled up without uttering anything other than basic pleasantries as if they hadn't just shared a special twenty-four hours. Okay, so she knew she'd said the wrong thing, that she'd hit a nerve, but she doubted very much that he'd listen to any apology and for goodness' sake, was she always going to be walking on damned eggshells around this man?

Chapter Twenty-Six

Andy had been polite and professional on the long drive home but the warmth that had been developing pre-Red Roaster had shifted. When she replayed the day in her head, she realised she'd been quite rude to him, chattering on incessantly with Lloyd and leaving Andy alone in the corner. She should have involved him more in the conversation – they'd probably have had a lot in common. Then to top it all she'd joked about getting him a major deal and that must have sounded just like his ex, the one who wanted to change him. Chloe knew from his reaction that she'd really hurt his feelings but he'd hurt hers too in assuming that's what she was like. Chloe wished she could take it all back but every time she tried to speak to him now they were back in Serenity, he suddenly found himself very busy.

Well, she was busy too. Now really wasn't the time to have to run after a man who seemed to constantly take offence at everything she said! Every building in Serenity had to be primed and primped ready for the cameras, every person had to be briefed and an entire marketing campaign had to be prepared so it could be launched the moment they had permission to reveal the location. For the past fortnight there'd been teaser trailers on TV highlighting the next series and showing pictures of the glorious beach, alongside the mountain retreat where the other group of celebrities would be heading.

Science v Nature – who can turn back the clock?

Every time that trailer appeared on the TV in the pub the whole room stopped and turned to watch it, giving it a huge round of applause at the end. Chloe was slapped on the back when she walked through to the bar and wasn't allowed to pay for any of her own drinks.

'You've put us on the map,' said Maggie, handing her an unrequested gin and tonic, courtesy of the owner of the ice-cream parlour.

In between the bouts of nervousness, Chloe couldn't help but feel a tiny bit chuffed with herself. It was actually happening and it was mainly because of her. Importantly, she'd stressed the cash-flow issues with Kareem and had secured upfront payment for Roisin and her own finder's fee. Having some money to hand, meant that Roisin would be able to start the negotiations to buy the farmhouse from Heather and therefore get the cousins off her back. Chloe sipped the ice-cool drink, letting the sharp zest of lemon refresh her; it had been a busy day but they were ready now. Her heart lurched from excited pounding to terrified plunging and she imagined it was like standing in the wings on the West End preparing to deliver a world famous speech. She had rehearsed and prepared like crazy but until the curtain went up and the cameras started rolling, she had no idea whether she'd trip over her feet and fall flat on her face.

'Will your folks be coming over for the shoot?' asked Maggie, startling her from her thoughts.

Chloe hadn't considered asking them. There was no room for them to stay in Serenity so it would have to be a day trip; all the accommodation in the village was taken up by the cast and crew but it would probably feel good to let them know what she was up to and it would help explain why she'd been too busy to visit. Landing a TV shoot by a major network surely had to trump being made senior stylist. Her mother always claimed to hate the reality shows but she seemed to know enough about the celebrities to suggest that she watched them and besides which, the show was bound to feature in the magazines that were always in hairdressing salons.

'Just like you, I can't actually tell them it's coming

here until the first episode,' replied Chloe, citing the confidentiality agreement the village had committed to. She knew that giving her mother inside information, even thirty seconds before the programme aired, would send her into a frenzy of excitement – she'd certainly manage to WhatsApp *all* her friends in that space of time. The thought of it made her giggle; she would definitely do it as soon as she could. Chloe finished her drink, thanked Maggie and the ice-cream shop owner and started back to the farmhouse. On the way, her phone rang: Kareem.

'Everything okay?' she asked.

'All ready to go this end,' he replied. 'But we've had a slight change and I need you to accommodate one more celebrity. I presume that won't be a problem?'

There was no option for it being a problem so Chloe simply agreed to it and took note of when everyone would arrive. There really was no room at the inn throughout the whole of Serenity and the only option at the farmhouse was for her to give up her bedroom. She was the only one who wouldn't be appearing in front of the camera anyway, so technically she was support crew. The crew were all staying at the pub but all the rooms were taken there too. The thought of sofa surfing or bunking in with her teeth-grinding best friend didn't appeal.

'There's a tent in the loft,' said Roisin when she got back and told her the news. 'It's a nice one, not one of those poky things Bear Grylls would have and there's a foldy-up bed, camping stove, kettle – the whole caboodle.'

They climbed up into the loft and pulled it out, putting it up in the garden. It was actually quite perfect: big enough to live in for a few weeks and far better than imposing herself on any of the villagers. Chloe could easily picture herself out here in the big sky, with the sound of the waves lulling her to sleep; it would be a little canvas sanctuary.

'I love it,' she said. 'And if we pitch it at the far corner of the field then I'll be out of the line of the cameras but still be able to see everything.'

Eventually, after days of prepping and re-prepping everything, the moment the whole village had been waiting for arrived. The camera crews had taken up residence under Maggie's watchful eye the day before and now the entire population of Serenity awaited the arrival of the helicopter housing the celebrities who would change their fortunes. The format of the show was that the celebrities were filmed stating which retreat they'd prefer – nature or science – but then they were blindfolded and not told where they were going. When the chopper landed, they'd be helped off and the retreat would be revealed.

'How on earth does that work?' asked Heather. 'Surely you know whether you've been in the air for one hour or two? And it's always bumpy over the Alps. Would they not guess then?'

'I don't think it's really a secret,' replied Chloe. 'It's for the dramatic effect.'

Heather humphed that for anything to be dramatic it at least had to be slightly realistic – then forgot all she'd said as the helicopter came into view and the crowd started cheering. Despite knowing how much of this had been scripted, Chloe was as delighted as everyone else. The blades of the helicopters scattered hats and lifted skirts as it landed and men dressed as bodyguards leapt out first, pushing the crowd back as if they were expecting royalty to disembark.

'Who do you think we've got?' asked Maggie practically piercing Chloe's arm with her newly painted nails as she gripped her excitedly.

'They're getting off now.'

And they did, as each blindfolded person was led carefully out, murmurs went around the crowd as they tried to work out who on earth they were.

'That's the influencer woman – Fliss something or other – you know that one who made millions when she lost half her body weight with ten minutes of exercise a day.'

'Oh my goodness is that Mozzy Black?' asked Heather. 'I had all of his albums when I was a girl.'

'Ha, Suzie Armstrong.' Maggie laughed. 'She's going to be gutted when she sees where she is.'

One by one they were lined up, still blindfolded, while the helicopter took off. Then came the moment for removing the masks. The cameras were in place for the close-up reactions as the celebrities finally found out where they were. Those who had asked for the nature retreat: Fliss Carter, a twenty-nine-year-old super slender picture of health; ancient rock star Mozzy Black, dressed appropriately in dark sunglasses and a long military style coat; and grand dame of British theatre, Dame Julie Penbury-Jones, in her usual flowing robes and scarves – looked delighted to see the enormous coastline and skies. When it appeared on screen they'd look even more delighted as the reveal wasn't quite as fulsome as the director wanted and they had to have three takes just to get the right reaction.

The three who'd asked to go to the science retreat: Sebastian Moon, the celebrity astrologer, in a white three piece suit; Rik Luboski, an American action-movie star, in tight jeans and an even tighter T-shirt (both from his own range); and Suzie Armstrong, a reality show regular, in a velour onesie – looked devastated. Especially Suzie. The camera panned from Dame Julie extolling the virtues of the stunning location to Suzie.

'What the f—!' she yelled. 'This is bloody Northumberland isn't it? I only live in Newcastle. If I'd wanted to come here I'd have caught the bus!'

With the cameras following, the six celebrities were led towards the farmhouse and their accommodation. Chloe wanted to check the footage with the director so hung back with the crew; after all, making everyone feel at home was

Roisin's job. The show wasn't live and the action would be televised in a once-weekly show so that anything untoward could be edited out. Chloe crammed herself into the editing booth that had been set up in the pub snug and looked over the editor's shoulder. The drones had captured the landscape perfectly, making the bay look like a Caribbean island before pulling back to reveal sand dunes and finally – distinctly British fields. The voice-over would have viewers guessing at the location and then a giant globe would spin, pinpointing the spot everyone was staying. The reactions of the celebrities also worked well and Suzie's comedic outrage finished it off fabulously. It was a brilliant opening sequence and although Chloe knew the arrival of the other team in Switzerland would be every bit as gorgeous, her heart simply soared, knowing millions of people would now know how beautiful this place actually was.

Chapter Twenty-Seven

It was just as well Chloe wasn't in front of the cameras as her first night in the tent wasn't exactly restful. She had sent Andy another text asking if they could talk but got no reply. Yet again. Exhausted from the day and worry that he'd never speak to her again, she had rolled out her sleeping bag onto the folding bed and had felt such physical relief as she snuggled down into it, she'd thought that despite everything she'd sleep like a log. The sound of the waves rolling in and out was hypnotic to begin with but then, against the silence of the night, they seemed to crash louder and louder until she could imagine the tide reaching the edge of the tent and whisking it away. There was rustling through the grass, fluttering of wings and frequent hooting as the nocturnal animals came out to play. The silent countryside was pretty darn noisy when you actually had to listen to it. Still, she thought, as she headed to the farmhouse after her first night, at least the celebrities should be well rested by now.

'My agent was specifically instructed to ensure I attended the Swiss clinic.' Sebastian Moon was in earnest discussion with Kareem. He was dressed in the white three piece suit he arrived in and his packed suitcase was by his side. 'I can't possibly be expected to improve my health in a place like this.' He waved his arms around the kitchen and then started pointing at a freshly baked loaf as if it were the accused standing up in court. 'I mean look at that, they are serving us *carb-o-hydrates* for goodness' sake.'

In the background, Suzie Armstrong was sniggering and wolfing down a loaf with scrambled eggs. She didn't look as if she'd had much sleep either and then Roisin appeared looking frazzled.

'Thank God you're here,' she said. 'They're a bloody nightmare.'

Chloe led her outside, out of earshot. 'What's happened?'

'Sebastian Moonface over there claims the stars aligned to have him amongst mountains for success; Suzie and Mozzy hit the pub last night and rolled home at around midnight; Fliss has turned fruitarian overnight and keeps asking if the fruit fell from the tree or was cruelly plucked. Only Rik and Dame Julie seem to be taking this whole thing seriously.'

Chloe looked across at the kitchen table where the grand dame was picking sparrow-like at the fresh fruit loaf. She was asking Heather to make sure she got the recipe before she left and although her mouth smiled politely, her eyes were aloof. A behind the scenes camera appeared to tape the discussion between the two women and Chloe watched in amazement as Dame Julie changed her expression almost immediately to portray affection and interest; it was incredible to see and certainly explained why she'd won all those Oscars. Chloe gave her friend a little hug.

'Don't worry,' she said. 'It's all part of the format. They have to set up their characters so the viewers start rooting for them. You'll see, Suzie and Mozzy will be transformed by the end and Sebastian will find that he's suddenly a water sign or something.'

'I hope you're right.'

'Let's get them outside and doing something – that should stop the bickering.'

The first activity of the day was a kayaking trip and Chloe smiled broadly at Andy as they approached the bay, but he looked away. He was standing on the beach with the kayaks lined up on the sand explaining the benefits of exercising outside. Chloe stood behind the cameraman as Andy was interviewed; he kept his gaze straight ahead, not once looking at her and she felt a sad tug on her heart strings. They'd grown so close in London and although she'd ruined it, she had to try again. What had he said that time about chemistry?

That you know it straight away? Well she did now and couldn't ignore it. The interview continued and she could see he would definitely become a favourite with the viewers. His passion for teaching these activities and his love of life shone through those hazel eyes and when he laughed, oh boy, when he laughed the whole world would want to be his best friend just as she did. With benefits obviously.

Rik grabbed Andy at the end of the interview and shook his hand; or rather gripped his hand in a show of strength. Andy told everyone to grab the small toggle at the end of their kayak and pull it down to the waterline; they weren't heavy and he had already placed them very near the water so it meant only a short drag. Nevertheless, Rik picked up three boats – his, Sebastian's and Dame Julie's. He carried one under each arm and pulled the third along behind him. The camera loved it, and the accompanying gratitude that flowed from the celebrities. Everyone patted him on the back except Fliss who stood fixed by Andy's side.

'It's not as if he even carried them to the beach,' Chloe heard her murmur to him. 'You did all the hard work.' Fliss lay her hand on Andy's arm for a tiny bit longer than was strictly necessary and a tiny bolt of jealousy shot through Chloe.

'Calm down,' she whispered to herself. 'Remember what you've just said to Roisin. What they are doing is all play-acting.'

Andy got them all into their wetsuits. Predictably, Fliss, and Rik looked fabulous while Mozzy and Sebastian looked quite like comedy walruses waddling along in neoprene with their paunches. Suzie insisted on wearing a T-shirt over the top of hers while Dame Julie draped one of her trademark scarves around her neck and the crew was expressly forbidden from shooting anything below the shoulders, so on TV she'd look as if nothing ever flustered her. She was to join Andy in a two-man canoe which would be easier to sit in, so she held his hand like royalty as he helped her take her seat and then got in behind her. She sat at the front with a paddle across the bow and a sunhat on her head like a maharaja's wife about to sail down the Ganges. Andy paddled for both of them until the camera was on them and asked for an action shot. The others soon found themselves propelled through the gentle waves as they got the hang of paddling. The initial cries of concern and fear evaporated into whoops of delight and excitement. Chloe watched the celebrities, camera crew and safety boat disappear around the bay and sighed with relief. The arrival and first morning were in the bag. She had time to run back to the editing suite and see last night's footage before they all returned.

'Is it looking okay?' she asked the editor.

He nodded and showed her what they had so far: the big helicopter arrival was ready to go and they'd added a head piece from each celebrity saying what they thought of Serenity at first glance. Each of them was fairly positive, even Rik and Suzie; Rik said that he'd wanted to go to Switzerland because he 'did this kinda outdoors stuff all the time' and it would have been nice to try something different, Suzie just doubted that a trip to the beach could help her but was happy there was a pub nearby in case she got bored of the others. Only Sebastian expressed real disappointment at the location but said he'd continue to watch the stars and consult the tarot in case things changed. It was the right balance of optimism, doubt and cookiness that the programme makers needed.

'When does it go out?' asked Chloe.

'Thursday week. The first show has the arrival, their starting results and settling in. That's when the tantrums tend to happen,' replied the editor.

'I'd noticed,' said Chloe.

The show was ten episodes long, with the big finale just before Christmas programming began. At the end of the series, the celebrity who'd turned back the clock most would win money for a charity and the best retreat would also get a cash prize and a publishing deal for a book outlining the best ways to turn back the clock at home.

Chloe asked to see the unused footage and stood open-mouthed as the editor showed her the scene at the pub. Both Mozzy and Suzie had obviously had a few too many when a local band brought in to entertain the crew invited Mozzy to play with them. He happily did so but at the end of the set must have forgotten where on earth he was and had taken the guitar lent to him and smashed it rock-star style against the wall. Chloe watched the scene as the band and crew tried to wrestle the guitar out of his hands before he did any more damage.

'Will you be putting this in?' she asked.

'Edited obviously, but it's pure gold,' said the editor. 'Viewers will love it.'

'I think I'd better go and see Maggie,' replied Chloe, thinking the landlady probably wasn't loving it.

'There'll be expenses to cover and it's a lot more mess than it looks,' said Maggie as Chloe asked her how it was going. 'I know you said there'd be cables but they're everywhere. I can't serve lunch without tripping over and near killing myself. Still you did warn us and I guess you can't make an omelette and all that.'

Chloe was relieved that Maggie was grinning and bearing it for now. She had tried to tell the village how disruptive a film crew could be, but that never prepared anyone for the real thing. She hadn't factored in any misbehaving from the celebrities but could see now that it would be part of the narrative of the show so the villagers had to be ready for that too. Thanking Maggie for her patience, Chloe started back to the farmhouse to find Kareem and ensure that Roisin was ready for the afternoon's yoga session. As she got closer, she saw everyone from the house piling out of the door and rushing towards the beach. She joined in the exodus, catching up with Kareem and yelling out to ask what was happening.

'They've capsized,' shouted Kareem.

Horrified, Chloe picked up the pace and got down to the shoreline as the kayaks were being abandoned – the celebrities gathered around Suzie who coughed and spluttered on the sand. Rik laid her on her side and thumped her back to get the water from her lungs and then, laying her back down, started mouth-to-mouth. It seemed rather unnecessary as Suzie was evidently breathing but it would look good on screen.

'What happened?' Chloe asked Andy, relieved to see that he was okay. He waved her away saying nothing as he returned to the water's edge and escorted Dame Julie from the canoe.

'Not sure this guy knows what he's doing,' Rik was saying to camera. 'It was a good job I was out there.'

He went on to explain how Suzie had got into trouble as the current got stronger. 'Your natural reaction is to keep paddling in the direction you wanna go,' he said, 'but unless you're strong that ain't gonna work. Suzie needed to go with the flow and that was gonna take her into the bay. From there I could take her rope and tow her to safety. Instead she panicked and rolled over. She never should've been out there on a day like this.'

Chloe listened then looked from him out to the calm flat sea, puzzled. There was nothing dangerous about the day and if there had been, Andy would never have taken the risk.

'What actually happened?' she asked Andy as the celebrities left the beach for the farmhouse. Andy shook his head in dismay and looked resigned to the fact he had to speak to her about this.

'She stood up in the kayak and started trying to dance.' He sighed. 'A ripple of a wave unbalanced her and she fell in. The safety boat was there in seconds but action man was having none of it and dived into the water after her. Then he dragged her back to Sebastian's kayak and tried to drape her over the hull. Of course that unbalanced him and he panicked so he was over too. Rik doesn't like being told what to do. At least not by me.'

This would definitely make the final cut; it was too dramatic to be edited out so Chloe hoped that Andy wouldn't be turned into the handsome baddie against Rik's celebrity superhero. She squeezed his arm and was pleased that he didn't shake it off. She helped him get the kayaks off the shore and onto the trailer for driving back to the shack. After they'd loaded them all, Chloe was about to get into the van to help at the other end when the camera crew asked her to get out of shot. She looked round to see Fliss, changed into a bikini with a sarong draped seductively around her hips, strolling down the beach towards them, her long blonde hair catching the breeze in a picture-perfect way. When she got there, she walked up to Andy and took both his hands gently.

'Don't worry, I'll tell everyone what really happened out there,' she said.

Before planting a kiss on his cheek as Chloe watched on through narrowed eyes.

Chapter Twenty-Eight

The summer humidity continued to build over the next few days making sleeping under a nylon sheet pretty impossible, so when Chloe emerged from her tent she was absolutely exhausted. Rubbing her eyes and sighing, she stood up inhaling what there was of a breeze, but even that was too warm. It was only seven o'clock in the morning so today would be a nightmare. She lit her little camping stove and started to boil up some water in a tiny kettle.

In the distance was the familiar sight of Fliss, bobbing on the gentle waves in a kayak. She'd taken to meditating out at sea every day before the rest of the celebrities had even stirred. The crew had been less than happy as they'd had to get up to record her mindful moments but as soon as they got footage from the first few days, they could re-use it so now they left her in peace. Chloe watched as Fliss raised her hands towards the sun before paddling back towards the shore. She pulled the kayak out of the water and then started teetering across the rocks and peering into rock pools. After a while she reached down and picked something up. The kettle started to whistle so Chloe made herself a mug of tea while still vaguely curious what Fliss had found. She imagined it was either a shell that would become a necklace or a variety of seaweed that would feature in one of the health guru's smoothies. The thought of a salty drink on a day like this made Chloe grimace; she sincerely hoped Fliss wasn't about to inflict one of her recipes on the rest of the group.

Not wanting to appear to be spying on the celebrity, Chloe left her to her seaweed searching and, carrying her mug with her, made her way to the farmhouse. Standing outside in the garden was Roisin looking pink-faced and harassed.

'What's up?' asked Chloe.

'Just this heat,' replied Roisin. 'And half a dozen celebrities getting up overnight and asking for the air conditioning to be turned up.'

'They do realise they're in an old farmhouse and there isn't any don't they?'

'They do now and they're not best pleased. They've just started breakfast. We've served it in the yoga room so we can keep the French windows wide open and they're still moaning; Jemima's gone with Andy in the van to try and buy some fans. Maybe that'll help cool them down.'

For a split second, Chloe wondered whether her friend was talking about the celebrities or Andy and Jemima, who seemed to have been seeing a lot of each other since filming began. It seemed that every woman on this set could get close to him except her.

'Guys, can we talk about today's agenda?'

They turned to see Kareem approaching them, clipboard in hand.

'We have baking on the programme but given the heat does that seem sensible?'

The ethos of the retreat included taking time over food preparation and meals; the message for both the celebrities and the viewers at home was that no food group should be excluded from anyone's diet. Roisin particularly wanted to showcase her gran's bread recipes and Chloe also knew that they'd have visitors flocking to the website. As they were deciding on the best course of action, Jemima and Andy burst through the garden gate carrying boxes of fans.

'Good job we were out early.' Andy laughed. 'We bought out the whole shop. Jem even tried to negotiate the one keeping the shop cool didn't you?'

Jem?

'I told him it was for a prime time TV show and would be used by big celebrities but he wasn't budging was he?' replied Jemima, her hand on Andy's back.

'They can 'ave their lackeys walk behind with parasols,' continued Andy obviously imitating the accent of the shop owner.

'Or waft 'em with those big fans the Egyptians used.' Jemima's attempted accent was very different but whatever the shop owner had sounded like, they had evidently been very amused. They went back out to the van and returned with more boxes; they certainly had enough for each room of the house now. Having delivered everything, the pair left in the van, still laughing.

'They're getting on rather well,' remarked Roisin.

So Chloe wasn't the only one to have noticed then.

Forcing some refocus, she looked around at all the fans and then back up towards Kareem. 'Is this enough to keep the baking in the show?' she asked.

'Let's see.' Kareem shrugged.

They walked back into the kitchen where Heather was ready for action with her apron on and sleeves rolled up.

'Okay, what about this,' said Heather. 'The bread making process, the selecting ingredients, mixing and kneading isn't that much work so if we set the fans up in the kitchen out of shot then the celebrities should be able to get on with that. Then when the dough is left to prove then bake, we get the guests out on the treasure hunt and we come back in the evening to eat al fresco. They won't be anywhere near the house when the ovens are on.'

Kareem and Chloe nodded along as she spoke and then agreed. They hurriedly opened all the windows and doors then set up fans on the floor and on surfaces that wouldn't be seen on the screen. Six mixing bowls were put out around the kitchen table while flour, oil, salt, yeast, water and a variety of nuts and seeds sat in the middle. The celebrities arrived back from their walk into the comparative cool of the newly aired kitchen.

'Ooh and what delights do we have in store here?' asked Dame Julie.

Heather gathered them around the table and explained that this morning they would be baking. 'There is a proud history of fabulous bread in this house and we wanted to show you that a freshly baked loaf is an absolute joy. It's easy to make, vegan and environmentally sound as there's no plastic bag. Our philosophy has always been that a little of what you love does you good and believe me you will love this.'

Fliss, Suzie and Dame Julie began investigating the ingredients with enthusiasm while Rik and Mozzy looked rather lost but followed their lead.

'I've never cooked in my life,' said Mozzy. 'Unless you count home brew when I was a kid – the demijohn exploded all over me dad's shed.'

Sebastian folded his arms and set his mouth in a petulant pout. 'How on earth is this healthy? Fliss, surely you can't be endorsing this? There's no way any of us will lose weight if we stuff ourselves with bread.'

Heather was looking rather wounded by his comments but Fliss smiled at her then walked over to Sebastian and put her hand gently on his shoulder. 'Actually there's a whole lot of evidence to show that you should have carbs in your diet. Lots of people put on weight because they try to compensate for not feeling full, then they eat sugar and snack too much. Plus, carbs increase endorphins and if you feel good about yourself, you might just feel more motivated to exercise.'

Chloe looked to Kareem, impressed with the speech; the cameras were rolling and it seemed everyone in the room was holding their breath waiting for Sebastian. He sighed and unfolded his arms then wrapped the apron Fliss held out to him around his waist. 'Let's just get on with it then shall we?' He shrugged.

Heather was making her first appearance in front of the camera today and now, as Chloe watched her through the lens of the camera, she looked like one of the Golden Girls;

her long silver hair shone, her cheeks oozed rosy joie-de-vivre and her eyes danced with delight as she saw everyone waiting with their mixing bowls. Chloe was so pleased that Heather's recipes were actually going to feature.

Heather declared, 'Oh this is wonderful, seeing so many people in this kitchen again all making bread for each other. I am honoured to have you all here.' She actually wiped a tear from her eye as some of the celebrities expressed their excitement as to what was in store for the camera.

'I have a theory ...' said Heather as she instructed the group in weighing out the flour and mixing in additional ingredients of their choice to make either fruit bread or a focaccia. 'That if you stir your ingredients with love and knead the loaves with happiness, those things come through in the taste. Bread made by someone who cares for those who'll eat it is simply delicious.'

'That's a precious thought,' said Dame Julie.

'Is that why no matter how I try, nothing tastes as good as the scones my Nan made?' asked Suzie and Heather nodded, telling her it probably was.

Under Heather's calm and affectionate instruction, the group slowed down, mixing the dough and sharing stories that echoed Heather's sentiments.

'I had a great-aunt who used to say she'd put wishes in her apple pies,' said Rik who by now had taken off his shirt and stood in a tight white T-shirt with the bowl tucked under his arm in a manner to help show off his biceps. 'When you ate a slice, you got to make a wish.'

'We should put together a recipe book,' declared Fliss. 'It could be called *Made with Love* and it'd be the things we remember from our childhoods.'

They all nodded and murmured their enthusiasm. Kareem checked his watch and ran his hand across his throat as the signal for filming to stop. They had to clean up, shoot their individual pieces to camera saying how they thought things were going and then be back down on the beach. While all this was going on, Heather and Chloe gathered up the dough the celebrities had been working on and set it aside to prove.

'How do you think it's going?' asked Heather.

'Well you were a superstar that's for sure,' replied Chloe. 'But I can't read them at all. One minute they're lovely and the next ...' She shook her head.

'I guess that's what they're paid for – to deliver the drama. Otherwise no one would watch if it was always lovey-dovey.'

'I guess not.'

'Anyway,' said Heather, 'what does your mum think of this? She must be very proud that you've pulled off all this.'

Chloe nodded and smiled meekly. She'd decided not to tell her mum until she was sure the show was going to be a success. TV programmes always have an angle and although they'd sold the retreat on its relaxed ethos, the on-screen narrator was in danger of making it sound more like Ibiza or Magaluf. The opening sequence was gorgeous and exactly how Chloe wanted people to see Serenity, but then after the partying in the pub, Sebastian capsizing and the bickering about the heat, it might look less and less like a place anyone would want to visit. She hoped these were just teething problems and the whole show would get back on track – when it did, she'd tell her mum she was behind it. After helping all she could with the bread, Chloe headed to the beach to watch the afternoon's activities.

The horizon was still thick with heavy clouds which kept the heat in and the humidity high, so it seemed perfect that Andy had everyone in the water, either swimming or on bodyboards. Dame Julie swam with a sunhat on her head; Mozzy, Fliss and Sebastian lay flat on their stomachs paddling out to sea and letting the very gentle waves bring them back in, while Rik and Suzie gave the more energetic stand-up paddleboarding a go. To Chloe's relief, they all seemed happy and relaxed. She also noticed that Andy was taking no chances this time and had positioned two lifeguards, along with himself and Roisin, at the seashore just in case. Chloe walked up to Kareem.

'It seems to be going well,' she said.

'Appearances can be deceptive,' he replied before being called away by one of the cameramen.

Chloe desperately wanted to know what he meant but at that minute, a roll of thunder started. It wasn't a threatening roll and still seemed very far off but they decided to call everyone in. The cameras kept rolling, hoping to get a flash of lightning as the celebrities were running out of the sea. They didn't get that. Instead they got Suzie screaming and swearing violently as she hopped around on one foot. Everyone ran to see what had happened; Suzie sank down on to the sand holding her leg up as blood ran through her toes.

'I've stood on something. I think it was glass.'

With fear and dread pounding through her body, Chloe traced back Suzie's footprints until she found a shard from a broken bottle lying on the sand. She picked it up and looked around but couldn't see any more. It was brown glass, the type found in medicine bottles and the edges hadn't been ground by the sea or sand so it had arrived here fairly recently. Chloe had never ever seen any litter on this bay and the thought crossed her mind that it could have been planted to sabotage the show but who would do that? Anyway, conspiracy theories weren't going to help things now. She returned, showing Andy the shard and he frowned, looking as puzzled as she was.

The incident ruined the evening meal. As soon as the weather looked threatening, Heather had gone to great lengths to bring the outside in, draping the kitchen with pretty lights and bunting. A fabulous cold buffet which complimented the home-made focaccia perfectly was laid out waiting for them after they'd showered and changed, but it was all in vain. The conversation was all about the glass and how many more disasters were going to befall them.

'This place shouldn't be called a health retreat at all,' Suzie was saying direct to camera. 'It's more like a hazard retreat. Honestly, they might as well have sent us to Chernobyl.'

Credit where it's due, thought Chloe, no matter how devastating her words were, that woman knew how to deliver a kick-ass sound bite.

Chapter Twenty-Nine

If anything, the next day was even hotter; the weather channel promised a break from the heat soon but they tended to forget about this little corner of the country so "soon" was a very nebulous notion. It was a big day too as the celebrities would get their first set of results. As they'd done little but bicker since they got here, Chloe doubted there'd have been much progress but she lived in hope. As she climbed out of the tent to make her way to the farmhouse, she noticed Jemima had joined Fliss on her morning meditation today and they were now making their way back to the retreat. Although Chloe had been slightly sceptical about the self-styled health guru to begin with, she was out there every day and certainly seemed to practice what she preached.

Up at the farmhouse the celebrities gathered to hear their results. All measurements had been taken before breakfast in both resorts and Kareem had the results for Serenity in an envelope which he handed to Dame Julie. She cleared her throat, stood tall as if making an Oscar speech and opened it.

'I will read out all of the results unless anyone would prefer to have them delivered privately,' she said to her fellow residents. None of them asked for a private conversation so she continued.

'Health is so much more than weight, although of course that is important in fending off so many illnesses.'

Chloe wished she'd get a move on and from the amount of toe-tapping going on under the table, so did everyone else.

'So the measurements taken look at blood pressure, flexibility, strength, lung capacity and stress levels as well as body composition and brain age ...' She paused dramatically. 'So here are the results.'

They weren't a complete disaster. In fact everyone had

improved in at least one area: Mozzy had seen his strength levels improve; Suzie had lost weight, and Rik, who was already very strong had improved his flexibility and was very happy about that. Dame Julie's heart rate and blood pressure had improved as had Sebastian's, but unfortunately he had put on weight.

'I'm not in the slightest bit surprised,' he said. 'It's all these carbs. I'll be enormous by the time I leave here.'

Chloe made a mental note to talk to someone about Sebastian's diet; the food regime at the farmhouse had been healthy with lots of fruit and vegetables at each meal so she couldn't understand how he'd actually gained weight. Portions were sensible and there hadn't been any alcohol served; Sebastian looked like the kind of man who normally enjoyed a half bottle with a meal and even cutting this out should have helped him. Dame Julie continued.

'But our star performer is Fliss, who has lost weight and body fat, improved her flexibility and lung capacity as well as having low stress levels.'

The celebrities gave her a round of applause.

'The only issue is apparently your resting heart rate, which is looking a little high, darling.'

'That's probably because I forgot about the tests and had a coffee just beforehand.' Fliss shrugged.

'Yes, that happens to me too,' replied Dame Julie. 'So collectively, sweethearts, we have turned back the clock fourteen whole years.'

This time the round of applause was muted and Chloe could see eyes and brows raised upwards as each celebrity mentally calculated what that actually meant: on average they'd lost just over two years each, which wasn't a fabulous performance.

'How did they do at the other place?' asked Rik.

'Twenty-one years unfortunately.' The dame sighed.

Shoulders dropped in disappointment until Fliss stood up

and spoke. 'Look, I know some of you would have preferred the science approach with all its gadgets and pills but improving your health naturally is better in the long term. You'll learn things here that you can take home and do for the rest of your lives. Science might get the instant results but nature will win out in the end – we'll show them.'

Rik, Suzie and Mozzy whooped their support but Sebastian just stood up and tutted. 'It's all right for you, you're still in your twenties. Some of us need the instant results.' He turned to Roisin. 'Come on then, what ludicrous activity are we doing next?'

Chloe could see that Roisin was struggling to stay upbeat. She knew it wasn't about a TV show or even the fee that came with it for her; her friend genuinely believed that a stay at Serenity could improve anyone's life and the thought of letting people down would be weighing heavily on her. Chloe watched as Roisin put on a big smile and told everyone they'd be riding bicycles along the clifftops to get some exercise and to enjoy the only likely breeze of the day as they cycled. The celebrities were generally enthusiastic, particularly about the possibility of a breeze on this stifling day and they cajoled Sebastian until he actually confessed that he'd enjoyed cycling in his youth and had always planned to get back on a bike one day.

They filled water bottles, selected helmets and began their journey. Roisin led the way while Chloe rode at the back with a pannier full of extra water and a bigger than usual first aid kit given the incidents that seemed to keep happening to this group. She looked up at the dark sky as she set off: the clouds were certainly thickening and had to break soon but it wasn't forecast until the early hours of tomorrow morning. That would make for an interesting night in the tent. If only Andy was still talking to her; he might have let her sleep in the van. As they rode along the clifftops, the tone of conversation amongst the celebrities seemed to lighten. Some of them hadn't ridden bikes for years so had wobbled when they'd first set off but now they were getting the hang of it and finding their own pace. Rik and Suzie raced ahead while Mozzy and Dame Julie sauntered at the back near Chloe. Mozzy had a set of binoculars around his neck and every now and then stopped to take a closer look at one of the birds flying over the fields or across the sea.

'I somehow never pictured the hardman of rock being interested in birds,' called out Dame Julie, echoing Chloe's thoughts.

'Magnificent creatures, Duchess,' replied Mozzy. 'Just imagine all that freedom, being able to take off whenever you wanted. They fly miles every year – see that one over there? It'll have flown from Africa to get here. Amazing ain't it?'

He turned to Chloe. 'You know you've got a helluva lot of species that are on the conservation lists around here. You should maybe set up some birdwatching sessions.'

'We do have a guy in the village who can do that,' Chloe replied. 'I'll introduce you to him. He's called Mick but be warned, he's a little odd.'

'Best sort normally are,' said Mozzy. 'Bloody 'ell, it's getting black over there. Better get a move on.'

He was pointing at the horizon where the dense clouds now resembled an angry army approaching the mainland. It looked as if the rain would be arriving a lot earlier than the weather channel had said. Chloe picked up the pace too then. Making a snap decision she started racing ahead to catch Roisin. Having had to keep up with Rik and Suzie, she was some distance away and Chloe was breathless and sweaty when she reached her.

'I think we should turn back,' she panted. 'I think the weather's going to break.'

Before the words were fully out of her mouth, the first big fat plop of rain landed on her head and then the next. The celebrities stopped and held out their palms to check what they'd all just felt. They didn't have to wait long to confirm their suspicions. In seconds the heavens opened and torrential rain hammered down on them – perfectly vertical torrents as if they were standing under a waterfall or someone up high was simply emptying a bucket on them. They were utterly drenched but there was no option other than cycling back – they hadn't got as far as the track where she could have asked Andy to pick them up in the van and there was no way the van could have made it across the fields in this anyway. All they could do was get their heads down and ride those bikes as fast as they could. Still keeping up the rear, Chloe gave her jacket to Dame Julie. It wasn't waterproof but it might help a little. Mozzy seemed to be enjoying it all, raising his mouth to the sky and taking in a drink of rain.

'Makes you feel alive doesn't it?' he cried.

Heather had hot comforting soup ready for them when they got back and although the day could have been construed as yet another disaster, when the celebrities sat down to eat with their hair towel-dried, their cheeks were rosy and the conversation was lively as they shared the excitement of the race back home.

The afternoon needed an indoor activity so Roisin announced there would be a class combining yoga and pilates to help stretch and strengthen the muscles they'd used in the morning. The celebrities went off to change and then gathered in the studio. Chloe needed the stretch as much as anyone so positioned herself at the back of the room, ready to join in. The rain stopped as quickly as it had started so Roisin opened the French windows and let the cooler air freshen the room. Over by the bay, a double rainbow glistened against the pewter clouds. The bright colours against the dark backdrop seemed to say 'It's not over yet. Fear not, there is hope'. Chloe wondered whether the rainbow was referring to the weather or the whole retreat.

Sebastian arrived the last, with a very large sports bag.

He found himself a space in the room, wiped the floor and then rolled out his mat. He was overdressed in his trendy leisurewear but Chloe wasn't going to suggest he take off the hoodie before they started. Roisin began and told them she was going to introduce them to some very simple moves that they could perform wherever they were. These moves would improve their core strength and yet no one would know they were doing them.

'People seem to think you need to do hundreds of sit-ups or crunches to improve your stomach muscles but balancing is actually one of the best ways to work your entire central region.'

She told everyone to pull in their stomach muscles and at the same time, just lift up one leg.

'Hold it and balance for as long as you can. If you're able to, bring that leg to your chest and then help it out to the side.'

Chloe, like others in the room, wobbled as she attempted this but it felt like a very elegant ballet move and as she noted Dame Julie doing the position with relative ease, she wondered whether this was one of the ways the actress maintained her wonderful poise. Roisin continued to demonstrate positions that were both challenging and interesting. Chloe had never really done yoga before coming here but had to admit, having to concentrate like this and pay attention to how her body actually felt was quite enlightening. She could feel the anxiety still nestling in her shoulders and even her jawline – how did she ever get a tense jaw? Roisin ended the class by asking everyone to lie down and relax.

'Now this is more my sort of class.' Suzie laughed.

By now, Sebastian had warmed up and stripped off his extra layer but on the advice of Roisin that their bodies would cool down during the relaxation, he dug around in his sports bag and pulled out a different sweatshirt. Chloe wondered how many outfits he'd brought with him. The curtains were pulled across the windows and they lay quietly in the semi-darkness with just a gentle breeze blowing in. On Roisin's instruction, they breathed in and out, in and out; holding the breath for a count of five and then letting it go, along with all the stresses and strains they might still be holding on to. It wasn't long before the sound of deep breathing turned to gentle snores; someone had fallen asleep. Chloe smiled as she lay there with her eyes closed. At least today had gone well. There had been no disasters and everyone was now calm and relaxed. She—

'AAAAAARGGGGGHH!'

The whole room was shaken with a piercing scream. Chloe leapt up to see Sebastian frantically waving his jacket at his bag, shooing something away. 'It's a rat!' he screamed.

Instantly there were screams around the room as even the action hero ran to the back, as far away from the potential predator as possible.

The terrified "rat" scuttled out of the doors and everyone relaxed slightly.

'This place is infested!' roared Sebastian. 'Let's get out of here while we can – rats never hunt alone.'

Everyone ran out of the door leaving a room of discarded mats, towels and sports bags.

'It was a field mouse,' said Roisin. 'We're probably going to be shut down and all for a panic over a field mouse.'

'Don't jump to conclusions,' said Chloe giving her friend a hug. 'The cameras will have caught it and they'll know it's not our fault.'

'It must have come in when I opened the windows to air the room. Of all people why did it have to target Sebastian?'

Chloe walked towards Sebastian's bag and pile of discarded clothes. 'Well his clothes look like a very comfy place to nest.'

Kareem appeared to collect the celebrities' belongings. 'That was a bit of a disaster wasn't it?' he said, opening Sebastian's bag to repack his clothes. 'Jeez,' he said, his eyes wide open.

'Oh no, don't tell me there's a nest in there?' asked Chloe, thinking the mouse might have taken her advice.

Kareem opened the bag wider and lifted out its contents: a secret stash of biscuits, crisps and chocolate bars. He handed them to Chloe and asked if she could get rid of them.

'No wonder the mouse made straight for Sebastian,' said Chloe.

'No wonder he's not losing any weight,' added Kareem.

Chapter Thirty

'I'm sorry but I have to take this seriously,' said Kareem. 'I have to ensure that there is no actual health and safety threat to our celebrities.'

'But you know that if you do, there'll be a headline across all the tabloids when the episode goes out – RAT INFESTED SERENITY. It'll completely ruin us before we're even off the ground,' protested Chloe. 'And you saw his bag. He's simply attracted a field mouse by offering it a year's worth of food. It was his fault in the first place.'

'I really am sorry but the celebrity is always right and besides,' Kareem was talking to Roisin, 'it's up to you as the person in charge of the retreat to keep these guys on course.'

Kareem took Sebastian's sports bag and left them standing, shoulders dropped in utter despair.

'What do we do now?' asked Roisin. 'That was so dramatic, it's bound to make the edit isn't it?'

Chloe nodded. A serene yoga class, an outburst and a rodent would most certainly make for entertaining viewing, especially as hardman Rik had been as terrified as the rest of them and leapt behind a chair.

'I didn't think it would be like this,' Roisin continued, slumping down on the floor. 'I thought people would come here and fall in love with the place like I did. I thought they'd want to improve their health, not fight me every step of the way.'

'Most people would,' Chloe replied, joining her cross-legged. 'But having celebrities on a reality show was probably the worst place for you to start. They have to rebel to make good TV. I'm sorry I got you into this.'

'No, it's my fault. I don't know whether I'm cut out for it. I like teaching yoga but I can't boss people around.'

Chloe pulled her friend towards her and kissed her on the top of the head. A hundred thoughts were whizzing around her brain. They had to get the celebrities back on track and perhaps one way of doing that was to get them to police each other.

'Let's have a word with Dame Julie,' she said, standing up and holding out her hand to pull Roisin back to her feet. 'They seem to respect her and if she can rally them, they might behave for a while.'

'Do you think that will work?'

'At this stage, what have we got to lose?'

Linking arms tightly, they went in search of the grand dame, but opening the door to the kitchen revealed Heather sitting at the table, deep in thought. She hadn't heard them come in and was completely focused on the letter she was holding in her hands.

'Gran, what's the matter?' whispered Roisin. Heather jumped but then composed herself and smiled at the girls.

'Shall we have a cup of tea?' She stood up and stuffed the letter in her pocket.

Roisin shook her head and pulled her back down onto a chair asking, 'Have you had some bad news?'

'It's nothing to worry about.'

'It obviously is, Gran. Tell me what's happened.'

Heather took the letter out of her pocket and handed it over. Roisin read it quickly then, slumping back on the chair, handed it to Chloe who did exactly the same thing.

'How can the valuations be so different?' asked Chloe. The letter was from the second surveyor appointed by the cousins and it told them that the property was worth more than twice the first valuation and that they knew of an interested party who could probably proceed quickly.

'And how can there be an interested party when no one else has been to see the house?'

'I don't know,' sighed Roisin. 'But I can't put my hands on

this amount of money to buy them out. Maybe this was just one big stupid idea.'

Heather reached across and squeezed her hand. 'No big idea is stupid, but it's rarely a smooth road if you really want to achieve it.'

'I know you're right,' said Roisin. 'But what can we do?'

'I think you have to contact this surveyor and find out why the valuation is so high and who this interested party is,' said Chloe. 'It seems very fishy that the two figures should be so vastly different.'

Heather and Roisin nodded, deciding to call Mr Bald straight away. Chloe left them to it, continuing to look for Dame Julie.

She could see her, in the distance, walking on the beach with Mozzy. They cut an unlikely pair, her scarves floating out and his long coat flapping in the wind. Against the dark clouds and stormy sea they looked as if they were starring in a Jane Campion movie. Chloe started walking towards them but was stopped in her tracks by the sound of a siren. It took her a moment to realise what it was; a few months ago they had been part and parcel of everyday life and she wouldn't have even noticed the blare but since arriving at Serenity, she hadn't heard one so this was extremely unusual. It was obviously just as rare for the villagers who gathered on the main street to see what was going on.

Chloe ran to the village and quickly took in the scene in front of her. An ambulance was taking someone away on a stretcher while a police car was stationed, lights flashing, outside the Surfshack. Chloe ran up to Kareem to see what was happening, just as two police officers emerged with Andy in handcuffs. Her instinct kicked in and she ran towards them trying to pull the police away from him.

'Get off him,' she said. 'He hasn't done anything.'

Kareem pulled her away from the scene as the police guided Andy into their car. 'I'm afraid it's over.'

'What do you mean? Why do they have Andy?'

'The show, the retreat. I can't rescue this one, I'm sorry.'

He led Chloe to the editing suite and sat her down. 'It was Fliss in the ambulance.'

'Is she okay?'

Kareem nodded. 'They think so but she's passed out. The clinic does some random additional spot checks after every progress check to make sure everything is above board and Fliss's blood came back with an anomaly. We know for certain she was losing weight because she'd been taking illegal diet pills.'

'Wow,' said Chloe. 'But what has that got to do with Andy?'

'They were hidden in a kayak. The one she took out every morning. The police think Andy was stashing them there for her to pick up.'

'No!' exclaimed Chloe jumping up. 'He's not like that.' She absolutely knew that. It wasn't just how he was with Heather or what Roisin had told her – she felt it deep within. He was one of the good guys. A genuinely good guy. Chloe knew at that moment she'd do pretty much anything for him. And if one day he felt for her even half as much as she felt for him right now then that would be enough. 'Trust me,' she continued. 'He wouldn't do anything like this. We have to tell the police. You have to come with me now ...'

Kareem held her arm to stop her leaving. 'Think about it, Chloe. How well do you actually know him? No one else has access to the shack – who else could it be? She didn't have them in her luggage when she arrived because it's all checked.'

Chloe hadn't realized that and frowned because if luggage was checked thoroughly then how did Sebastian get his stash of biscuits in?

'I do know him, Kareem, and Andy would never do this. He believes passionately in the power of the outdoors and he just wouldn't take any kind of drug. There has to be another explanation – and I'm going to find it.'

'You're welcome to look for one but I can't see another outcome for you. This will be on the news before we know it. I can't control mobile phones and social media uploads.'

Sure enough, as Chloe left the editing suite, her mother was on the phone.

'Have you got anything to do with this reality programme they're filming? It's in Kyrrby isn't it?'

'Mum, yes, I am working on it but it's not how it seems.' Chloe sighed.

'I should hope not. I hope you have nothing to do with those drug pushers,' her mum declared loudly and with such a disproportionate level of outrage that Chloe wondered whether she was in the hairdressers while making the call. 'Why you'd want to give up a top London job to promote a village like that ...'

Chloe hung up on her mother before she said something she would really regret. She didn't have time for this – Andy needed her. Her friends needed her. The news would most certainly have reached the farmhouse and Roisin would be devastated.

The farmhouse kitchen was stiflingly hot as the humidity had reached boiling point and even though every window was open, it wasn't helping. Warm air blew across the room, fanning the flames of an already overheated scene. It was how Chloe imagined a bad day on the stock markets would look. The celebrities were shouting across the room at each other, or on the phone to their agents, waving their contracts in the air. At the centre of all this stood Roisin trying to shout louder than all of them, asking them to calm down – it was absolute chaos. Heather walked in, wiping her eyes. Seeing that the old lady had been crying simply broke Chloe's heart all over again. She'd caused all of this with her idea about making Serenity famous. Roisin and her gran had been perfectly happy before she'd interfered. Heather sat down without saying a word and signaled Chloe to do the same. Then Mozzy joined them and after a short while, the silent protest was noticed by the others who calmed down and finally took a breather from all their anger and outrage.

'I'm going to leave tonight.' Sebastian was the first to speak. 'I've told the crew to order me a car and it will be here within the hour if anyone would like to join me.'

'Doesn't seem much point in staying,' replied Suzie. 'I knew I should have gone to the Swiss place.'

They both started to get up from the table when a horrendous crash of thunder stopped everyone in their tracks.

'That has to be directly overhead,' said Rik, heading to look out at the evening sky.

A flash of sheet lightning lit up his profile and he jumped back, grabbing the window handle and struggling against the wind to pull it shut. Mozzy and Chloe leapt up and ran to the other windows, closing them as quickly as they could. Across the field, Chloe could see her small tent being shredded and tossed in the air by the gale force winds that had so suddenly arrived. She would never sleep another night in that but her first thoughts were to hope it wasn't going to harm any creature unfortunate enough to be in its path. Torrential rain hammered down on the house as bolt after bolt of lightning launched an attack. Thunder roared and bellowed overhead as each crash shook the house and Chloe could feel the noise actually reverberating through her body.

'Could this place get any worse?' said Sebastian.

The heavens answered. The lights went out and the farmhouse was plunged into black darkness punctuated only by the flashes of lightning. There were screams around the room then the sound of chairs scraping and people scrambling around looking for phones. Heather flashed on a torch and shone it around the table; Suzie was gripping onto Rik as if her life depended on it.

'Don't worry, we have candles somewhere,' said Heather.

She disappeared into the pantry and came back with

a couple of old-fashioned storm lanterns which she lit and placed around the kitchen. It would have been a very cosy scene if the mood had been different. 'We'll wait until the storm calms then we can take it in turns to use the lanterns to get to our rooms,' she said. 'There are candles in each room so it won't be that bad, quite romantic really.'

'I've always liked storms,' said Mozzy. 'All that energy in nature.'

Sebastian sighed and rolled his eyes. 'Candlelight and a good restaurant, that's romantic. Not being stuck in the back of beyond with a drug dealer on your doorstep and in the pitch black while waiting for a monsoon to take you down. Still, it's not for long now thank God.'

Chloe turned to berate the astrologer for what he was saying about Andy but the phone rang and startled them all. Roisin picked it up and as she listened, Chloe tried to gauge from her expression whether it was good or more bad news.

'Thanks, and at least no one was hurt,' said her friend before saying goodbye.

'What's happened?' asked Chloe. 'No one was hurt in what? Has there been an accident?'

Roisin shook her head. 'The good news is that Fliss is okay and getting the care she needs and equally good, no one was hurt when the power cables came down – that's why we don't have any power.'

'Is there bad news?' asked Rik.

'They came down over the main road along with some trees,' replied Roisin, cautiously eying Sebastian as she spoke. 'There's no way in or out of the village tonight. I'm afraid your car has had to turn back.'

'Brilliant, bloomin' brilliant!' cried Sebastian, throwing his arms in the air. 'I asked whether tonight could get any worse and it looks as if it just did.'

Chapter Thirty-One

With no way out of the village, Chloe couldn't get to Andy and because it was both black dark and cordoned off by the police, she couldn't search the Surfshack for evidence of his innocence. She'd sent text messages that she knew he wouldn't get and called the station for updates but she wasn't family so had been told nothing. Picturing him alone and wishing she could just hold him, she'd scrunched up on the sofa and sobbed herself to sleep feeling utterly useless.

As Chloe opened her eyes she saw a glimmer of light peeping through the top of the curtains. Her body was aching and her eyes puffy but despite that, the day looked bright and hopeful. She walked to the window and pulled them back fully, then stood in awe at the scene in front of her: the most stunning sunrise she had ever witnessed. The tide was out and the gentle ripples in the sand seemed to mirror those in the light stratus clouds above. The roaring orange sun sat on the horizon getting ready to rise and its light sent the sky above all shades of lilac and red. The sea was gentle, just waking up or perhaps recovering after a night of frantic crashing waves. It was glorious, and Chloe thought back to that day out at sea. Kayaking at dawn with Andy, watching the sun rise together, feeling safe with him and completely at peace. Nature was telling her what she had to do.

Chloe dressed and left the house quickly. It was only six o'clock so there was no danger of her running into anyone now that the morning meditations had stopped. Heather had brought out the brandy when the lights went out and suggested they have nightcaps; they'd had quite a few of them in the end but judging from the singing that went on until after midnight, at least the celebrities had gone to bed on friendly terms. Chloe tried the police station again but once more was not allowed to speak to Andy. She had to think of a way of proving his innocence but remembering the most recent letter Heather had received, she also had to see Kareem and try to save the income from the show. She doubted he had time to replace them but surely they couldn't simply disrupt the schedule unless there was a contingency retreat waiting in the wings. Film crews had to get up early to prepare equipment for the morning shoots so there was a chance they'd be up even if Kareem were still in bed. Chloe strode towards the pub with her heart in her throat. She couldn't plan what she'd say to Kareem when she didn't know what he was thinking.

The crew was up and out and had their backs to her filming the beach; surely this was a good sign if they were capturing the dawn after the storm? Chloe tiptoed up to them but her efforts to stay quiet for the shoot went to pieces when she saw what the cameras were focused on.

'No!' she cried as she saw her little beach hut beaten to smithereens across the sand, the leaflets and bunting soaked and filthy. She barged through the crew and started gathering them up in her arms, the tears that had been her lullaby were back and trickling down her cheeks once again. Chloe rubbed them away and, in that instant, realized how completely and utterly defeated she felt. They'd tried so hard to make this work but maybe the sunrise wasn't the sign after all, maybe this wrecked beach hut was. It was a sign that this dream was over and she should just go back to what she knew. Going back would keep her mother happy that's for sure. A hand reached out and started picking up the pieces of litter alongside her; she turned to see Kareem looking at her with deep empathy but sadness. They continued tidying up the remnants of the hut in silence and when it had been thrown to one side, Kareem turned to her.

'Come and have breakfast with me. We need to talk,' he said.

They walked back to the pub where Maggie was ready to

serve a full English to the crew. As she placed a plateful of food in front of Kareem and Chloe, she put her arm on her shoulder as if to say 'You tried'. Chloe had the feeling that this would be one of those days when everyone would be looking at her with pity, as if she were at a funeral, which in some ways she was – it could be the death of her life here. As Kareem tucked in, she started picking at the food in front of her until she took a mouthful and noticed her stomach growling gratefully. After that she couldn't stop herself and didn't take in air until the plateful and the extra toast had been demolished. Maggie came to take the empty dishes from them both and replenish their coffees.

'Good on you, girl,' she said, noting the completely clean plate Chloe handed to her.

Kareem sipped his coffee and then looked up at Chloe. This is it, she thought. 'We've had to report everything that's happened,' he said. 'The mouse, the glass, the capsize, the drugs and I've asked Jemima to speak to head office later this morning to see what they want to do about it. I have to warn you that I don't think they'll want to continue. They won't put the celebrities in danger.'

'And they shouldn't.' Chloe shook her head. 'No one should feel at risk, especially when they've actually come to improve their health.'

They sat silently, stirring coffee that didn't need stirring.

'Is there another health resort that you'd move these celebrities to?' asked Chloe.

'Not at this stage,' said Kareem. 'So the plan is to tell the story of what's happened here, making a point about the dangers of diet pills and then fill each entire episode with what's happening in Switzerland.'

'I'm sorry. I know I really pushed you for this.'

'It's not all your fault. You didn't know Fliss was taking diet pills, none of us did. Although I bet you're pretty shocked it was your friend supplying them.'

Chloe shook her head adamantly. 'No, I won't accept that. It wasn't him and however this pans out you'll see that it wasn't him. He's not like that and I will prove it.'

'I imagine Fliss was paying him pretty well to help her win – it's important to her brand and followers that she does. There are very few people who'd turn down the offer of thousands of pounds and besides, you haven't really known him that long have you?'

'You don't always need to know someone for long to know them well,' replied Chloe, feeling incredibly protective of Andy.

Kareem needed to get to the farmhouse to check in on everyone and asked Chloe to join him but when they arrived they found that Roisin had taken everyone out for a morning walk. Heather sat alone at the kitchen table reading through the contents of a very formal looking letter. From the expression on the old lady's face, Chloe knew it had to be more bad news but she couldn't let Kareem know there was anything else going wrong while there was still an extremely slim chance that head office would continue the show.

'Do you want to catch up with everyone on their walk?' asked Chloe. 'It might be less inflammatory to talk to people when they're out in the fresh air.'

'You're right,' replied Kareem. 'Sitting down makes it seem like an interview or interrogation. Are you coming with me?'

Chloe shook her head and took Kareem to the edge of the garden, pointing out the path they'd have taken. She returned to the kitchen and sat down beside Heather. 'What's happened?'

Heather handed over the letter which was a confirmation of the new valuation. It said that the land accompanying the house was significantly more valuable than they'd first thought.

'But you don't have to sell,' said Chloe. 'This is your home, surely you can do what you want with it.'

'You'd think so wouldn't you,' replied Heather. 'I can sell it to Roisin, that's not a problem but I have to do it at the full market value apparently otherwise it's seen as a tax dodge or something. Whether I sell it to her now or leave it to all of my grandchildren to divide up, this is what Roisin will have to find.'

'She loves this place,' sighed Chloe. 'It'll break her heart to see it go.'

'So I guess I'll just have to stay here until the day I pop my clogs and let them fight it out when I'm gone,' said Heather. 'It's the only way to give the retreat a chance.'

Chloe was surprised to hear the resignation in Heather's voice. 'It sounds as if you were thinking of leaving.'

Heather got up and started washing cups that were already clean. 'I'm old,' she said without looking at Chloe. 'But I hoped I still had one last adventure in me.' She walked across to the window and looked out. 'One day I'll be scattered out there with my daughter so I'll always come back but it would be nice to have a little change of scene before then. I can't look out at that bay without seeing her.'

'Roisin doesn't know any of this does she?'

Heather shook her head but didn't turn round.

'Is that why you don't paint seascapes anymore?'

Heather nodded and her shoulders dropped as she pulled the curtain across the window. 'Let's not talk about this,' she said. 'I'm a very lucky woman, living in a beautiful place with a granddaughter who loves me. I've no right to grumble.'

A knock on the door jolted them from their thoughts. It was Jemima.

'How is Fliss?' asked Chloe.

'She's had her stomach pumped and she's still under sedation,' replied Jemima. 'So she'll recover, thank goodness. It's hard to believe this was all Andy's doing and to think I really liked that guy.'

Not enough to give him the benefit of the doubt, thought Chloe.

'Anyway, I've had word from head office,' continued Jemima. 'So I need to speak to Kareem.'

Chloe noticed that Jemima looked slightly nervous as the room filled with Kareem and the celebrities. The production co-ordinator cleared her throat and started to speak but only a tiny croak came out. Heather brought her a glass of water and Jemima nodded her thanks then spoke.

'Everyone at MediaFifty really believed in this place,' she said. 'Kareem and I had a fabulous weekend and we really hoped you'd all have the same experience. We promise you that we never intended any harm to come to any of you.'

'Sweetheart, none of this is your fault,' Sebastian simpered. There was definitely a tone of hope in his voice and Chloe knew he'd be furious if he found out he had to unpack.

'But with all that's happened, especially to you, Sebastian, the company feels that we can't continue. The beach is obviously hazardous with all the glass around, the farmhouse has rodents – even if they are natural and wild – they're still rodents who seem particularly attracted to half-price chocolate hobnobs.'

The celebrities laughed and Sebastian shrugged in a coquettish way. 'Busted.' He smiled.

'But obviously the key concern is the drugs. Although Andy has been detained, there is no telling whether he's the only source in the village and we simply can't risk that.'

'Hang on,' said Roisin, grabbing Chloe's arm before she thumped Jemima. 'Are you suggesting that one of us might be supplying diet pills too?'

'I'm not implying anything,' replied Jemima, her palms raised to calm Roisin and Chloe down. 'But the prize is significant for both the winning resort and celebrity – it can become a big temptation. And we know you need the money.'

The disdainful glance around the kitchen was the straw that broke the camel's back. Chloe was angry when Jemima started her implications – by the end of the speech, where blame was being placed firmly at their feet, she was completely incandescent. Something in what the woman had said was bothering her and she tried to focus while Jemima explained the closure of the show and what they'd be telling the media.

What was it? She ran through the irritating speech trying to remember each exact word.

'Half-price Hobnobs,' she muttered, getting a quizzical look from Kareem. Chloe closed her mouth. Now was not the time to tell him. She had to think this through first but then she'd get him on his own and ask him how it was that Jemima had known the biscuits in Sebastian's bag were Hobnobs when they alone had removed them before anyone saw them and hadn't mentioned the brand at all. Chloe had even been the one to pop them in the bin. And the price tag hadn't been remotely obvious at first glance!

Chapter Thirty-Two

Chloe imagined everyone could hear her heart pounding as she tried to sneak out of the kitchen. Only when she reached the courtyard did she take a deep breath, and then another. What was she actually thinking about doing? How was all this related to Andy? And would it do any good anyway? Was it too late to save this day? The words of her odious ex-boss came to mind.

'*Choose your battles, Walsh.*'

Well she'd made up her mind and was choosing this one; she was determined not to give up without one last charge. No one was going to hurt all the people she loved. No one was going to accuse Andy of something she knew he hadn't done, no one was going to destroy the reputation of Serenity and *absolutely* no one was going to tear down her best friend's dream by whipping away the farmhouse from under her feet. These people were her world and it was time to show them all just how much they meant to her.

Chloe checked her watch, wondering how much time she had and what to do first. It was just past 11 am and she guessed it would take at least a couple of hours to clear the fallen trees from the road, so the celebrities wouldn't be able to leave yet, unless of course they were lifted out by helicopter. Surely that would take some organizing? They couldn't move the show yet and the most critical thing was to prove that Andy was innocent and get him out of that police cell. Evidence, she needed evidence. She practically sprinted to the pub and the editing suite where the crew was sitting waiting for instruction. Chloe sighed with relief that they weren't packing up and decided to act as if everything was normal.

'You know the cameras you have set up to capture the

beach and seascape shots?' she asked innocently. 'How much of the bay do they actually record?'

'Most of it, why?'

'Can I take a look at it?'

'There's hours of footage – what day do you want?'

Chloe wasn't sure what she needed so had to take an educated guess. She guessed that Fliss had to have taken the diet pills shortly before being admitted to hospital so she had to have been given them within the past forty-eight hours.

'I need the past three days, but just between the hours of midnight and six in the morning.'

The technician cued up the footage and told her to knock herself out, leaving her on her own while he went to a meeting with the rest of the crew.

In just half an hour Chloe had fast-forwarded through hours of nothing happening, just the tide ebbing and flowing, until she finally saw something. A small light in the darkness of dusk – the light of a torch on a mobile phone? She rewound the footage a little and then played it through. The person was wearing a big overcoat with a hood that practically swamped her body but there was no mistaking who it was – Jemima. Chloe sat back, her breathing was still rapid and she tried to calm the adrenaline racing through her body. She was determined to clear Andy's name but showing that Jemima had access to the Surfshack wasn't enough; after all the production co-ordinator could legitimately argue that she was checking out something for the next day's recording, even if she was doing it out of hours. Chloe pictured Andy lying on a single bed in a police cell and Fliss similarly stretched out on her hospital bed. Fliss was the only person who could tell people the truth if she decided to but, in any case, not until she was well enough to do so. And that might be too late.

The technician returned and told her what she already knew, that he had to start packing up. Chloe feigned surprise and left him to it. She needed a moment to think through her next move. She sat on the harbour wall, watching as the tide ebbed and flowed without a care in the world.

'The sea is a good metaphor for life,' said a voice behind her. It was Mozzy, carrying a bag from the chocolate shop. 'A raging storm hits it one night but it copes and then gets back to normal.'

He opened the bag and offered her a chocolate – the salted caramel that she'd found so intoxicating when she first arrived. She took a piece and let the endorphins flood through her.

'The sea doesn't have a mortgage to pay,' she said and Mozzy nodded that she'd made a good point.

'Had to buy some of this,' he said, taking another piece of chocolate. 'My daughter will love it. That's if there's any left for her by the time I see her.'

'Are you married?' asked Chloe. 'Sorry, maybe I should know that. You might be one of those celebrity couples.'

Mozzy laughed. 'I could find someone called Keeto and we'd be moz-keeto.'

'Or someone called Chief and be Moz-chief – that would suit you.'

'She was the chief in our house,' said Mozzy sadly. 'Always kept me in line. She'd have had a laugh at this – me trying to improve my health. Although she'd have loved the place.'

Chloe looked out at the sunlight dancing on the gentle waves. Thinking again of Andy and his passion for the sea, she said, 'It would be hard for anyone not to love it.'

Mozzy held out his hand to pull her up and together they started walking back to the farmhouse. Chloe thought for a moment about what she was going to ask and then, deciding she had nothing to lose, went for it. 'I need to ask you a favour,' she said. 'Could you ask Sebastian who gave him the biscuits he had in his bag?'

'I don't need to,' replied Mozzy. 'He told me last week he couldn't cope with all this healthy food and needed a junk food fix. He was whingeing every day and then one day he stopped. I asked whether he was getting used to it but he just winked and said someone had come to his rescue.'

'And he told you who?'

'Yeah, Jemima. Why?'

That meant she was encouraging one person to lose weight and another to gain weight but surely Jemima had to benefit from Fliss winning for it to make any sense? Once again, Chloe felt trapped in a corner with the only two people who could answer her questions being the only two she couldn't or wouldn't ask.

As they reached the farmhouse, Kareem stood outside making a call. He looked very earnest as he listened, nodding along and then as the call ended he sighed with relief. 'Good news. Fliss is awake and doing okay.'

'Has she said anything,' blurted Chloe. 'About who gave her the drugs? Have the police interviewed her? Has she told them it wasn't Andy?'

'Hold your horses, she's only just stirred. They're going in later this afternoon.'

'Can I go? To see how she is?'

'I doubt they'd let you – even if you could get there. Have you forgotten the giant tree trunk lying on the road?'

Chloe had momentarily forgotten that small fact; it was both a blessing and a curse. As long as the celebrities had to stay, she felt there was a chance of rescuing the situation but if she couldn't get out then there was little chance of rescuing Andy. She looked around the courtyard for a sign, a solution, an idea, anything. Bingo! There it was – a bicycle leaning against the wall. She couldn't really cycle the whole distance down the dual carriageway to the hospital but she could get to the tree, climb over it and then arrange for a taxi to pick her up on the other side. It was doable.

Chloe said a frantic goodbye to Mozzy and Kareem and then grabbed the bike. She pedaled as fast as she could through the village and onto the main road leading out of Serenity. It was steeper than she'd imagined and her initial burst of energy turned into a laborious slog but she couldn't give up. Finally she reached the tree, an enormous old sycamore which lay pitifully slain. Some workmen were trying to remove boughs and branches before tackling the main trunk and warned her to stay back. Chloe rested the bike against the hedgerow and realized she wasn't going to be allowed to climb the tree. On the other side, she could see the taxi she'd ordered pulling in. The driver got out and scratched his head, then approached the workmen. They were signaling that he should turn around. Quickly Chloe phoned the taxi company and yelled down the line, 'Tell the driver to stay exactly where he is! I'll be right there.'

If she couldn't get over the tree, she'd have to go around it. That meant climbing through hedgerows and over barbed wire into the field. The tree had brought some of the fence posts down meaning that the wire closest to the fall wasn't as high. She threw her jacket over the worst of the spikes and looked for something fixed to hold onto as she climbed. There was nothing. 'Okay girl,' Chloe said to herself. 'Core stability.'

Remembering what Andy had taught her in the paddleboard lesson, she picked up one of the sawn-off branches and faced the wires of the fence. She held the branch as if she were pole vaulting and as quick as a flash, propelled herself onto the top wire with both feet and launched herself off into the field. She landed with a few scrapes but at least she was over. Looking quickly along the edge of the field, the other side of the tree, was a five bar gate. She ran towards it, climbing over, and waved at the taxi to drive down to meet her.

Once at the hospital, with her disheveled hair and bloodied scratches, she likely looked as if she should be being admitted but Chloe paid no heed to the stares she was getting and, flashing a MediaFifty ID card that she'd snuck out of the editing suite, asked the way to Fliss's ward. The young woman lay in a private room but looked so pale and exhausted with hydration drips and machines attached to her that Chloe forgot her desperation for answers for a moment and simply sat beside the bed and squeezed her hand.

Fliss turned her head towards her and mouthed, 'I'm sorry.' A tear rolled down her cheek and Chloe squeezed more tightly.

'It's okay,' she said realizing that Fliss was as much a victim in this as Andy.

A nurse came into the room and checked all the machines then handed Fliss a drink with a straw and waited until she'd drank all of it. Fliss asked to be propped up so Chloe and the nurse plumped up the pillows and helped her to sit. Chloe asked whether the police had been to see her yet and Fliss shook her head. 'I'm not ready for them. I feel such a fraud. The world expects me to be perfect. Or the world I've created does anyway.'

Chloe said nothing but let her speak.

'I needed to win this before refocusing my career. My agent said that if I went out on a high from this then I'd be more likely to get the presenter job on the next series. And once you get one presenter role, you start to get offered more. I'd be able to get off this guru bandwagon once and for all.'

Fliss started coughing so Chloe refilled the drinking cup and held it out for her to drink from the straw.

'Thank you. But I wasn't losing any weight, not surprisingly as I don't really have a lot to lose but I needed to.' Fliss turned and held both of Chloe's hands tightly. 'Then one morning I was offered something that would help. I need you to know that I'm not normally like this. I do believe in a natural route to health and I was told those pills were made from homeopathic ingredients. But I'm not stupid. Deep down I knew.'

Fliss lay back down, exhausted. She closed her eyes and started to drift back to sleep. No matter how much sympathy Chloe felt right now, she couldn't waste another moment. Proving Andy's innocence and saving Roisin's retreat depended on what this woman knew. She perched herself on the side of the bed and gently shook Fliss who half-opened her eyes.

'You said you were *offered* the pills,' said Chloe firmly but gently. 'Who by? Who offered them to you, Fliss?'

Fliss shook her head slowly. 'I can't say,' she murmured. 'Don't want to get them into trouble.' She closed her eyes again.

Chloe wasn't giving up and shook her slightly harder. 'The thing is,' she said, 'someone is already in trouble and I know they're not responsible.'

Fliss looked away but Chloe kept hold of her arms, willing her not to fall asleep. 'Look Fliss, they've arrested Andy for supplying you with these pills but he wouldn't do a thing like that. They've said he kept them stored in the Surfshack, hidden in a kayak and that you collected them every morning when you went for an early morning paddle.'

Fliss still had her head turned but opened her eyes on hearing this.

'Correct me if I'm wrong,' said Chloe. 'I think you liked Andy. He's a really decent guy and he doesn't deserve to have his name, his reputation and his business destroyed if it wasn't him. Please Fliss, you have to do the right thing.'

Fliss took a deep breath and turned to look Chloe directly in the eye. 'You're right, it wasn't him. Get me a phone and I'll call the police. Andy is completely innocent.'

'If I tell you who I think gave you them, will you just shake your head if I'm wrong?' Fliss gave a tiny nod so Chloe continued. 'I think it was Jemima.'

Fliss kept her head completely still and a tear rolled down her cheek. Chloe grabbed her in such a tight hug that both women winced from their respective injuries. After Fliss had made the most important call, Chloe left her to rest and rang Kareem on the way home. 'Please don't let anyone leave just yet,' she pleaded. 'Remember what you said to me? The show must go on? And I really think it can.'

Chapter Thirty-Three

Chloe took the waiting taxi straight to the police station and asked the driver to wait for her yet again. She saw Andy in the reception – he looked exhausted and vulnerable and as he stood up to shake the hand of the constable behind the desk, she couldn't help herself. Chloe rushed over to him and held him tight, pressing herself into his chest and breathing him in. He gave her a gentle squeeze in return then untangled himself from her grip.

'You look as if you've been dragged through a hedge backwards,' he added, picking a leaf out of her hair.

'I have, kind of,' she replied and slightly embarrassed by the hug that she'd given, explained her climb over the fallen tree.

'I might have misjudged you when you arrived,' he said. 'I'm sorry for that.'

Although she dismissed his apology with a wave of the hand, inside she was glowing and wondered whether this could be a fresh start together. She took him to the cab and asked the driver to get them to Serenity as fast as he could; it seemed to Chloe that she'd been living in an action movie for the past twenty-four hours and with the role of Andy played by himself. She looked across at him. He had the window open and faced the breeze with his eyes closed. Chloe couldn't imagine how it would have felt for a man like him to have had his freedom threatened. She reached out to squeeze his hand but the cab chose that moment to hit a pothole and he was jolted out of his seat, out of reach.

The heavens are telling you to leave the poor guy alone, Chloe thought to herself. She sat on her hands in case they started to develop a mind of their own.

The fallen tree had now been cleared and lay in a field.

Andy whistled as they drove past and told Chloe he was even more impressed by what she'd done now he'd seen it. By the time they arrived back in the village that afternoon, Kareem had heard from the police, and Jemima had been taken in for questioning. The celebrities learned that she'd been jeopardizing their chances from the start because she'd been promised a lot of money from Fliss's agent to make sure Fliss won.

'Fliss was guaranteed the presenting role in the next series if she won this one,' explained Kareem. 'That would have meant a large commission for her agent but because all luggage is searched, she needed someone on the crew to bring the pills in. Jemima was happy to take money to do it.'

'And giving me biscuits was a way of making sure I didn't win?' asked Sebastian.

'Partly,' replied Kareem, 'but it was also about creating more drama and making sure the ratings were really high so that Fliss was part of a successful show. The glass on the beach from the pill bottle was probably just an accident but that and the capsized kayak showed the celebrities in some kind of danger and viewers loved it. Winning a dud TV series helps no one.'

'But surely it went too far? She didn't plan on making poor Fliss ill did she?' asked Dame Julie.

'No, that was just a reaction Fliss had to the pills,' replied Kareem. 'Anyway, the agent told Jemima she'd still get the cash if she got the show closed down as soon as possible to let the publicity die down. So when she spoke to head office, she told them you all wanted to leave. That's why it's over.'

Although their bags were packed and piled up ready to go, all the celebrities took seats at the table, enthralled and waiting for the next instalment.

'This place is like a soap opera,' said Suzie.

'Yes,' exclaimed Chloe suddenly. 'It's *exactly* like a soap opera and that's why the show must go on. Now that we know all of this, we can't let Jemima and Fliss's horrible agent win.'

Kareem sat down with the celebrities and signaled her to continue – it was like facing the selection panel all over again. 'The first episode was glorious, happy faces and beautiful scenery. The second brought some friction because the residents weren't enjoying the new regime and didn't seem to be making much progress. Then in the third, well in the third there was thunder, lightning, stormy seas and stormy arguments. We've had a drugs bust, a biscuit hoard and a mouse! I bet they didn't have any of that over in Switzerland.'

'You can say that again,' replied Kareem. 'Don't forget the tabloid coverage of this. They know about Fliss and that can't be simply glossed over.'

'So work with it. Viewing figures will be enormous with everyone wanting to know what happens next. Whether we like it or not, we've created a cliffhanger. Fliss should apologise and then be welcomed back with open arms and everyone should vow to commit to the programme properly.'

Chloe turned to the celebrities. 'It isn't fair that my friends should suffer because of the actions of two people. And it isn't fair that you leave here without getting the full benefits of a naturally healthy resort because, trust me, it will work and we can beat Switzerland.'

Silence fell around the room as the celebrities looked from one to the other. Finally Mozzy spoke. 'Well I don't have anything I need to get back to. I'll stay.'

'Me too,' said Dame Julie. 'I'm beginning to think it's rather beautiful here.'

One by one the celebrities made the commitment to give it a go, even Sebastian, who got the biggest round of applause. Then, while Kareem went to phone his boss, the crew was called in and they did it all again for the camera, with Suzie making Chloe's passionate plea and Rik ending with a fist punch and a *Let's do this guys*.

'I'm still not sure I can continue,' said Roisin as she pulled Chloe and Andy to one side. 'I'm so glad we're not losing the fee and that people will see what we're really about but I know now that I'm just a yoga teacher. I'm not some strict drill sergeant. What if I can't keep them all under control?'

Andy put his arms around her and then held one arm out for Chloe to join them. It felt good but Chloe knew Roisin needed more than a group hug. Suddenly Andy let go of them both and looked directly at her. 'Your friend,' he said. 'The coffee guy. Didn't you say he was a personal trainer? A big guy with a deep voice like that would make people listen.'

'Of course!' cried Chloe. She grabbed hold of his face and, pulling him down towards her, planted a big kiss on his forehead. 'Have I ever told you how utterly brilliant you are? Roisin, wait here.'

Chloe disappeared into the living room where her sleeping bag still lay discarded on the sofa; she'd left its snuggly confines only hours earlier but it felt like a lifetime ago. Chloe found the contact she needed and dialed the number; it rang out for such a long time, or at least it felt that way. Finally, his face appeared on the screen, sweaty and, with trees and a park in the background, evidently out on a run.

'Double-Shot, how y'doin'?'

Lloyd was hooked on all the goings-on at Serenity through the TV show but was still amazed to hear the full story. 'What can I do?' he asked.

'Come up here,' Chloe replied. 'Please. Roisin hates giving orders but that's what they need – some good old boot camp discipline from a qualified trainer. You'll be on TV.'

It didn't take Lloyd long to consider her request and agree to it; he could sort out everything he needed to then get a train tomorrow afternoon and be there by 7pm. Chloe rushed back to her friends and quickly told Roisin all about Lloyd. Andy said he'd go with them to pick him up from the station the following day and Roisin held both of their hands, thanking them and looking incredibly relieved. They all had things they had to get on with so said their goodbyes. Chloe sighed with relief – it felt as if she was juggling several spinning plates at once. The show and her friends were looking fairly steady but there was one at the end that looked like it would tumble at any moment. That's the one she had to spin now.

When she reached the gift shop, Louise was putting a picture of Mozzy holding up a bottle of Serenity craft ale in the window display. 'He said he enjoyed it,' she told Chloe. 'And that he didn't mind me using his name.'

'I'm sure he wouldn't. I should tell Tony to do the same. When I met Mozzy he was scoffing bags of the salted caramels. Some health regime eh?' Louise smiled and invited her to sit down. Chloe explained the situation up at the farm, that Roisin was hoping to buy it from Heather but the latest valuation seemed extremely high. 'Heather said something about the land attached being more valuable than they'd originally thought.'

'Hmm, that probably means they've found out there are no building restrictions in place. The surveyor is potentially valuing it as a property with development potential and they might even know of companies looking for land. Companies often put out word that they're looking for land and pay finder's fees for any they eventually buy.'

'That doesn't sound good,' replied Chloe. Is there any way of finding out who might be looking ?' Louise said she'd ask around some of her old colleagues. 'Meanwhile,' she said, nodding towards the wreckage of the beach hut, 'where are you thinking of setting up shop until that's fixed?'

Chloe shrugged and shook her head; she hadn't had time to think about it.

'Come and set up in here,' continued Louise. 'I can move the paintings to the back room and create a gallery. Having the tourists coming in for leaflets can only be good for business and there's a flat upstairs that isn't used if you're planning on staying.'

'I am, and as I have no idea where my tent actually vanished to in the storm, that seems like a pretty attractive offer,' replied Chloe. 'How much is the rent?'

Louise told her and added, 'I can wait until you're up and running if you need me to?'

'No that's absolutely fine. Now that the show's back on track I'll get my fee and I really want to pay my way. It'll feel as if I officially live here.'

'Then that's agreed.' Louise smiled, holding out her hand and shaking on the agreement. 'Come on up. I was about to close the shop so I'll show you round.'

By the time dusk rolled around and the sky began to drift into a gentle darkness, Chloe had explained Louise's offer to Roisin and Heather, got their blessing and moved the few belongings she had into the flat above the gift shop. It was a little bigger than she'd thought it would be and as Louise had left a bed, a kettle and a chair up there, she really did have everything she needed for now. The front of the flat looked out over the sea and that evening as she spent her first night in her new home, Chloe could imagine spending hours simply watching the changing colours and seasons.

The following day, Chloe woke refreshed and ready for action. Yesterday had been so long and so dramatic, she'd almost collapsed into sleep the moment her head hit the pillow. Today she was with Louise searching through planning documents, just in case any companies had been refused permissions recently and might therefore be looking for alternative land. It felt like looking for a needle in a haystack and was just as fruitless. She stretched and checked her watch – she'd been at this for hours and it was already time for them to collect Lloyd; right on cue, Roisin and Andy pulled up outside the shop in the jeep.

'I'm terrified,' Roisin said as Chloe climbed into the back. 'What if this guy thinks I'm a complete flake?'

'Then we'll tell him flakes are good things,' replied Chloe. 'I have them in ice-cream cones all the time.'

Roisin laughed out loud but visibly relaxed as they started the journey to Newcastle station.

They dropped Andy off at his little terraced cottage behind the high street and went straight to the farmhouse with Lloyd where his arrival caused quite a stir. The celebrities were having supper and, as Chloe introduced him to each of them, she could see them weighing him up for one reason or the other. Rik puffed his chest out and gripped the trainer's hand, shaking it firmly as if weighing up who was stronger while others took a good long look for very different reasons. Lloyd joined them at the table answering their questions about his background amiably but professionally.

'God, he's lush,' Suzie whispered to Chloe. 'Wouldn't mind a bit of one-to-one with him.'

'Remember the agreement,' Kareem scolded her quietly. 'Everyone sticks to the rules from now on.'

After supper, Lloyd asked that he and Roisin be allowed to discuss the health data for each celebrity and the results from the other retreat. He told everyone that they'd talk to them individually after that. 'Roisin here knows how to get you healthy and it'll be my job to make sure you don't slack. I'll be the bad cop to her good cop.'

Chloe watched her friend blush a little and then show Lloyd into the yoga studio where Kareem followed with his laptop. Back in the kitchen, the evening was drawing to a calm close so Heather suggested a game of cards which Mozzy and Dame Julie agreed to while the others yawned and drifted off to do their own thing.

Although she should have felt tired, Chloe was still buzzing so, decided to pop into the Fiddler's Arms for a nightcap; after all, it was on her way home now. She smiled at the thought that she now had a proper home. Inside the bar, the gentle murmur of the last few customers and the warmth of the fire made for a very relaxing atmosphere. Chloe was about to take up a stool at the bar when someone called over to her.

'That drink is on me,' said a warm deep voice she knew belonged to Andy. A wave of happiness washed over her as she ordered a red wine. She lifted her glass to him in a toast before walking over to join him. As she sat down at his table, she could see that he'd had a couple too many.

'It was pretty scary you know,' he slurred. 'Being locked up for something I didn't do. I kept thinking, how can I prove it wasn't me? Who's going to believe my word against some world famous celebrity?'

'I believed you,' whispered Chloe, glancing up into his eyes.

Andy clinked his glass against hers. 'I know you did. You were the one who climbed trees and hedges to prove my incense, I mean my *inn – o – cence*. For that I thank you, from the bottom of my heart.' He hiccupped.

She completely understood his need to have a few drinks after all he'd been through but he looked exhausted and probably needed a night's sleep more than anything. She helped Andy to his feet and nodded goodbye to Maggie as she led him towards the door.

'I was wrong about you, you know,' he muttered as they staggered along the road. 'I thought you'd be like all the others – come here and try to fix us, fix me then … *poof* … you're back to the bright lights and big city.'

They reached the door to his house and Chloe took his key off him and opened it, pushing him inside and onto the sofa. She took off his shoes and filled a glass with water, making him take a drink before putting it on the floor beside him. He lay down.

'But you care about this place don't you?' Andy continued. 'And you know what? I care about you.'

He took hold of her hand and kissed it gently before falling asleep. Chloe put a coat over him and locked his door as she left, posting the keys through the letterbox.

As she walked back to her flat she pressed her lips to the spot he'd kissed. It had been the action of someone overwhelmed by events as well as a little too much beer but she knew she'd go to bed tonight hoping that he'd meant it.

Chapter Thirty-Four

Chloe waited until she was just about to leave her flat before trying Andy's number. She wanted to check that he was okay but guessed there was a chance that he hadn't woken up yet. He had.

'I'm sorry about last night,' he said wearily. 'A bit too much to drink.'

'Don't worry about it,' replied Chloe. 'Anyone would have done the same after what you'd been through.'

'Thanks for getting me back home. You seem to be rescuing me a lot these days. I didn't say anything embarrassing did I?'

'No,' said Chloe unable to stop the smile in her voice. 'In fact you were perfectly lovely and said all sorts of fabulous things about me.'

Andy let out a pained groan so she told him to get back to sleep before ending the call. She picked up her things and practically skipped down the road.

The farmhouse courtyard was abuzz with activity when Chloe arrived. The cameras were trained on Lloyd and Roisin who stood in front of the blackboard like drill sergeants. The celebrities were all kitted out in extremely smart matching sports gear, although Dame Julie had added her trademark sunhat and silk scarf.

'Where did the kit come from?' Chloe whispered to Kareem.

'Lloyd ordered everything before he left and it arrived this morning. He says it turns them into one team.'

Roisin was speaking to the group. 'I have always believed that Serenity can improve your health by helping you to find a love of life that you want to maintain. Whether that's walking in the fresh air, meditating or getting out onto the water – whatever you love doing will keep you young.'

'And that's the key,' continued Lloyd. 'You have to love it or it won't do you any good. Over the rest of the time we have together, you're gonna stick to what you love but you're gonna give that activity one hundred per cent. *Not* eighty percent, not ninety. If you enjoy it, go for it and see how good you can be. Trust me, it will be a whole lot better than you think.'

The celebrities nodded, looking in awe and slightly nervous.

'So, who wants to tell me what they've loved most?'

Roisin stood poised ready to write down the activities and goals for each person.

'I'd love to do more walking and to find out about the flora and fauna of the area,' said Dame Julie.

'Yeah, me too,' added Mozzy. 'Do a bit of hikin' and bikin'.'

'Good,' said Lloyd as Roisin wrote it down. 'That's your thing. And if you can do ten miles now, I want thirty miles out of you by the time you head home. Okay, who's next?'

Rik raised a hand. 'If your guy Andy is still in play after all that stuff, I want to get out there exploring. It's a great resistance workout, paddling against the ocean.' He flexed his arms as if to make the point.

Lloyd looked at Kareem. 'Is kayaking still in play?'

'Of course,' he said. Chloe silently whooped, happy to have a real excuse to go and see Andy later.

Sebastian opted for a more spiritual approach, saying he wanted to learn meditation to help keep his mind young and stress-free; Suzie, probably with her eye on a different type of prize, asked Lloyd if he could teach her some boxercise moves. He avoided her flirtatious glances and agreed immediately.

With everything written down, Roisin once again addressed the team. 'Thank you,' she said. 'These activities will keep you young. The natural diet will keep you healthy and the daily stretches I lead you through will give you strength and flexibility. These three things are all anyone needs.' She pressed her palms together and bowed her head, inviting them to stand up and begin the day with a sun salutation. The celebrities almost looked professional as they moved from one position to the next without groaning or toppling over.

Chloe approached Lloyd. 'They seem to be happy with this approach but it's not going to win us the competition is it?'

'Does that matter?' he replied. 'This is what Roisin wants this place to be. Let her live that dream while she can – besides, the results might just surprise you.'

He was right, they'd started this with a vision of what Serenity could be and there was no point in winning if those values were destroyed. And yet winning might be the only way of keeping the retreat; it was a fine line to tread and Chloe's role in all of this had to be keeping both the public and the media on their side. Fliss was getting out of hospital today and Kareem had arranged a press conference alongside Fliss's new agent to re-launch the young woman, save the show and assure any potential advertisers out there that Serenity wasn't some drug dealer's ghetto.

As she arrived back at the village with Kareem, it was already teeming with camera crews and presenters waiting for the conference to begin. They were wandering in and out of shops, obviously buying the local gifts and crafts, so, Chloe thought to herself, whatever came of the meeting itself, at least the village would have had a good day's business.

Fliss's new agent approached them to get the story straight. 'Fliss wants to make a statement about the pressure of being thin,' she barked at them. 'How it doesn't equal healthy or beautiful.' Kareem and Chloe obviously weren't expected to say anything so they simply nodded and the agent continued to talk at them. 'How the world is self-obsessed now and if we focused more on what's going on around us, we'd all be healthier both physically and mentally.' Again, they nodded. It made sense. 'Today we're launching a campaign to end selfies,' said the agent.

'Wow,' Chloe replied. 'That will get attention. Is that what Fliss is planning to do herself? To stop taking selfies?'

'For a month at least. There'll be a hashtag obvs, something along the lines of #lovelifenotselfies.'

'I have to say, I genuinely like it,' said Chloe. 'I think you'll get lots of coverage and if Fliss could encourage less introspection, it will probably do her followers the world of good.'

'Yeah well, the followers are getting older anyway. I'm also trying to fix her up with a new show where she tries things she's never done before so we need to work towards that while she's here. She needs to be using senses other than sight, you know, tying in with how it's not always about how things look?'

Fliss's relaunch was music to Chloe's ears; they could promote all the other activities they'd listed on that blackboard when she first arrived. 'We can absolutely fill her days and you can come back to film the new show if you like.' Chloe couldn't help herself but got a sharp glance from the agent.

'I think her followers want to see other parts of the world, no offence.' She turned on her extremely high heels and started click-clacking down the road towards the village hall in a manner that said 'we're finished for now'.

Kareem and Chloe followed her, dutifully keeping a few paces behind. 'I get why she thinks I'm no one, but she does realise you're the producer doesn't she?' Chloe whispered to Kareem.

He laughed and replied, 'Oh I'm only just above you at the bottom of the pile. The talent is king don't you know.'

The village hall was packed to the rafters with vloggers and big social media influencers at the front and mainstream media seated behind them. Kareem began by announcing that everyone connected with the show going forward was completely without blame. Inevitably there were questions about the kayak where the drugs had been found but Kareem convinced the press that it had simply been a convenient hiding place.

'Doesn't this prove that these types of programmes encourage unreasonable pressures? I mean you win a lot of money if you lose weight in a few weeks.'

Kareem was saved from answering that by the appearance of Fliss. Instantly cameras started flashing and it wouldn't have mattered what he said, they wanted to hear it from the horse's mouth.

'I'll take that question if I may,' she said.

Chloe noted that she wasn't wearing a scrap of make-up but her long blond hair shone under a spotlight which seemed to have been set up in the perfect position to achieve that effect. No filter but clever lighting. She had to admit, Fliss's new agent knew her stuff.

'Serenity was never about weight and neither was the show,' Fliss continued. 'The retreat here is about health and turning back the clock because you're feeling less stressed or you feel more mentally alert. I was the one who mistook health for weight but I've learned my lesson.'

An image of Dame Julie was projected onto the wall behind Fliss and she stood aside to let everyone see it. Chloe recognized that it had been taken on the bike ride; the dame was smiling, her hand clutching her sunhat which was about to blow off. Then the image changed. It was Rik baking bread, then Suzie laughing as she wobbled on a paddleboard and Mozzy biting his tongue in concentration as he attempted the tree pose. They were beautiful images that had the room smiling so when the final picture was projected – Sebastian in a kayak with his mouth wide open in astonishment as a seal popped his head out of the water to stare at him, the entire audience simply laughed.

'They're great aren't they,' continued Fliss. 'Compare those images with these.'

This time the projections were all selfies taken by the young woman; pouting, hips strutting out, contoured selfies. It was an absolutely perfect way of making the point. Fliss didn't look happy in a single one of them and despite them having been taken in exactly the same environment, there was no joy and no adventure.

'If all you portray is yourself, you miss out on so much,' said Fliss. 'And you put pressure on yourself to look a certain way. I am calling for all my followers to ditch selfies. Maybe just for a week or a month to start with, but instead fill your posts with adventure and experiences. Tag me, but remember no selfies. It's time to #lovelifenotselfies.'

The hashtag was projected up on the wall and instantly had phones and cameras raised to record it. Fliss bowed to the crowd and left to an affectionate round of applause. Her agent fielded some questions and it was finally time for Chloe to take the stage. As she did she noticed Andy sneaking in at the back and waving sheepishly at her. She gave him a little wave back, her confidence boosted just from seeing him.

The majority of media had come to hear Fliss so Chloe wasn't surprised to see people leaving when she got up, heading out to get their interviews – at least the bay would be in the background. Some of those that remained in the room were obviously checking the footage they'd taken had been posted so she looked out upon a sea of downturned heads. Apart from Andy there were three people who strode in against the tide of people leaving and sat down at the back. They looked directly at her, focused and paying close attention; one of the three was Mr Bald. The sight of him put Chloe slightly off her stride and she had no idea who the others were but they had to have something to do with the new valuation, she was sure of it. For a millisecond she was torn; her speech was all about how wonderful Serenity was but perhaps she should be saying something to put these people off, whoever they were. There was no way of doing both so Chloe swallowed and, though her throat was now dry, she started extolling the virtues of the bay and explaining the activities Fliss would be taking part in over the rest of her stay.

'This all sounds wonderful,' said someone sitting with Mr Bald. 'So would you say that Serenity is a great place to work, live and play?'

It was obviously a loaded question and given Louise's theory about the increased valuation possibly being linked to development, Chloe decided to make a point while at least one or two cameras were still rolling. 'You can see it's a fabulous place to work, live and play right now and that's because of the unspoilt landscape and the families that have loved this village for generations. We have everything we need here and we're looking forward to welcoming visitors who want to see nature at its very best.'

The man said thank you and another man sitting to his left, who had evidently been filming her speech, nodded. Chloe saw him mouthing 'got it' to the first guy and her blood went cold. What had he "got"? Had she said the wrong thing? She shot a look at Andy who was frowning at the guy. He looked up at her with a concerned look on his face. He nodded at her and silently mouthed, 'It's okay,' and followed the men out as they left.

After the speech, Chloe was approached by a few magazines who wanted to feature Serenity in return for promises of advertising so by the time she got back outside the hall, the three men were nowhere to be seen. Andy however was rushing towards her with Louise behind him.

'Do you know what they're up to? Did you speak to them?' asked Chloe.

'I'm sorry, I didn't get the chance,' replied Andy. 'But Louise knows who they are.'

'My friend at the council has heard the jungle drums,' said Louise catching her breath.

'Is it bad?' asked Andy standing very close to Chloe and bracing for the news.

'They're making enquiries about changing the land use to include categories A and D – that's shops and leisure facilities.'

'So someone does want to build here?'

'It explains why the valuation is so much higher.'

'*Woah*, have you seen this?' Kareem appeared holding his phone out to her. He pressed play on a video clip and Chloe was puzzled to see herself there.

A great place to live and play. Families that love this village need work and look forward to welcoming you.

'That's not what she said,' protested Andy. 'That's been edited. Why would they do that? Surely they can't without her permission. I'm going to make them retract it.'

Chloe grabbed his arm and pulled him back. She wasn't sure how that might turn out and couldn't risk any more trouble for him.

'It's posted on a private twitter feed,' continued Kareem. 'It'll take some time to get them to take it down.'

'Louise,' said Chloe calmly turning to her and holding her by the shoulders. 'You have to find out who's making these change of use enquiries. We have to know who we're dealing with.'

'Oh I have a name,' said Louise pulling a scrap of paper from her bag and unfolding it carefully. 'But I've never heard of them. Here it is, someone called GLP?'

Chapter Thirty-Five

Andy googled the name and showed the results to Chloe.

'*THIS IS NOT HAPPENING!*' She raised her face to the sky and yelled as if she was summoning Thor himself. Around her Kareem, Andy and Louise took a step backwards.

'I take it you know them?' asked Andy.

'I knew them as GlobalLezure,' she replied.

She explained how she'd been sacked for refusing to work on their account. As she spoke, Chloe noticed Andy's expression changing; his eyes seemed to sparkle and a big smile broke out across his face. It wasn't the reaction she was expecting but nor was the huge embrace that came next.

'I'm proud of you,' he said when he eventually released her from the bear hug. 'I didn't know you were always such a warrior for the small guy.'

'I'm not really,' murmured Chloe finding herself in a strange state between confusion, anger and delight. 'I just don't like to see companies ruining life for others and they definitely have.'

Kareem cleared his throat loudly and Chloe pulled her gaze from Andy back to the matter in hand.

'I know this is important,' Kareem said, 'but so is the show and Louise is due to teach Fliss how to make aromatherapy candles as part of her new experiences programme.'

'You're right, I'm sorry,' replied Chloe. 'Please go and do Serenity proud. I'll find out what they're up to.'

'You're not going anywhere without me,' said Andy.

'Promise me,' she said looking directly into his eyes, 'that you won't deck them as soon as you see them – for my sake?'

Andy crossed his heart then laughed. 'Not as *soon* as I see them anyway. Now where are those sneaky toads?'

Louise said she thought she'd seen them going into the pub then left with Kareem in order to get back for Fliss's class.

Chloe and Andy swung round, marching down the high street like avenging angels. Inside the pub, Mr Bald and his companions were being served lunch by Maggie.

'I want to know what you lot think you're doing here,' said Chloe, folding her arms as Andy stood in the same pose right beside her. 'We know about the Global proposal and we're not leaving until we get some answers.'

The man who'd asked her the question at the meeting looked up at her. 'Happy to talk but would you mind waiting half an hour or so?' he said smugly. 'We're just about to start this rather tasty looking steak pie.'

'I think you mean *very* tasty looking,' said Maggie before getting a look from Chloe that made her retreat back behind the bar.

'You'll talk to us right now,' said Andy moving the plate away from him.

'Who are you all? I know you,' said Chloe nodding to Mr Bald. 'What does everyone else have to do with the farmhouse?'

Mr Smug, as he was now named in Chloe's mind, reached into his pocket, pulled out a business card and handed it to her. He looked very entertained by her reaction.

Chloe felt Andy steady her as she wobbled on reading the card. The moment had a feel of déjà vu. It said that this annoying person was Campaign Director at Delaney & Finch Advertising. She gave him the card back quickly as if it might spontaneously combust in her hand.

'He has my old job,' she said explaining her reaction to Andy.

'That's right.' Mr Smug stood and held his hand out to them both but neither of them took it. 'I was recruited when you turned down this account. Although funnily enough, you actually inspired the change in strategy for GlobalLezure. The brand name was a problem as you pointed out but a brand called Serenity Leisure, based here in beautiful

Northumberland, won't have any of the connotations of the old name. I guess this is what you'd call karma. They'll be part of your life every day now when the sale goes through.'

Chloe could feel her heart pounding and had to reign in every emotion whizzing around her body.

'Not if we can help it,' Andy was saying, squaring up to Mr Smug but she knew that wouldn't help matters.

Chloe felt sick that she had led this monster to their doorstep, sad that the dream might be over, foolish for thinking she could make a difference to Roisin or Serenity and angry that the big guy looked like winning this battle despite everything she'd tried. It was the anger that she tried to harness. It wasn't over yet but she needed more details before she could act. Swallowing back her fears she rested her hand on Andy's arm and said calmly, 'It looks that way, but I hope Global will bring something to the community. Do you know what the plans are?'

Mr Smug pulled a glossy brochure wallet from his briefcase and handed it to her. On the front was a theme park styled gate with "Welcome To Serenity Leisure" emblazoned across the top. 'It's a very ambitious project and one that'll create employment and bring a lot of visitors to the area so everyone will benefit.'

Chloe speed-read the papers inside the wallet and handed them on to Andy to do the same.

Meanwhile, Mr Smug continued. 'They'll build on the publicity from the show and make this their most natural leisure complex yet. They'll focus on activities as you've done. They might even give you some surfing contracts,' he said looking at Andy and smirking. 'Subject to regular drug tests obviously.'

Chloe grabbed Andy's hand just in case but Andy shrugged, evidently refusing to be riled any more by this guy. They listened carefully to the cavalier way in which Mr Smug described the complex they had planned with its bars and restaurants. To achieve this, they'd have to destroy the farmhouse and the surroundings. Chloe kept her expression neutral but inside she was bubbling up and within a few minutes, she'd heard enough. Andy might be staying calm right now but she had to get out of there.

'I know the type of complexes they mean,' said Maggie who was having a quick vape outside as they emerged. 'They tell you that it'll bring more people into the area and local businesses will benefit but they have all the shops anyone needs on the campus. The local area never sees a penny.'

'Surely Heather won't sell to them when she finds out what they want to do with the place?' said Andy.

'She won't. She'll tell her grandchildren that they have to wait,' sighed Chloe. 'But that's not what she or anyone else wants. Besides that the Global proposal buys up the fields around the farmhouse and its own land so they could go ahead and just hem Roisin in. That'll kill the dream too.'

None of them spoke for what seemed like ages.

'I wish I could think of something,' said Maggie. 'Maybe we can all petition the council and object to it? I'll go and get that started.'

Maggie went back inside and Chloe turned to Andy with fire in her eyes. 'They're not taking anything they want from us. In fact they're not coming here at all. Somehow we're going to find a way to stop them.'

'We are,' he replied. 'So what's the plan, partner?'

Chloe checked her watch. Andy was due to be out kayaking with Rik soon and after everything that had happened, she wanted him acting as normal, showing that he was innocent. She sent him on his way and strode to the farmhouse, her mind working overtime with how she'd tell Roisin and Heather what they'd found out.

How could they raise the money they needed? Perhaps a crowdfunding campaign would work; they could offer people yearly retreats in return for a contribution towards buying the place? That might also help raise awareness of why they needed the money. But it would take time and wasn't guaranteed to succeed. Maybe they could stage a sit-in, or a sit-on. She could imagine all the residents of Serenity seated on coloured deckchairs as the tide came in, vowing not to move until Global pulled out of the purchase. Charlie and Heather were quite old though and it didn't seem fair to subject them to the elements, besides which Kareem wouldn't be too pleased if she drew any more controversial attention to the show.

There was no one in the house when she arrived but the blackboard told her where everyone was: Roisin was teaching meditation to Sebastian, Fliss was doing an aromatherapy session with Louise, Rik was obviously on his way to the kayaking session, Suzie was out jogging with Lloyd while Heather had joined Mick's nature walk with Dame Julie and Mozzy. Chloe headed to the yoga studio and popped her head around the door very quietly and saw that both inhabitants of the room were in a very deep state of relaxation so she left them to it. Coming back out of the house she spotted Lloyd trying to teach sprint training on the sand but Suzie was bent over with her hands on her thighs gasping for breath. Lloyd egged her on and she picked herself up, giving everything she had to get to the finish line.

Chloe thought it best that Heather hear the news before Roisin and then perhaps they'd think of a way to tell her together. Besides, a little more fresh air would do the thinking process some good. She made her way towards the cliff tops where, in the distance, four people were strolling along slowly. They looked as if they didn't have a care in the world and when she reached them, they were so lost in the beauty of the place that Chloe couldn't bring herself to ruin Heather's day with the news she'd just heard.

Mick the Mouth had finally been recruited to take the walking tours and Dame Julie had taken his arm and smiled as he pointed out wild flowers and birds. Behind them, Mozzy was photographing butterflies and grasses while Heather suggested compositions and angles that might look good. The show's cameraman had taken the footage he needed earlier and now the four septuagenarians were simply enjoying each other's company. After walking a little further, Mick laid out a blanket and the ladies sat down while he went with Mozzy to help him identify some seabirds in flight.

'You all seem to be having a lovely day,' said Chloe.

'Oh we are,' replied Dame Julie. 'Michael is simply wonderful, so knowledgeable.'

'Has he actually said anything to you?' asked Chloe.

'He doesn't need to.' The dame smiled. 'His eyes speak volumes. They simply shine when we come across something beautiful. It is such a blessed relief to be with someone who doesn't blabber all day.' It looked to Chloe as if the world famous actress was actually rather smitten with the guide.

'And Mozzy has such a wonderful sense of composition and colour,' said Heather. 'Musicians often do. I love the work of Bob Dylan and Ronnie Wood although I've never met Bob.'

Chloe gave her a look. 'Meaning that you have met Ronnie Wood? The Rolling Stone?'

'I wasn't always an old lady who just bakes bread you know.' Heather nudged Dame Julie and the two of them laughed but Chloe couldn't bring herself to. Heather put her hand lightly on Chloe's back. 'You've found out something haven't you? About the new offer, I'm guessing? Why don't you tell me?'

Despite her best intentions, Chloe let out one big fat sob then quickly got hold of herself before any more tears managed to escape. She explained who Global were and what they were doing. 'And it's my fault. They wouldn't have even heard of this place if it weren't for me.'

'My dear, no one would have heard of this place if it weren't for you,' replied Heather. 'And then I wouldn't have met Julie or Mozzy.'

'And I wouldn't have met Michael or any of the other lovely people here,' added Dame Julie.

Chloe looked at their contented faces etched with history; like everyone else she'd seen today, they looked so healthy. The wellness retreat was finally delivering everything Roisin thought it could, just when it might be too late.

The two men returned, and while Mick picked up Mozzy's camera and flicked through the images they'd taken, the wild man of rock plonked himself down on the blanket. 'Why all the miserable faces?' he asked.

'That was tactful,' teased Heather. 'We might have had the most dreadful news.'

'Have you?' prompted Mozzy.

'Not the most dreadful. I've already lived through that, but it is very sad especially for Roisin and Chloe. We might have to close the retreat.'

Chloe found herself explaining her problems to a rock star, with a reputation for excess and debauchery from her dad's era. He took off his dark sunglasses after she'd spoken and without them he just looked like a kind old man. 'How can we help?' he asked.

If the celebrities were here under their own steam, there would be a number of ways they could help; they could launch campaigns or put the word out how evil Global were on their own social media accounts but they were under contract and for the next few weeks, they had to stick to the script. Global had big advertising budgets and the network would not be happy if they were badmouthed on national television.

'Surely there is really only one way you can all help – we simply need to beat the Swiss resort,' said Heather. 'I know they're way ahead of us in turning back the clock but maybe they peaked too early. If everyone puts in the effort and we focus on getting results, without cheating or jeopardizing anyone's health, then Roisin will get another year's income and maybe some advance bookings.' Both Mozzy and Dame

Julie said they'd certainly try and get everyone to knuckle down.

'I think we have to do more or it'll happen at some time in the future. If it isn't Global, it'll be someone else,' said Chloe despondently. 'We need to be so famous, they actually can't touch us. Like someone suggesting they build on the Galapagos Islands or knock down the Albert Hall. When they apply to the council for planning permission, it simply has to be turned down or there'd be uproar.'

'I'll book my daughters in for a week pre-Christmas,' said Dame Julie. 'And tell some magazines I'm doing it.'

'My kids would kill me if I booked them into a health spa.' Mozzy laughed. 'What use am I?'

Mick let out a gasp, which astonished absolutely everyone. They turned and waited to hear his first words – there weren't any. Instead he showed everyone the photo he was staring at.

'It's a flower, mate,' said Mozzy. 'Nice but won't win any awards.'

But Mick's eyes grew wide and Dame Julie grabbed the reference book he was holding out and thumbed frantically through the pages. The couple was communicating in a frantic silence, but no one else had a clue what was going on.

'That's his expression for very rare,' explained the dame. 'Very, very rare.'

Chapter Thirty-Six

'Are you sure about this?' asked Chloe getting a look of disdain from Dame Julie.

'If Michael says it's rare then I'm very sure he's right,' she replied, sidling up to the silent man protectively. 'And look, even the book says the *Spiked Orchid* is critically endangered.

'Sorry, no offence intended, but could it help us? Could it mean the area would be protected so no one can build on it?'

They all looked to Mick but he simply shrugged; no one knew the answer to that question. Chloe started looking around the grass they were sitting on. 'We're not accidentally squashing our best chance of saving Serenity are we?'

The group hobbled to their feet as quickly as they could, which wasn't particularly fast. They looked around their feet and under the blanket and breathed a sigh of relief when all they saw were gentle buttercups and not the delicate spiked purple petals of the rare bloom.

'Can you remember where you photographed it?' asked Chloe. 'We need to find it again and put a protective barrier around it or something.'

Mozzy lead the group to the edges of the meadow where he'd been taking the pictures and they gently swept their hands through the grasses and wildflowers to look for it, anxious not to cause any damage.

'Here he is,' called Mozzy kneeling down and brushing back the grass so they could see the small flower.

'How on earth did you spot this?' asked Heather.

'Dunno, just thought it was hiding in all of this lot. And I liked the spikes. It's not a girly flower is it?'

'No dear, you're absolutely right. It's a very masculine flower,' mocked Heather causing Mozzy to laugh at himself and hold his palms up in surrender.

Chloe was trying not to be distracted by all the flirting that was going on. 'Guys, pay attention – we need to mark the area off somehow and then get an expert in, someone who can verify its rarity and tell us if the area can be protected.' She took off her jacket, the dame untwirled a bright red scarf and Mozzy offered his belt; they created a little clothing fence around the flower. 'I'll fetch something more secure from the house,' said Chloe. 'But at least we'll be able to find it again now.'

On Heather's recommendation, Mozzy took more photographs. Chloe pulled up a digital copy of the day's newspaper to prove the date of the picture, then took one of the rare flower and the two celebrities.

'We should get it out on social media soon as,' said Mozzy. 'Tell everyone it's here.'

'No!' cried Chloe. 'Not yet. We don't want anyone trying to find it and trampling it by accident. Let's get a professional in first.'

Quite who that professional was, no one knew. As they turned to walk back, Kareem was heading towards them, urging them to hurry up. Their interim results were due to be revealed and they all needed to be camera ready to hear them.

'I'd almost forgotten we had to win a competition,' said the dame, linking arms with Mick and squeezing his. 'I was having such a lovely time with my new friends.'

'Me too,' added Mozzy doing the same to Heather.

Kareem looked at the loved up foursome in disbelief. 'If you can't beat 'em, you might as well join them,' said Chloe holding out a bent arm for him to link into. He laughed at her but took it anyway and the pair took the lead, picking up the pace to urge the lovers on.

'We still have a show to produce!' yelled Kareem. 'Quick step not waltz if you don't mind.'

The six arrived back at the house just as Rik and Andy were

coming back from a swim in the sea, towels draped around their shoulders.

'You all look very cosy,' said Andy, glancing at Chloe and Kareem.

'Oh it's been such a wonderful day,' said the dame. 'And so romantic.'

'For some of you anyway.' Chloe smiled, unlinking arms and raising her eyebrows to Andy. 'We were feeling left out weren't we, Kareem.'

Andy smiled and nodded. There was definite relief in his face. Chloe explained what had just happened.

'Will it help get rid of them?' he asked.

'I don't know,' replied Chloe, 'but it's worth a shot.'

'Let's do it then.'

While the celebrities were being primped for the camera, Chloe grabbed Roisin's laptop and, together with Andy, retreated to the yoga studio and started searching for organisations who might want to protect a flower. They discovered a few promising leads like the Wildlife Trust and Natural England but also read that the planning authority would be the people to ultimately decide whether or not the area was worth protecting. The authority would consult several experts as well as put advertisements in the local paper before making any commitment. Once again it sounded like an awfully long time but they had to start the ball rolling. They filled in as many of the official forms as they could online but they'd need to follow up with an official verification of the flower. First things first, they each rang a conservation charity and asked whether anyone could come out and verify it. Both charities were extremely excited by the potential find and they arranged to meet Chloe first thing in the morning.

'I guess that's all we can do for now,' said Chloe after the call. 'The conservation people will hopefully confirm it's a spiked orchid, then we can finalise that protection request.'

'I hope this works,' said Andy. 'It's all our livelihoods on the line here.'

It was time to start filming again so Chloe packed up the laptop and they headed back to the kitchen. Chloe stood at the back of the room out of shot while Andy joined Lloyd. They stood side by side, the two instructors together behind the celebrities who sat around the kitchen table. The mood was very different to the first results session; the celebrities giggled and chatted with each other but there was a spark of nervousness in the air. It seemed to matter to them. This time each celebrity was handed a separate envelope which they had to read to the group. Roisin stood by the blackboard with a stick of chalk at the ready to record their *turning back the clock* results. Rik stood up first and ripped open his envelope.

'I've been focusing on strength training in the kayak with Andy over there but the yoga we've all done is something new for me. It says both my flexibility has increased and my lung capacity – that'll be due to exercising outdoors.' Everyone in the room was on the edge of their seats as he read the note. 'I'm four years younger.'

Whoops and cheers filled the room and Lloyd gave Andy a slap on the back. Chloe calculated that he was a pretty fit guy so if he'd improved his health some of the others must have better results. Suzie leapt to her feet saying she couldn't bear the tension. She shredded the envelope and her eyes scanned the piece of paper inside from top to bottom. Her eyes widened in delight and she started leaping up and down then hugging Lloyd. He took the paper from her and read it out. 'Suzie has increased muscle tone, lost body fat and six pounds in weight. She's seven years younger.'

Roisin wrote down the number and looked over at Chloe who had her fingers crossed on both hands. The excitement was rising and one by one each celebrity unveiled their scores. Sebastian had lost weight by cutting out all the snacks and improved his blood pressure significantly through the yoga and meditation so he was a whole nine years younger. All the walking had improved Dame Julie's muscle tone so she'd dropped five years and to his astonishment, Mozzy had lowered his brain age by seven years. 'Now that is what I call turning back the clock. How the hell did that happen?'

'Learning something new – the photography,' replied Heather.

'Well I have you to thank for that,' he replied, ignoring the cameras and kissing her hand.

Fliss stood up and the room went silent. Given all that had happened, she was always going to read out her score last. The drama of this episode would focus on her fresh direction in life so the results had to be good. Her new agent had been refused permission to see anything in advance and was standing in the corner of the room, biting her fingernails. Fliss held the envelope up but unlike the others, didn't tear it open.

'You guys accepted me back even after I'd cheated and let you down. I will always be grateful to you for that. Since then, I've been eating the delicious and healthy food here and I've been learning to focus on my other senses to find beauty. At the chocolate shop I tasted the difference between Nicaraguan and Colombian beans – I mean I really could taste the landscape of those two countries and it was amazing. The world is so much better when you love life not selfies.' She glanced over at her agent who gave her the thumbs up.

'Come on then,' said Suzie. 'Less of the smushy stuff – how've you done?'

Fliss said a little more about the destination not being as important as the journey as she opened her envelope and waved its contents at them. 'Well, I've put on some weight so I'm not underweight any more.' She smiled and the room cheered. 'But I've also improved on all my other key stats – I'm two years younger!'

The celebrities gathered round her, hugging and congratulating each other on the results. They certainly looked like a healthier, happier bunch of people; not even Sebastian had anything to complain about. Roisin added up the scores on the blackboard and waited for everyone to calm down.

'I'm very pleased to say that adding everything together, you lovely people are collectively thirty-four years younger!'

Chloe could see the relief stinging her friend's eyes and wanted to go over and hug her but she wasn't allowed in the camera shot. To her relief, Lloyd noticed it too and put his arm around her. She put her hands around his waist and, visibly taking a deep breath, smiled up at him. Chloe glanced at Andy who smiled broadly back at her ... then blew her a kiss. She couldn't help herself. She giggled delightedly and blew one back.

'What about the other place?' asked Sebastian. 'How did they do?'

Kareem handed that critical piece of information over to him. 'Thirty-nine years,' Sebastian told the group with an air of despondency.

The room went quite for a moment and then Rik piped up. 'That's a much smaller gap than last time.'

'They've slowed down. They might even have peaked,' added Dame Julie.

'Yeah, and we're just getting going. We can still win this,' cried Suzie, punching the air.

The celebrities huddled, debating strategies to win the show.

'I could definitely lose more weight than any of you,' said Sebastian.

'And my brain is still technically older than me – I could lose years still,' continued Mozzy.

The cameras stopped filming but the conversation continued. 'I think they really want to win this for you now,' Chloe said to Roisin.

'I hope so,' replied her friend. 'I heard about the development.'

Chloe took hold of her friend's hands and Andy walked up to stand beside her. 'I didn't want to worry you with it, and we may have found a way of stopping it anyway.' She told her about the rare flower find and how they had two experts coming in the morning to see it.

'It's a bit of a long shot,' sighed Roisin. 'And we're running out of time.'

The celebrities and instructors were being taken out for an evening of celebration – a glass of wine at The Fiddler's Arms and a night of country dancing. Chloe waved goodbye to Andy, Roisin and Lloyd, remembering the evening with Will, Kareem and Jemima on their first visit. She smiled – it seemed like another lifetime. She would have loved to see them all attempt to jig but couldn't join them as she had a far more important mission this evening: protecting the orchid.

She didn't want to cover the flower in case it shriveled up and died without light so had to find something with which to build a fence around it – something slightly more robust than a belt and a scarf. Wishing that they hadn't thrown out so much of the clutter, Chloe searched the cupboards and outbuildings but there was nothing really suitable. She looked out towards the sea hoping for inspiration.

'A circle of pebbles,' she said to herself. Picking up a large rucksack, she walked down to the beach and started filling it with smooth white stones that would be visible when she brought the experts to the meadow in the morning. She wasn't exactly sure how many she'd need so kept going until she could barely lift the bag then, pulling it onto her back, made her way back to the orchid. She grunted under the weight, realising that two pebble gathering trips would likely have been better than one.

The red scarf had blown across the field and now lay across some ripening blackberries but the jacket and the belt were still in place marking the territory. She emptied the rucksack and started building the stone circle around the precious plant.

'I really do hope you're the answer to our problems,' she told it, thinking that Roisin was right and pinning their hopes on something so small was madness. Still, she kept laying out the pebbles until the orchid had three stone rings around it. She sat back and looked at her work. 'I'd camp out here to protect you if my tent hadn't been destroyed,' she said to the plant.

A noise across the field made her jump.

'Is anyone there?' she shouted out and then listened to the silence. A bird suddenly flew up from the grasses and she put her hand to her heart before calming down. 'Or maybe I wouldn't camp out here,' Chloe continued to talk to the orchid. 'I was terrified in a tent by the house and out here would be ten times worse.'

She stood up and brushed off her clothes, picking up the rucksack and stuffing in the clothes that had been left. She had a definite feeling of being watched and looked around the meadow again. 'This whole situation is making me slightly paranoid, little flower,' said Chloe. 'So I think we have to call for back up.'

Andy arrived with his camping equipment. 'I'm so sorry,' she said. 'I feel a bit silly asking you.'

'I don't want to risk this little guy any more than you do,' Andy replied.

'Will you be okay? On your own I mean?' Chloe asked tentatively, wondering whether he could hear her heart as it pounded in her chest. Those hazel eyes looked down at her and he reached towards her to tuck a loose lock of hair behind her ears.

'As much as I would *love* the company,' he said softly, 'I don't think I could concentrate on anything else if you were with me.'

Chapter Thirty-Seven

Unsurprisingly, Chloe slept very little, picturing Andy out there, re-playing his words and imagining how she might have affected his concentration?

Forcing focus back to the task in hand, she really didn't know if they actually had enough, with one small flower, to make any claim in the first place. And then, would preventing any development change the value of the land enough for Roisin to be able to afford it anyway? The thought of her friend hemmed in by fences was simply horrific.

Her phone rang. It was Andy saying 'all was quiet on the western front', the flower was blooming and the pebbles were still protecting it so if she was okay with it, he'd get back for his morning session with Rik. And that he hoped she'd slept well.

'Oh thank you,' Chloe replied. 'I slept okay but I know something that could have made it better.'

'Me too,' said Andy in that deep whisper.

She dragged herself away from the call and leapt out of bed, putting on a pair of jeans and a fleece. She didn't know what the conservation guys would want to do but it could involve standing around in a field for much of the day. At least they weren't looking for a needle in a haystack and the white pebbles would lead them straight to the right spot on the verge.

At nine o'clock when she left her flat, the village was already up and buzzing. The show had attracted a few celebrity spotters who had already emerged and had their cameras at the ready. She waved at Andy who was just pulling up to the Surfshack and Rik was walking towards him ready for a day on the waves. The camera crew was leaving The Fiddler's Arms carrying a myriad of equipment and Fliss was heading towards her. 'Hello there,' said Chloe. 'What does today have in store for you?'

They were interrupted by fans asking for a picture. 'No selfies,' Fliss reminded them so Chloe had to take the photo and the fans left happy. 'I'm so excited about today,' replied Fliss. 'I've another session with Louise and am simply loving everything I'm learning. I'm thinking about developing candles based around the seven chakras as they each have an essential oil associated with them – what do you think?'

Chloe's first thought was quite a cynical one, after all it would be an ideal licensing opportunity for the young health guru but everyone deserved a second chance so she simply told her it sounded fabulous and wished her well.

The conservationists pulled up at the farmhouse on time and together they trekked to the field. With each step Chloe's heart seemed to pound heavier with nervous anticipation.

'We're very excited by this find,' said one of the conservationists. 'If it is a Spiked Orchid, they haven't been seen in the county for thirty years or more.'

'So how would it get here now?' asked Chloe wondering whether they had actually identified the plant correctly. 'Surely after thirty years, they just vanish.'

'There've been rare sightings in Sussex and pollen carries, so do insects, birds, it could happen in a number of ways but until now it hasn't.'

'We're nearly there,' said Chloe, seeing a flash of white pebble up ahead and the guys with her started taking their cameras out of their cases in anticipation.

Before reaching the spot, Chloe knew something was wrong. She'd built three stone circles around the flower last night but here there were only two. It hadn't been windy last night and even if it had, the wind wouldn't have removed a perfect circle of pebbles. Looking around at where they stood, it didn't feel right either. They hadn't walked far enough.

The conservationists looked at the flower that bloomed

in the centre of the circle and their shoulders dropped in disappointment. 'That's not a Spiked Orchid,' they said to her. 'It's a scabious and I'm afraid they're quite common.' They started packing the cameras away.

'No, this is not the spot,' said Chloe looking at the grass nearby which should have still been flat from Andy's tent but wasn't. 'And Mick wouldn't have made a mistake like that. It's been moved.'

'The orchid's been moved?'

'No, but this isn't my stone circle. Let's look a bit further along. It was here and we guarded it all night I promise.'

They walked slowly and methodically along the verge. Andy had said it was still here when he woke up but there had been noises last night. Had someone been watching and waited until he'd left? 'Is a rare flower worth anything?' she asked. 'I've heard of people paying a lot for orchids.'

'They can be. I know people will pay around five thousand pounds for a Rothschild's Slipper Orchid but not for a wildflower.'

Chloe suddenly spotted a scattering of pebbles up ahead and ran towards them. She was sure this was closer to the spot but it looked as if the pebbles had been kicked into the field. Whoever did this obviously hadn't had the time or inclination to move all three circles worth of stones. Chloe knelt down at the verge, checked the picture on her phone and then looked back at the blooms blowing gently in the breeze in front of her. The Spiked Orchid wasn't there.

'Someone's taken it.'

She stumbled backwards and sat down, her knees pulled tightly to her chest. Inside her ribcage, her heart was breaking. For weeks now it had felt as if someone kept throwing them a rope only to pull it away at the last moment. That comfortable job with a nice agency she'd been offered, why had she ever thrown the opportunity away? She loved it here but nothing seemed to ever go right. Was it finally time to admit defeat?

'Oh this is interesting,' the conservationist's voice interrupted her self-pity and Chloe crawled over to see what he was looking at. He'd pulled aside some of the foliage and revealed a small plant with no flower just a base of leaves. 'You were right,' he said. 'These are the leaves of the Spiked Orchid so it was here. Whoever did take your flower simply plucked the bloom and left the rest of the plant. It's a dreadful thing to do because without the bloom, it can't attract pollinating insects.'

'So it'll die?'

'We don't know but it would be safer to take the whole plant out carefully and nurture it somewhere more protected.'

'What about just protecting this field? That's what we wanted anyway.'

The conservationist explained that it would take too long but they would monitor the area from now on, in case there were more sightings. Chloe thanked them for coming out and left them to their work. They promised to come and fetch her if they found another example of the orchid but in her heart she knew they wouldn't. If only she knew what had happened here.

Chloe wracked her brain for what to do next but could only think of one thing and that was to make a personal appeal to Global to build elsewhere. She'd explain how much the resort meant to Roisin and hope that they would listen. Her only way to them was through her old agency so she put aside her pride and called her old boss, the one who'd sacked her in the first place. His secretary, Lucas, answered the phone and was delighted to hear from her.

'I've been watching the show,' he said. 'I so want Suzie to win, she's hilarious.' She'd got on very well with Lucas and at any other time she would have loved to gossip with him but time was of the essence.

Lucas put her through to Mark who answered the call by gloating. 'I'm afraid there are no vacancies, if that's what you're calling about. I can't imagine you'll be marketing your little village for much longer when Serenity Leisure launches.'

Quite how she managed to restrain herself, she would never know but this was for Roisin, Andy and the rest of the village. She clenched her jaw, and in the most constructive tone she could muster, told him about the rare flower find and advised that if Global went ahead, there could be a backlash from environmentalists.

'But the plant's not actually there is it?'

'How do you know that?'

'It's my business to know everything that might impact my client,' he replied. 'Look, Walsh, I know you don't like them but they're not that bad. They'll bring jobs to the area and they'll put something in place to protect plants or whatever. This is a relaunch for them. They're not about to rebrand themselves then ruin it. My guys have worked for months on this. We're not changing now.'

'Can you at least tell them what's at stake or let me call th—' Chloe didn't manage to get the words out before the phone was put down. 'How did I ever work for a piece of dirt like you?' she said staring at his photo on her contacts list. As she pressed delete, she decided that the best revenge wasn't only a life well lived after all, it was also about taking down the people who tried to stop it happening for others.

Back at the retreat the mood was still high as out in the garden, Suzie was doing a piece to camera about her latest achievement: a hundred metre sprint in thirteen seconds. Sebastian was demonstrating his newly found ability to balance on one leg in a rather wobbly warrior III position and, as anticipated, Fliss had lined up seven little candles with colours and scents to reflect the chakras while her agent photographed them and loaded them onto her Instagram account.

Inside, Lloyd and Roisin were planning the next day's activities while Heather showed Mozzy how to sketch from his photographs; they looked up expectantly as Chloe entered the room and all spoke at once.

'Was it an orchid?'

'Will they protect it?'

'And am I going to be famous as the person who discovered a long lost part of the British countryside?' asked Mozzy smiling. 'I might get Attenborough's job when he's done with it.'

Chloe didn't join in the joke. 'What's wrong?' asked Heather.

She explained that Andy had slept out last night but somehow the flower had been stolen this morning. Seeing the last ray of hope vanish from her friend's face, she simply couldn't stop the tears appearing. She wiped them away quickly but her friend rushed to her and hugged her tightly.

'What do we do now?' asked Roisin who seemed to have aged ten years in ten minutes.

'Bloody vandals,' added Mozzy. 'But look, love, there's no point getting upset. You hadn't even heard of it before yesterday and the conservation blokes said it might grow back didn't they?'

'It's more important than that,' said Roisin, telling him about the sale of the estate and their hope that the plant would mean the area could be protected.

'Why didn't you say?' asked Mozzy looking to Heather.

'Global are a really big advertiser,' Chloe told everyone. 'And with everything that's happened at the retreat we thought we'd be able to solve things without making any waves, but I've tried talking to their agency and they won't listen.'

'Well let's make them listen! I like making big waves,' replied Mozzy, thumping his fist down on the table. He picked up his phone and stabbed a contact. 'Duchess, get yourself down to the pub and bring Mick – I'll fetch the others.'

Chloe, Roisin, Lloyd and Heather followed the celebrities through the village. On the way they picked up the rest of the troupe so with Kareem, Rik and Andy they all sat down at a long table in The Fiddler's Arms with only glasses of mineral water as refreshment to show they really meant business. Mozzy explained what he wanted to do.

'This photography, walking and nature stuff has made all the difference to me,' said Mozzy. 'I want this week's show to tell everyone what I found and how it was destroyed. I want people signing them online petitions to keep this place as it is.'

Chloe felt Andy reach for her hand and squeeze it reassuringly.

'It's not really within the remit of the show ...' started Kareem.

'Surely it can be part of it?' said Dame Julie. 'How can we improve our health in the natural environment if that green space is destroyed?'

'Or polluted,' added Rik. 'We cleared up some plastic when we were out on the sea today.'

'Besides, how will it look if we all improve our health here and then let down the very place that helped us achieve it?' protested Fliss. 'Surely you want Serenity to flourish rather than flounder.'

Kareem looked towards Chloe and Roisin. 'You're all right and I had a brilliant time here too. Okay, let's do it.'

Chloe worked with Kareem to plan as much of a campaign as they could in the time they had available. They needed the celebrities' agents, their social media accounts and the key magazines working together. When the episode finally aired that week, it re-enacted the events and played out more like a murder mystery. Dame Julie, Mick and Mozzy were filmed hiking along the coastline noting the plants and birds while Mozzy's beautiful photography was loaded onto all the show's social media simultaneously. They extolled the virtues of fresh air and reminded viewers that everyone could turn back the clock with a simple walk every day. Then, with a little more drama than had happened originally, Dame Julie swept down to the ground and pointed at an imaginary flower, asking what it was. Mick showed her in his book and they looked overawed for the cameras.

'The next day, in the early hours of the morning,' said Mozzy in a piece to camera, 'the plant was destroyed. It matters because we can't keep destroying our environment and expect no consequences. So we all want to know who did this. Who stole Spike?'

Chapter Thirty-Eight

#WHO STOLE SPIKE?

'Have you seen all of this?' Roisin gawped, fanning out a rainforest of magazines and newspapers which seemed to have decided that, for today at least, getting the nation behind the theft of a rare wildflower was more important than world politics. 'And at least this time it's not about mice in the yoga studio.'

'Yeah, it's amazing how quickly we've gone from being the villains to the heroes but it always helps to have outraged celebrities promoting the cause,' replied Chloe, unable to hold back a giggle at the photo of Sebastian and Mozzy, an unlikely duo with their arms folded, looking like warriors ready to take on the world.

Social media channels were just as active and it helped that several of Mozzy's aging rocker friends were now heavily into conservation so had shared Serenity's posts to their hundreds of thousands of followers.

'Will it do the job?' asked Andy looking up at her from his seat at the table. 'Will Global pull out now?'

Chloe could only shrug. 'I really don't know. I guess we have to make sure that it's not just tomorrow's chip paper or salon fodder.' She could imagine the entourage in her mother's hairdressers picking up the magazines in a few months' time saying *'Oh wasn't this the campaign your daughter started? Shame it never got anywhere'*. That couldn't happen, it had to get somewhere.

'Come on,' she said. 'We need to get down to the village.'

Andy leapt up like a knight ready to do battle for her. She smiled across at him. *I could get used to this*, she thought.

*

Overnight, Heather and Olly had worked to put together a digital exhibition of Mozzy's photographs in the craft shop and the media were now starting to crowd in to get pictures and talk to the man himself about his transformation from Rock God to nature lover.

'They've done a fabulous job,' said Louise, slightly in awe as all photographs were beamed across the room. 'Pulling all of this together in such a short space of time – I didn't even know you could project all these things at once.'

'Me neither,' replied Chloe. 'It looks amazing doesn't it?'

Mozzy sidled up to them to talk to Heather. 'They're asking if they can buy some of the prints. What should I charge?'

Heather was about to walk off with him when Roisin held her gently by the arm. 'Gran, I don't want to be a complete killjoy here but if the focus becomes the photography then we risk them forgetting the main message – saving Serenity.'

Chloe looked at her friend and although she knew she was right, her heart skipped a beat waiting to hear how the world famous celebrity would react. To her relief, he nodded at Roisin. 'You're right, this ain't about me – yet,' he added with a mischievous smile. 'Let's get this party started shall we?'

He walked into the centre of the room and raised his hands for silence. One by one the crowd noticed and a hush descended on the room.

'Imagine,' he said quietly, 'when I were a nipper. I had a dream. I wanted to play in a rock and roll band. I wanted to be like Elvis Presley or Bill Haley so I got a paper round and saved up every penny I had. I spent it all on a second hand Fender Stratocaster and practiced like crazy. I got a gig in a pub playing with this covers band, borrowed the money from my dad to get there and promised I'd pay it back. The gig was everything I hoped it would be and I might not have set the world alight with my playing that night but it certainly set my world alight. I knew I was where I wanted to be.'

He looked around the room and held his hand out for

Roisin to join him. Puzzled, she did as he asked. 'You're wondering what this all has to do with Serenity aren't you? Well my guitar got nicked that night and I thought my world had fallen apart. I couldn't do the one thing that meant everything to me and I couldn't afford to get a new one. I thought I'd lost everything.' He put his arm around Roisin and pulled her closer. 'This woman has put everything into creating a kick-ass retreat. Hell, it's even got me out taking walks and photos of plants.'

The crowd laughed with him.

'And now, her dream looks like it might be destroyed because some scumbag nicked the very thing that could stop development on that field. The very thing that could keep her dream alive. When I got my guitar nicked, I also got my bus money nicked 'cos I'd kept it in the guitar case. I was wondering how the hell I would get home and what my dad would say when I got there. Then, this old guy, a technician for the band, stepped in. He gave me a lift home and when I told him what had happened, he lent me one of his old guitars so that I could keep playing until I could afford one of my own.'

He turned to face Roisin and holding both of her shoulders said, 'Well now I'm going to repay that favour and this old guy is gonna help you out. You lot want to buy my photos? Well every single one of them is for sale and the proceeds will go to finding the bugger who stole Spike and saving the land around Serenity so no one can build on it.'

Chloe whooped and intuitively turned to hug Andy. He didn't resist.

'Heather over there will tell you the prices,' Mozzy finished off – causing the woman herself to go into a bit of a panic. She looked over at Andy and Chloe, they unfurled themselves and Chloe reached out to hold the old lady's soft hands.

'How on earth do you price photographs?' asked Heather.

'Find out what David Bailey's go for and add ten per cent,'

Louise interjected, smiling and completely swept up in the maelstrom.

'What can we do next?' asked Andy as the two women went off to price the pictures.

'Come upstairs with me,' replied Chloe.

They retreated to her flat and Andy walked over to the window that looked out onto the waves. 'I can see why you chose this place,' he said.

'I didn't really choose it,' said Chloe stepping beside him, 'but it has its advantages. I can spy on you every morning for a start.'

'Can't think why you'd want to do that.' He laughed.

Chloe turned to face him. It was time to stop all the joking and find out where she really stood with this guy. 'Can't you?' she asked. 'Understand why I would want to see you every morning?'

Andy stood saying nothing but Chloe noticed he was breathing more deeply.

'I know we didn't get off to a great start and I'm sorry, I know I've said some stupid things ...'

'I have too,' said Andy. 'I've been a pain in the neck and I'm surprised you're even still speaking to me.' He took a step closer and ran his hand down the side of her arm. The sensation was electric and she lifted her face towards his. 'Can we ...?'

They were interrupted by a huge cheer from downstairs.

'I guess we should see to business first.' Chloe smiled. She took a deep sobering breath as they moved from the window to sit down near the coffee table where Chloe explained the next move. 'If they're doing their job properly,' she explained, 'my old agency will be upfront about the backlash and advise their client to either pull out of the sale or lie low until the publicity has waned.'

'So what do you want me to do?'

She rummaged around her papers for Mr Bald's business

card. 'This is the agent. Call him and tell him you're our representative. He might recognize my voice and besides, I'm sure I'll lose it with him if he won't listen.'

'And you think I won't?' replied Andy. He took the card and, sitting up straight, dialed the number. He cleared his throat and with a strong, deep voice asked for an update.

'I've had no instruction that the offer has been withdrawn,' said Mr Bald on speakerphone. 'It looks to us that the conservation order is unlikely to happen so I imagine they will proceed, but of course they'll take advice and if there are rare species to be protected then they will do that. They do run nature courses at their retreats.'

Chloe looked despondently at Andy. She hadn't really expected a fairy-tale phone call where the evil interloper simply backed down at the first sign of trouble but it would have been nice. They must be lying low if they weren't backing out. The celebrities would be leaving Serenity very soon and after that, she very much doubted the reporters who were here now would ever set foot in the place again. Andy mouthed the words 'anything else?' but she shrugged, unable to think of the next step.

'Mr Lindell,' said Andy suddenly. 'What if my clients could match Global's offer? Maybe not right now but over a few weeks?'

'Put it in writing.' He sighed. 'But I'll need to be assured that you actually have the funds.'

Andy thanked him and ended the call. 'I just thought it might buy us some time,' he said. 'How close to the offer do you think we can get?'

'I have no idea,' sighed Chloe, standing and reaching out for his hand. 'Shall we go and see how Mozzy is doing?'

Woah! The heat of the gallery hit her like a warm weather cloud as they walked back into the furore. The place was heaving. They stood watching for a moment as Heather and Louise were taking orders and processing credit card transactions while Roisin told her story to every journalist that asked. Mozzy stood by her side to ensure that she was the focus and when he spotted Chloe, he winked at her as if to say everything was going okay.

'I have to get out of this heat,' said Chloe pulling Andy with her. Outside on the pavement was just as busy. They walked up to Lloyd who was manning long tables selling home-made sandwiches wrapped in cellophane and drinks to the hordes of tourists who seemed to have arrived. 'Maggie says the pub is full,' he said to them both. 'She sent me to man this.'

'You're doing a great job.' Chloe laughed as he threw a tuna mayo at Andy who caught it and unwrapped it to share with her.

Kareem was standing by a cameraman taking everything in and shaking his head.

'I'm sorry,' said Chloe when they reached him. 'This probably isn't how you expected the show to go.'

'It certainly isn't,' he replied. 'I should have gone to Switzerland. Apparently it's all running smoothly over there.'

Fliss approached the group. 'I'd like to do a piece to camera,' she told them and led them to an artfully arranged space by the Surfshack where a rainbow-coloured selection of candles had been placed.

'I want to offer the profits of my new signature aromatherapy range to the save Serenity fund.'

From the side glance both men managed to throw towards Chloe, they knew as well as she did that this contribution wasn't as selfless as Mozzy's had been but that didn't matter right now. Every penny counted and Fliss had millions of followers, so millions of pennies would definitely add up.

'How much do we actually need?' asked Andy. Chloe told him the number and he whistled. 'I hope she sells millions of those candles in that case.'

'Hey, you're the ones who got TruNorth to film their ads up

here aren't you?' said Rik, approaching them as they walked on.

'Yes but they've still to make a decision on who's going to be the new face of the fragrance,' Chloe replied back in work mode.

'Well they've decided,' said Rik pointing to himself. 'My agent's just called. They saw me on the show and I got the gig. Thanks.'

'Wow, that's great,' said Andy shaking his hand. 'I'm genuinely made up for you and it'll be good having someone I know out on the water.'

'Look, if it wasn't for this place and you getting me out there, I wouldn't have this job so I want to make a contribution too. How does ten percent of the fee sound?'

'It sounds brilliant,' Chloe exclaimed. 'Can I hug you?'

He reached out and wrapped his extremely strong arms around her, squeezing her tightly. *I'm being embraced by a movie star*, her mind was screaming in excitement.

'Ahem, do you two mind?' Andy coughed.

Chloe turned to him. He didn't mind did he? Surely not? Why would he after what they'd very nearly said?

'Can't have you getting all the attention!' He laughed before hugging Rik himself – one of those man-hugs – in congratulations.

Chloe laughed too as Andy pulled her in for a quick squeeze around the waist. A wolf-whistle separated them all and they turned to see the other celebrities approaching.

'Everyone seems to be offering something,' wailed Sebastian. 'What can we do?'

He was with Dame Julie and Suzie who seemed equally at a loss as to how they could help. Chloe had to think quickly to keep them engaged and get the most from their celebrity. 'Can you sign some of the photographs and auction them to your followers?'

They seemed happy with the idea and left to announce

their contributions to camera. Rik asked Andy if he would come and join him to announce the TruNorth deal and they walked away together.

As the evening rolled on, many die-hard fans and some of the media remained in the village and were now enjoying Maggie's hospitality. It had been a phenomenal success in raising the profile of the village and the cause. Even Kareem was happy with the tangential publicity and had found an angle for the show about pursuing your passions to help turn back the clock. They'd raised a huge amount of money with more to come from online sales and Fliss's range so it was time to add up the numbers. Rather than use the blackboard this time, Chloe invited Heather and Roisin up to her flat where they opened up a spreadsheet, putting together the definite contributions from the day and forecasts of money still to arrive. It was a pretty substantial number and although it didn't exactly match the offer from Global, it was worth putting to Lindell.

'I'll do it,' said Heather. 'I'm getting a bit fed up with some of my relatives. We're here doing all we can and all they can think about is the money. I'm going to tell them how much it means to us all and that if they don't back down I'm going to leave all of this to a conservation charity. They'll get nothing. I'm sorry, Roisin.'

Roisin put her hand on her gran's and smiled. 'I'd rather that happened than have the place destroyed.'

Heather started writing an email telling them her feelings and ending: *"This is an opportunity to have the meadows named after our family forever, so that we never lose our place in the history of the region."*

Having made her plea and their final offer, Heather let the girls read it and together they poised their fingers above the send button. They were just about to press when there was an urgent knock at the door. Andy called out, 'Chloe, Roisin, get yourselves down here right now!'

They took the steps two at a time and were ushered into the back of the gallery where, to their astonishment, Mr Smug was being pinned against the wall by a couple of journalists.

'What's going on?' Chloe asked Andy.

One of the journalists loosened his grip and walked towards her with a very sorry-looking bloom.

'Spike,' cried Mozzy, rushing up and taking it from him.

'I don't understand. What's happened?' asked Roisin.

'This guy was trying to give me the other side of the story,' said the journalist. 'About Global and all that they could do for the area, jobs and development wise.'

Chloe hadn't seen Mr Smug arrive in the village and was horrified to think that he'd try to hijack this for Global's benefit.

'I can't deny,' continued the journalist, 'I like to get both sides of the story, so I asked him for his business card. He reaches into his pocket and pulls it out but something comes out with it – this flash of purple that I know I've seen somewhere.' He pointed up at all the images around the room.

'You stole Spike?' growled Mozzy, going to grab Mr Smug by the collar. Heather reached him just in time to stop that photo opportunity.

Within seconds, the watching world had been told exactly who the #SpikeThief was and within minutes, Roisin received a call. Chloe watched as the relief took years off her. 'Global have pulled out,' she said. 'And the estate will accept the previous offer we made.'

Chloe grabbed her and they danced around the room hugging each other and gathering others until there was a bundle of people hugging, smiling and bouncing up and down on the spot.

'We made it!' cried Roisin.

'We certainly did,' replied Chloe, her heart simply bursting with joy.

Chapter Thirty-Nine

'Tonight should be pretty spectacular,' said Andy as the day was drawing to a close on the final night of the celebrities' stay.

'I know and I can't think of a more perfect way for the show to end,' replied Chloe. 'After everything that happened yesterday I really believe we're all going to enjoy this and no one will ever forget it.'

The revelations of yesterday had been so dramatic that it would have been very easy to forget the show itself. Mr Smug didn't confess. He said that he'd picked the flower because it was beautiful and if he'd known what it was, he wouldn't have touched it. He made a contribution to the conservation fund but it wasn't enough to save his job. Global "parted ways" with the agency and they, in turn, parted ways with Mr Smug. The money the campaign had raised was accepted by the estate and Mozzy's people were establishing how the land around Serenity could be protected in perpetuity. After the publicity, the planning authorities were rushing through the work to put Serenity Bay in big letters above Kyrrby on the village sign. Chloe had discussed Tony's comments with the rest of the village and agreed that it would be good to keep the Norse name too. The retreat website was pinging with future bookings and Roisin was delighted. Chloe had been assured that Northumberland Tourism would look into the possibility of funding a development officer for the area and meanwhile they were fielding most of the new visitor enquiries generated by the show. There was a huge amount of work to do if Chloe was going to really build a career here and she'd get down to it as soon as the show was over but right now, she had to make sure Kareem had the grand finale he needed.

The final set of results was due to be read out soon. Chloe had put the upcoming evening's ritual in her very first proposal as the big finish and she knew it had swung the votes for her with the network.

'I'll go and make sure everyone's ready,' said Andy. 'Meet you down there.'

She'd called in a specialist team to manage the event and they'd been on the beach for a couple of hours so Chloe couldn't wait to see everyone's reaction. She didn't have to wait long. The ritual began and a long line of flames roared up on the beach. The reporters and fans that had stayed on in the village panicked slightly and then stood in awe as the celebrities walked calmly towards the fire. Chloe had taken them through the events of the evening in fine detail and they knew exactly how to behave for the camera. They walked in a line, hand in hand, to the blazing sands.

'This is beyond my wildest dreams.' Kareem smiled, looking at the camera footage.

The celebrities sat cross-legged as the flames died into glowing embers and Roisin began explaining the fire-walk ritual to them and to camera. 'Serenity was founded by Vikings who settled here and made it their home. This ritual was their way of overcoming limiting beliefs and accepting that they could do anything they set their minds to.

'You have overcome beliefs that held you back and in doing so have changed your lives and bodies. You are physically younger than you were when you arrived. In a short while we find out how young but right now, we walk the fire and we thank ourselves for bringing us to this point.'

When she'd designed this finale, Chloe could never have guessed how much it would have meant to her personally. She had changed so much in these past few months – mind, body and spirit.

The specialist team was now inviting everyone to stand and line up in front of the hot coals. 'You don't make a wish when you walk,' said Roisin. 'You make a vow. Because you have the power to make that vow happen.'

Unsurprisingly, Rik was at the front of the queue but Fliss touched his hand gently and asked if she could go first. Chloe bit into her clenched fist. It was one thing arranging all of this and quite another watching a young woman about to step bare-footed onto burning hot rocks. Fliss briefly closed her eyes.

'I vow to use my gifts to make this world a better place,' she declared.

The tension as she took her first step and then hot-footed across the coals was almost unbearable but she made it and everyone breathed again. One by one the celebrities took their places, made their vows and walked the fire.

'I have never felt so fabulous in my life,' said Sebastian to camera. 'No matter what the results are, I feel alive again. The twenty-year-old me wasn't half as healthy as I am now.'

Chloe watched Mozzy take Heather's hand and lead her to the front of the fire. 'Your turn,' he said, giving her hand a kiss before letting her go.

'I wonder what she's vowing,' said Roisin.

'I don't know exactly,' replied Chloe as Heather reached the end and, with her face full of amazement, went straight back to Mozzy. 'But I think you should get ready to say goodbye.'

Kareem called an end to the shoot and the celebrities started moving towards the retreat for the final results. Their silhouettes disappeared slowly against the washed-ink sky and the last glow of the fire-walk.

'The embers are still hot.' Chloe turned to see Andy walking up to her. 'Do you want to give it a go?'

'I will if you will.'

'Let's do it together.' She watched as Andy took position and held out his hand to her. She took it and stood at the edge of the coals. Seeing other people do this hadn't prepared her for the real thing; the smell of burning that rose up and hit her nostrils seemed to be warning her off – after all, wasn't walking over a fire in your bare feet an insane thing to do? She pushed her fear to the back of her mind. She could do this and moreover, she *wanted* to do this. Andy looked at her and she nodded. She was ready.

Chloe closed her eyes, mentally made her vow then tentatively lifted her foot and together they stepped onto the coal and bolted right the way across the embers. They both burst out laughing as they finally exhaled at the other end.

'We did it!' exclaimed Chloe. She grabbed Andy and hugged him as if both of their lives depended on it.

A small cheer rose out of the shadows.

Chloe peered through the dusk to see who it was as most of the crowd had left with the celebrities.

'We're so proud of you,' said her dad, running towards her with his arms outstretched.

'So very, very proud,' added her mother with tears rolling down her cheeks. 'I always knew you'd be a big success.'

It was as close to saying she'd been wrong that her mother would ever get but it was enough. Chloe hugged them and then turned back towards Andy, introducing him to her parents.

'Very pleased to meet you,' he said, shaking their hands.

'And we're even more pleased to meet you,' said her mother, giving Chloe a knowing glance. 'We only came down to watch the finale so we'll head off now but I hope you'll *both* visit us soon – cheerio sweetheart.'

'Oh! We're … We're not … We're …'

Her mother simply tapped the side of her nose and blew her a kiss goodbye as both of her parents scampered off.

'Sorry about her,' said Chloe as they walked up the beach together. 'About her assuming we're an item.'

'Aren't we?'

The evening breeze was picking up and blew her hair

around her face. She grabbed at it, trying to tame it, and get it back into it's scrunchie.

'What I said in your flat,' continued Andy. 'About being sorry for the way I've behaved, I meant it.'

'I did too,' replied Chloe.

'When I think back to the way I treated you at times ...' Andy shook his head in despair. 'I think I was just jealous. You always seemed surrounded by good-looking blokes.'

Chloe stood to face him. 'There's only one good-looking guy I'm even remotely interested in. And just to be clear, there is *nothing* I would ever want to change about him.'

'I know that now.' He turned to face her and took hold of her hands. Then he untied her hair, let it fall around her shoulders, before gently lifting her chin towards him.

'What did you vow?' she whispered, breathing him in.

'To never ever let you leave Serenity.'

He kissed her lips tenderly. Every inch of her body wanting more as he pulled her in close.

But *no!* She heard their names being called. Andy chuckled against her lips and shook his head as he stepped back.

'Will we ever get some alone time?'

'The show isn't over,' she said.

Chapter Forty

They entered the kitchen to find Kareem handing the golden envelope to Mozzy. Chloe looked over to Roisin and held up her hands with her fingers crossed.

'Whatever happens,' said the rock star to the anxious group, 'we've had a life-changing time here and we're all winners.'

He tore it open and read through the findings. 'Suzie – congratulations, girl, all that running and boxing has given you muscles in places you probably didn't know you had and you're nine years younger.

'Rik, big man – not sure how you could get any fitter but you have and your body is now seven years younger. Fliss, you were always gorgeous and I'm happy to say you've lost five years and revitalized your brain.

'Duchess, apparently all that time out on the meadows with me has done you good and you're a sprightly sixty-four-year-old now – you've gone and lost eight years.

'Sebastian, bloody hell, mate, you're slimming down before our very eyes and you've lost thirteen years.'

The round of applause that started with Suzie reached a crescendo with Sebastian.

'And myself, I might have turned back the clock eight years but I feel as if I've found the next eight.' He winked at Heather. 'So in total that's fifty years we've lost just by having a bloody good time in this amazing place. Thank you.'

He raised his hands to Roisin and the others did the same. Chloe felt the most enormous sense of pride in her friend as Roisin hugged Lloyd and thanked him for his help.

'Okay,' said Suzie. 'Now tell us what happened in Switzerland. Did we win?'

Chloe found herself between Heather and Andy squeezing

their hands. Mozzy took the second envelope from Kareem and opened it. He'd been directed not to give the game away with his expression and he absolutely delivered on that. Chloe could not tell what had happened. Mozzy swallowed and handed the results to Suzie who could not keep up the poker face and her disappointment was immediately written all over it.

'Bummer,' she exclaimed. 'They won it by one measly year.'

Shoulders dropped around the room and there was silence for a moment. Then Sebastian stood up. 'You know what, it doesn't matter. I meant what I said. I feel like a winner so I am.'

One by one, the celebrities all claimed their personal victories and Kareem brought in a bottle of champagne to celebrate the end of the show. Leaving the celebrities to their celebrations with their coaches Andy and Lloyd, Roisin and Chloe took a glass each, walked into the garden and plonked themselves down on the bench.

'I'm sorry we didn't win,' said Chloe. 'It would have secured this place forever.'

'It already is,' replied Roisin. 'The land is protected and we have bookings through to next summer. To be honest, I couldn't cope with more celebrity publicity. Here's to them safely back where they belong.'

'How will you manage the bookings, if Heather's not here? It did sound like Mozzy might have plans for her.'

'She definitely won't be here. She asked me tonight if it was okay that she heads off. She's going around the world with Mozzy on a tour of his music and art.'

'Blimey, that's amazing,' said Chloe, thinking back to the conversation she'd had with Heather and how she'd wanted an adventure. This would certainly fit that description. 'I'm really pleased for her. They're good together.'

'So,' continued Roisin. 'Lloyd has said he'll stay on and help me run the retreat. He'll put together the programmes and keep people on track while I stick to what I love.'

Chloe turned to her friend and could tell, even in the darkness, that she was blushing. '*Woah*, when did that happen?'

'Oh, you know when he was practicing his downward dog.'

They laughed and linked arms. 'So talking about people being good together ...' continued Roisin. 'Any news?'

It was Chloe's turn to be coy. 'Well you're the one who predicted it would happen – the city girl with the gorgeous local and I think it might. But I still can't make cupcakes.'

Roisin squeezed Chloe in delight. 'I'm soooo pleased,' cried Roisin. 'And Heather will be thrilled. We've been rooting for you two for months!' She clinked her glass against Chloe's.

'Remember that night on the beach when we said this place was magical? Well I think we proved that now,' Roisin continued. 'Here's to us and to Serenity.'

'To Serenity Bay.'

Andy's tall shape appeared in the doorway and Chloe looked at her friend. 'Would you mind?' she asked. 'I kind of have some unfinished business.'

Roisin smiled and wandered off as Andy walked towards Chloe and she stood to meet him. He stroked her cheek softly as Chloe looked directly into his eyes.

'Now where were we?' he said.

Epilogue

'Serenity Bay Marketing, how can I help you? Yes we can accommodate advertising shoots but the village is busy. When were you looking at?'

Louise was working out the best way to display the new stock while Chloe managed her business from the front desk and in the background Smooth Radio gave the whole place a, well, Serene ambience. The women, like the rest of the village, had mellowed into a busy but contented routine since the TV crews had left. The bell above the door jingled and Andy walked in, waving at Louise then approaching Chloe's desk and kissing her lovingly.

He handed her a postcard and she smiled. Heather was the only person in the world who still sent these things but Chloe had to admit, they were a delight to receive. The gallery now housed a map of the world and every time they received a card, they put a little pin in the map to show where Heather and Mozzy were. The card featured a baby koala as the tour was currently in Australia but Chloe already knew that as she'd been one of the millions following this second stage of Mozzy's career online with affection. Heather was truly having the adventure she'd always wanted. Chloe showed Andy an email she'd received that morning. 'They're looking for another kayaking shoot,' she said. 'Have you got time to look into what they need this afternoon?'

'Yes, sure. I'm just delivering new yoga mats to the retreat then I can get onto it. Dame Julie's back with some of her actress friends. They're launching a YouTube channel.'

'Good on them, and I imagine she'll be catching up with Mick when she's here.'

'The ladies love that strong silent type.'

'Well in my case strong at least,' said Chloe pulling him

towards her for another kiss. 'Oh, I must remember to book a room at The Fiddler's – my mum is coming up for the weekend.'

'She's never away from the place. Who is she bringing this time?'

'Marjorie and her daughter, you know, the "*Senior Stylist*".' Chloe laughed. 'She's showing them all the celebrity hangouts.'

'Amazing that stuff really matters to people, but great for us.'

He left her to her work and she hummed along to the radio as she whizzed through the social media questions and emails as she watched him walk out the door, sure she would never tire of that body. One email was from Lucas telling her that he'd found a new job and thanking her for the reference. After the GlobalLezure fiasco, her old agency issued a profit warning and many of her old colleagues, including Lucas, lost their jobs. Despite all the wonderful things that eventually happened, Chloe could still remember the pain of losing her job and wouldn't have wished this on anyone so she offered references to all those she'd respected and contacted agencies she now had links with to try and find them positions. Blue Banana had offered to hire Lucas and Chloe couldn't be happier for him; they continued to give her work so now she would be able to stay in touch with her old friend.

Chloe's phone rang and when she saw who was calling, a big smile broke out across her face. 'Kareem, it's so good to hear from you. How is it going? I saw you at the TV awards looking very *smart*.'

Turning Back the Clock had won the Best Reality Show award and while Suzie had accepted the gong and made the speech on the night, the producers and directors had been up there on the stage too. Kareem had looked uncomfortable being in front of the camera but Chloe and Roisin had commented how photogenic he was. He'd been promoted to head the company's drama division shortly afterwards.

As soon as Chloe realized it wasn't simply a social call, she moved into the back gallery away from the radio and the bell on the door which was jingling more frequently now they'd hit lunchtime.

'Yes there is a village church, behind the pub. You must have heard Maggie telling everyone the vicar gets his holy wine from her? It's one of her favourite jokes. Why do you need a church?'

Chloe listened and as she did her eyes grew wider. She could see Louise was serving a young couple so simply had to keep a grip on the excitement bubbling over.

'We wouldn't let you down, Kareem. It would be an absolute honour. My mum has watched that show forever and just loves guessing whodunnit.'

Louise was handing the couple their change so Chloe ran to the door and held it open for them, thanking them for their custom.

'You couldn't get them out quick enough,' said Louise as Chloe turned the shop sign to closed and gave her an enormous hug.

'*The Montgomery Mysteries*,' she exclaimed. 'You know how the detective always goes to different villages and somehow stumbles on a crime he has to solve?'

Louise nodded slowly.

'Well they're coming here! They're shooting their Christmas special right here in Serenity Bay!'

Thank You

Dear Reader,

First of all I'd like to thank you, dear reader, for choosing *Serenity Bay*. I really hope you've enjoyed it. Although the village of Kyrrby is entirely fictional, the idea for the novel came from my regular dog walks along the Northumbrian coast. It's a truly beautiful part of England and I hope you get the chance to visit on day.

If you've enjoyed *Serenity Bay* please leave a review for the book on Goodreads or the website where you bought the book. You can also follow me on Twitter for news on my next book and perhaps to share photos of your favourite beaches! Looking forward to hearing from you.

Helen x

About the Author

Helen Bridgett lives in the North East of England.
Outside of writing feel good fiction, Helen loves
the great outdoors and having a good laugh with
friends over a glass of wine. Helen lives with her
husband and their chocolate Labrador, Angus; all
three can often be found walking the Northumberland
coastline that inspired *Summer at Serenity Bay*.

To find out more about Helen,
follow her on social media:

www.twitter.com/Helen_Bridgett
www.facebook.com/HelenBridgettAuthor/

More Ruby Fiction

From Helen Bridgett

One by One

When practising what you preach is easier said than done ...

Professor Maxie Reddick has her reasons for being sceptical of traditional policing methods, but, in between her criminology lecturing job and her Criminal Thoughts podcast, she stays firmly on the side lines of the crime solving world.

Then a young woman is brutally attacked, and suddenly it's essential that Maxie turns her words into actions; this is no longer an academic exercise – this is somebody's life.

But as she delves deeper, the case takes a sickening turn, which leads Maxie to the horrifying realisation that the attack might not have been a one-off. It seems there's a depraved individual out there seeking revenge, and they'll stop at nothing to get it ... little by little ... one by one.

Visit www.rubyfiction.com for details.

More from Ruby Fiction

Why not try something else from our selection:

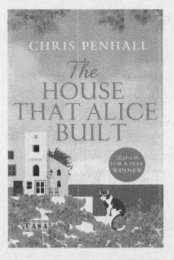

The House That Alice Built
Chris Penhall

Book 1 – Portuguese Paradise series

Home is where the heart is …

Alice Dorothy Matthews is sensible. Whilst her best friend Kathy is living it up in Portugal and her insufferable ex Adam is travelling the world, Alice is working hard to pay for the beloved London house she has put her heart and soul into renovating.

But then a postcard from Buenos Aires turns Alice's life upside down. One very unsensible decision later and she is in Cascais, Portugal, and so begins her lesson in 'going with the flow'; a lesson that sees her cat-sitting, paddle boarding, dancing on top of bars and rediscovering her artistic talents.

But perhaps the most important part of the lesson for Alice is that you don't always need a house to be at home.

The Purrfect Pet Sitter
Carol Thomas

**Introducing Lisa Blake,
the purrfect pet sitter!**

When Lisa Blake's life in London falls apart, she returns to her hometown rebranding herself as 'the purrfect petsitter' – which may or may not be false advertising as she has a rather unfortunate habit of (temporarily) losing dogs!

But being back where she grew up, Lisa can't escape her past. There's her estranged best friend Flick who she bumps into in an embarrassing encounter in a local supermarket. And her first love, Nathan Baker, who, considering their history, is sure to be even more surprised by her drunken Facebook friend request than Lisa is.

As she becomes involved in the lives of her old friends Lisa must confront the hurt she has caused, discover the truth about her mysterious leather-clad admirer, and learn how to move forward when the things she wants most are affected by the decisions of her past.

Visit www.rubyfiction.com for details.

Introducing Ruby Fiction

Ruby Fiction is an imprint of Choc Lit Publishing.
We're an award-winning independent publisher,
creating a delicious selection of fiction.

See our selection here:
www.rubyfiction.com

Ruby Fiction brings you stories that inspire emotions.

We'd love to hear how you enjoyed
Summer at Serenity Bay. Please visit
www.rubyfiction.com and give your feedback or
leave a review where you purchased this novel.

Ruby novels are selected by genuine readers like yourself.
We only publish stories our Tasting Panel want to see in
print. Our reviews and awards speak for themselves.

Could you be a Star Selector and join our Tasting Panel?
Would you like to play a role in choosing which novels
we decide to publish? Do you enjoy reading women's
fiction? Then you could be perfect for our Tasting Panel.

Visit here for more details ...
www.choc-lit.com/join-the-choc-lit-tasting-panel

Keep in touch:
Sign up for our monthly newsletter Spread for all the latest
news and offers: www.spread.choc-lit.com. Follow us on
Twitter: @RubyFiction and Facebook: RubyFiction.

Stories that inspire emotions!